It was several minutes before Charlotte realised she was not being taken to Piccadilly.

The chairmen had turned down a dark alley and were trotting at a pace that was bone-shaking. She put her head outside and commanded them to stop. They ignored her; if anything their pace increased. She shouted at them again, but it soon became evident that they had no intention of obeying her. Now she was very frightened indeed. Where were they taking her? And why?

Captain Carstairs's warning came to her mind. She was being kidnapped!

After several more minutes they stopped outside a dilapidated ⬛⬛⬛⬛⬛ let down the chair. She hurried t⬛⬛⬛⬛⬛⬛⬛⬛⬛⬛⬛e. But they had anti⬛⬛⬛⬛⬛⬛⬛⬛⬛⬛ arms and dragged ⬛⬛⬛⬛⬛⬛⬛⬛⬛ to the building, alo⬛⬛⬛⬛⬛⬛⬛⬛⬛dark as pitch, and into a candle⬛⬛⬛

A woman rose from a chair to face them. 'You got her, then?'

'We did, Molly, we did. 'Twas as easy as winking, though she made a deal of noise.'

He was a big man, with a weather-beaten face, a moulting bag wig and bad teeth. He was also the man who had grabbed her bridle in Hyde Park. Captain Carstairs had been right in saying they might try again. Oh, how she wished she had listened to him…

AUTHOR NOTE

This is number five in my *Piccadilly Gentlemen's Club* series, in which club members solve crimes in Georgian society. Previously I have featured murder, deception, coining and smuggling. This one explores kidnapping—but it is an unusual kidnapping, which involves sailing the high seas. Captain Alexander Carstairs, recently elevated to Marquis of Foxlees, being a Master Mariner, is just the man for the job.

The 'kidnapped beauty' is the daughter of a coachmaker. It was fun researching the coachmaking business, which was once very lucrative; the best coachmakers would have been multimillionaires in today's terms. Anyone who was anyone needed a coach or carriage to get about, and the richest had more than one—just as today's millionaires will have several different cars.

Henry Gilpin, father of my heroine, has become exceedingly wealthy in the coachmaking trade. The trouble is that it is trade—and tradesmen were not admitted to the society of the nobility. He is doing his best to find his daughter a titled husband when she is kidnapped.

I would like to acknowledge the help of Clive Gilbert, Chairman of The British Society of Portugal, in researching this book.

THE CAPTAIN'S
KIDNAPPED
BEAUTY

Mary Nichols

First published in Great Britain 2012
by Mills & Boon, an imprint of Harlequin (UK) Limited.
Harlequin (UK) Limited, Eton House, 18-24 Paradise Road,
Richmond, Surrey TW9 1SR

© Mary Nichols 2012

ISBN: 978 0 263 89278 9

Harlequin (UK) policy is to use papers that are natural, renewable
and recyclable products and made from wood grown in sustainable
forests. The logging and manufacturing process conform to the
legal environmental regulations of the country of origin.

Printed and bound in Spain
by Blackprint CPI, Barcelona

Born in Singapore, **Mary Nichols** came to England when she was three, and has spent most of her life in different parts of East Anglia. She has been a radiographer, school secretary, information officer and industrial editor, as well as a writer. She has three grown-up children, and four grandchildren.

Previous novels by the same author:

RAGS-TO-RICHES BRIDE
THE EARL AND THE HOYDEN
CLAIMING THE ASHBROOKE HEIR
  (part of *The Secret Baby Bargain*)
HONOURABLE DOCTOR, IMPROPER ARRANGEMENT
THE CAPTAIN'S MYSTERIOUS LADY*
THE VISCOUNT'S UNCONVENTIONAL BRIDE*
LORD PORTMAN'S TROUBLESOME WIFE*
SIR ASHLEY'S METTLESOME MATCH*
WINNING THE WAR HERO'S HEART

*_The Piccadilly Gentlemen's Club_ mini-series

And in Mills & Boon®:

WITH VICTORIA'S BLESSING
  (part of *Royal Weddings Through the Ages*)

**Did you know that some of these novels
are also available as eBooks?
Visit www.millsandboon.co.uk**

Chapter One

1765

The regular meeting of the Society for the Discovery and Apprehending of Criminals, popularly known as the Piccadilly Gentlemen's Club, was drawing to its close. Led by James, Lord Drymore, they were all gentlemen of independent means dedicated to promoting law and order in a notoriously lawless society. Some called them thieftakers, but it was a soubriquet they rejected only because of its unsavoury connotations. In general thieftakers were nearly all as corrupt as the criminals they brought to justice, but the members of the Piccadilly Gentleman's Club were not like that and refused payment for their services.

Today each had reported on the case on which

they were working. Jonathan, Viscount Leinster, was trying to trace two notorious highwaymen who had escaped from prison while awaiting trial and not having much luck. Harry, Lord Portman's particular interest was counterfeit coiners and he often went in disguise to the rookeries of the capital in search of information, though to look at him, you would hardly believe it; he was the epitome of a dandified man about town. Ashley, Lord Cadogan, was chasing smugglers with the help of his brother-in-law, Ben Kingslake, and Captain Alexander Carstairs had just returned a kidnap victim safe and sound to her distraught parents without it having cost them a penny in ransom money. James himself was tied up with their sponsor, Lord Trentham, a Minister of the Crown, in maintaining law and order in an increasingly disgruntled populace.

'Allow me to offer condolences on the loss of your uncle and cousin,' James said to Alex as they prepared to disperse. 'To lose both together was a double tragedy.'

'And felicitations on your elevation to the peerage,' Harry added. 'Marquis of Foxlees, no less.'

'Thank you,' Alex said. 'It was a great shock and I have hardly had time to gather my wits. A peerage is something I never expected and I'm not at all sure I like the idea.'

'The same thing happened to me,' Ash said.

'My cousin was the heir and he died out in India and his father, my uncle, soon afterwards. It was an upheaval adjusting to it and just before my wedding, too.'

'At least I don't have a bride waiting for me,' Alex said.

'That will soon be remedied, my friend,' Harry said, flicking a speck of dust from his immaculate sleeve. 'Sooner or later, everyone in the Piccadilly Gentleman's Club succumbs to falling in love.'

'Not me. I will have my hands full sorting out my uncle's affairs. It is just as well I have no case on hand at the moment.'

'That, too, can be remedied,' Jonathan put in.

'I think we can allow Alex a short respite to sort out his affairs,' James said with a smile.

They stood up, replaced hats on heads and headed from the room in Lord Trentham's house where they held their meetings and emerged on to the busy thoroughfare of Piccadilly, where they went their separate ways.

Alex set off on foot to Long Acre because he wanted to hire a carriage to carry him to Norfolk and his newly inherited estate. He had not visited it in years, mainly because his uncle and cousin were so rarely there. They were seafarers, just as he was, just as his late father had been and his father before him. His uncle, his father's older brother, had bought Foxlees Manor when his wife had decided, after a half a lifetime of following him all over the globe, that she had had enough of travelling and living in hot, uncomfortable places and wanted to stay at home.

That did not mean his uncle had given up his voyaging; the sea was in his blood and, being captain of an East Indiaman, he found it a lucrative business. He simply came home at the end of every voyage to spend a little time with his wife and their son, Harold, until Harold himself became a seaman and followed in his father's footsteps. The marchioness had died soon afterwards and his uncle and cousin rarely visited Foxlees Manor after her demise. When not at sea they lived in their town house on Mount Street.

They had both been lost when their ship foundered in a storm while rounding the Cape of Good Hope and so Alex found himself a Marquis and owner of the Mount Street house and the Foxlees estate. It was something he had neither expected nor wanted, but he admitted the town house was a great deal better than the bachelor apartments he had hitherto occupied.

He enjoyed his life as Captain Alexander Carstairs, member of the Piccadilly Gentleman's Club; it fulfilled his sense of adventure at the same time as he was doing some good in society. He had a full social life and many friends—what more could a man ask? But with his elevation to the peerage and the acquisition of an estate came responsibilities and these he could not shirk.

He emerged from Newport Street and crossed the road into Long Acre, looking for the coach-making premises of Henry Gilpin.

'The Earl of Falsham has failed to pay his interest again this month, Papa,' Charlotte said, looking up from the ledgers on which she was working. 'Last time I wrote to remind him, I warned him that if we did not receive at least some of what was owed, we would take him to court. He did not even favour us with a reply.'

The Earl had bought two carriages two years previously, a splendid town chariot for two hundred and ninety pounds and a phaeton for seventy-two pounds, borrowing the money from her father to pay for it. For the first six months he had diligently paid the five per cent interest on the loan, but since then nothing at all. Charlotte, who kept her father's books, had written every month on behalf of the company to remind him, but the Earl had ignored her letters.

Henry Gilpin sighed. 'You know how I hate taking customers to court,' he said. 'It ruins their reputation. As soon as news of the case gets out, every dunner in the country beats a path to their door. Let's not forget that the Earl did introduce me to his cousin and *he* pays promptly.'

'I am persuaded his lordship is counting on you remembering that.'

Henry chuckled. 'No doubt you are right. Send the Earl another stiff letter. Give him seven days to reply and if he does not, then court it shall be.'

It was not that Henry Gilpin was in need of the money—he was one of the richest men in the kingdom—but his wealth was built on sound business practice and allowing bad debts to accumulate was not one of them. He did not in the least mind people owing him money so long as they paid the interest. To make sure of that he always insisted his debtors take out a bond for double what they owed in the event they reneged. The bond was backed by their assets which could, and sometimes did, include their estates.

Charlotte looked up from the desk at which she was working and looked about her. The Long Acre premises had been much enlarged over the years and were now big enough to house the whole coachmaking business, a workshop for the construction of the undercarriages, another for the body, one for the wheelwright, furnaces for the metal working, paint shops, leather shops, design rooms and offices, huge stores for the timber: mahogany, pine, birch and deal; racks of cloth and lace for the interiors—everything necessary for constructing coaches of every description. And in each department there were men to do the work, two hundred of them.

Charlotte was the only woman and she had had to plead with her father to allow her to work there. He had no son and she was his only child, so one day she would own it all. She needed to know how it operated and she loved the cut and thrust of business, the smell of varnish, paint and hot metal, loved watching the new coaches taking shape under the skilful hands of their operatives and derived huge satisfaction from the pleasure of their customers for a job well done. Since her mother had died, it had become her father's whole life and hers, too. Not for her the round of meaningless social gatherings intended to unite eligible young men with suitable brides.

'But you do not need to concern yourself with it,' her father had told her when she first broached the subject of working at Long Acre with him. 'One day you will marry and your husband will take over.'

'I may not marry.'

'Of course you will. You are a considerable heiress and that alone would secure you a bridegroom, even if you were not so lovely.'

'Lovely, Papa?' she queried.

'Of course you are. You are the image of your dear mother, God rest her. You can afford to be particular. A title, naturally, and the higher the better. I do not have a son to make into a gentleman, but I am determined you will be a lady.'

'If I am not already a lady, then what am I?' she had demanded with a teasing smile. 'An hermaphrodite?'

'Do not be silly. You are a lady, do not doubt it, but I meant a titled lady, a countess, a viscountess or a baroness at the very least. I may be able to mix with the best in the land and you may be admitted to every drawing room in town, if you would only take the trouble, but it doesn't make us gentry. That is something for the next generation.'

'Hold hard, Papa.' She had laughed. 'I am not yet married. And supposing I don't fancy any of the eligible titles? I might fall in love with a man of the middling sort, a businessman like yourself, someone I can respect.'

'Bah!' he had said. 'Falling in love is an overrated pastime and does not guarantee happiness, quite often the reverse. If you must fall in love, then make sure he is worthy of you. A title he will have, even if I have to buy one for him, though I'd as lief he came with a respected family history.'

'I might decide I would rather stay single and keep my independence. You need someone to help you run the business and that is what I most like to do. I should hate to see it ruined by a profligate son-in-law who does not understand how important it is.'

'Then you must make your choice carefully. I will not always be here to guide you.'

'Papa, let us have no more of that. You are good for years and years yet.'

He had given in and allowed her to accompany him from their mansion in Piccadilly to Long Acre every day to assist the accountant with the book-keeping, a task which gave her a great deal of satisfaction. It was better than sitting at home looking decorative, reading, sewing or paying calls and listening to the latest scandals. And it gave her an insight into how the business was managed. If she had her way, she would do much more.

Their discussion about the Earl's debt was interrupted by a shout and a resounding crash coming from the main workroom. They both dashed out from the office to see what was amiss.

Joe Smithson was lying at the bottom of the stairs to the upper floor and was struggling to rise. The stairs were wide and had a detachable banister because the coach bodies were constructed on the first floor and they were let down with ropes when complete and it was this task which had been occupying him when he fell. Charlotte had once said that the workrooms should be rearranged in order to construct the bodies on the ground floor, but her father had pointed out that to do that the metal workers, decorators and the upholsterers and all the other ancillary workers would have to be moved upstairs and how could they do their work if the coach on which they needed to work was downstairs? She was obliged to admit the logic of his argument. There was a completed shell of a town chariot on the upper workshop floor and Joe had been readying it for its descent to the ground which had meant removing the banister.

Charlotte and her father dashed forwards but someone beat them to it, a tall stranger who had come in from the street and reached Joe a fraction of a second before they did. He bent down and put his hand on Joe's shoulder to stop him struggling to rise. 'Be still, man,' he said. 'We need to know what damage is done before we get you to your feet.'

'Yes, Joe, keep still,' Charlotte said, as other workers crowded round them. 'We will send for a doctor.'

'Miss Charlotte, there's no need for that,' Joe said. 'I'm not badly hurt, just shook up a bit. I'll be right as ninepence when I've got me breath back.'

The stranger squatted down beside Joe and began feeling along his arms and legs. When he reached Joe's left ankle the young man winced.

'I am sure it is not broken,' he told Henry who hovered nearby. 'But if I were you I should send for the sawbones to be sure.' He put Joe's arms about his neck and hauled him to a standing position, then flung him over his shoulder. 'Where shall I take him?'

'Into the office,' Henry said, leading the way. Charlotte sent the messenger boy for the doctor and the rest of the workforce back about their business before following.

She found Joe deposited in a chair, her father fussing round him and the stranger dusting down his coat. He looked up as Charlotte entered.

She was struck by his looks. She was not particularly short, but he overtopped her by a head at least. His complexion was tanned and there were wrinkles each side of his eyes as if he had spent hours out of doors, peering into the weather. A mariner, she surmised, and this was confirmed when he bowed to her.

'Captain Alexander Carstairs, at your service, ma'am,' he said, sweeping her a leg, a very elegant leg, she noticed.

'I thank you for your assistance, Captain. It was lucky you were passing.'

'I was not passing, I was heading here and just entering when the young man fell. It is surely dangerous to have stairs with no handrail?'

Henry started to explain the need for it, which

made the Captain turn towards him and that gave Charlotte an opportunity to study him more closely. He was wearing a dark blue kerseymere suit of clothes, very plain but superbly tailored, a long pale blue waistcoat with large pockets and silver buttons, a white shirt and a neatly tied white muslin cravat. His stockings were white and his shoes had silver buckles. Besides being very tall, he was broad of shoulder and slim of hip. His hands were strong and capable. Her gaze travelled upwards. His dark hair was his own, worn long and tied back with a narrow black ribbon. He was most certainly not a fop. He turned back to her again and her breath caught in her throat. He had the most penetrating eyes, neither green nor brown but something in between, and they seemed to be looking right inside her, as if her skin and flesh were transparent and he could see secrets about her she had never even been aware of.

'My daughter, Miss Gilpin,' Henry said, waving a hand in her direction. 'She likes to come and see her old father at work sometimes.'

Alex bowed to her again. 'Miss Gilpin, how do you do?'

'Well, thank you, Captain,' she answered, resolving to have words with her father about the condescending way he had presented her.

Likes to visit her old father, indeed! 'How can we help you?'

'I need to drive into the country and came to hire a carriage for the purpose.'

'I am sure we can accommodate you.' She held his eyes with her own, letting him know she was not the insignificant daughter her father would have him believe and that she was part of the workforce, but it took all her self-control. Being businesslike when one's heart was definitely not behaving in a businesslike manner, but skipping and jumping about, was difficult. 'What had you in mind?'

The doctor arrived before he could answer and as the room was not large enough for everyone, Charlotte led the Captain back into the main workshop so that her father could deal with the doctor. He hesitated, taking a look at Henry who was watching the doctor examine Joe, before deciding to follow her.

'Now,' she said, turning to face him, once more in command of herself. 'Tell me, what do you have in mind?'

'Do you not think we should wait for your father to join us?'

'No. Do you suppose I am not capable of conducting the simple business of hiring out a coach?' It was said with some asperity and served to disperse her last lingering discomposure.

'Well...' he began and then hesitated as her eyes challenged him.

'I am a female and therefore useless, is that what you were about to point out to me?'

'Oh, most definitely you are female—as to being useless, that I could not say.' Now there was a teasing look in his eyes and it was most disconcerting. Was he laughing at her? She did not care for that at all.

'Nevertheless,' she told him. 'I have been running about these workshops ever since I learned to walk and I also keep the books, so you can trust me to know what I am about. Tell me about the journey you wish to make. How far? Are you in some haste? What will the roads be like, smooth or rough? Do you go alone or will you have passengers and much luggage?'

'You need to know a great deal considering all I came to do is hire a coach to take me to Norfolk.'

'Ah, that has answered one of my questions,' she said with a smile meant to disarm him, which it very nearly did. 'And probably a second. I believe the roads to that part of the country are devilishly bad.'

'*Touché.*' He returned her smile with one of his own. It softened his features and she realised suddenly that the lines on his face had not all been made by wind and weather, some were laughter lines. The erratic heartbeats began all over again. She took a deep breath to steady herself.

'Do you need a large conveyance for passengers and luggage, which will be slower, or something lighter to carry you swiftly?'

'I might have a passenger for part of the way,' he said. 'And little luggage, but as you so rightly pointed out, the roads to Norfolk, once away from the capital, are dreadful, so the vehicle will need to be sturdy enough to withstand the jolting if we are to travel at speed.'

'And do you intend to make just one journey or will you be coming backwards and forwards to the capital?'

'Does it matter?'

'If you hire a coach, you will need to return it by the arranged time and hiring over a long period will be more costly than buying an equipage. We have several second-hand coaches for sale, which I can show you or, if you are not in a hurry, we can construct one to your own specification. We can also supply you with horses.'

'Do not tell me you are an expert on horseflesh as well,' he said, laughing.

'I know a good horse when I see one.'

'And no doubt you are a bruising rider, to boot.'

She let that pass without comment. 'There is a very good chaise in the yard, taken in part exchange for a newer model, which might very well suit you. Shall you take a look?'

'Yes, I might as well see what you have to offer while we are waiting for Mr Gilpin to join us.'

She was annoyed by his attitude, but it was not the first time and she did not suppose it would be the last when customers treated her with condescension as if she were just out of the schoolroom and needed humouring. She was twenty-two years old; many ladies of her acquaintance had been married for years at that age and already had a brood of children. It was the only thing she regretted about her single state, she could not be a mother.

She conducted him outside, crossed the yard which had standing for a least a dozen coaches, and into another building, a vast barn-like area which contained a host of vehicles: town coaches, travelling coaches, phaetons, landaus and landaulets, gigs and tilburys. There was even a magnificent berline. Some were plain, some highly decorated, but all bore the hallmark of the Gilpin works, meticulously finished and polished.

'This chaise is a sturdy vehicle,' she said, indicating a travelling coach in forest green, its only decoration lines of pale green about the body work and round the rims of the wheels. It was highly varnished, elegant but not ostentatious.

He walked all round it, rocked it on its springs,

jumped on the coachman's box with its red-and-green-striped hammercloth and sat there for a few moments before jumping down and climbing inside. The interior was upholstered in green velvet and there were light green curtains at the windows. He sat a moment and stretched out his legs. There was little leg room for one so tall, but that was not unexpected; he had yet to ride in a coach which allowed him the luxury of stretching out.

Charlotte watched him without speaking. He was undoubtedly athletic, climbing up and down with consummate ease, and the way he had climbed on the box suggested he was no stranger to driving a coach. He was self-assured and would not be easy to gull. Not that she intended to deceive him; that was not the way Gilpins did business. Their reputation for honesty and fine workmanship had been well earned over the years and she would do nothing to jeopardise it.

He emerged from the coach and rejoined her. 'I think it will do me very well,' he said.

'Would you like to look at others before you make up your mind?'

He agreed and she showed him several more, some more sumptuous, others well used with scuffed paint which she told him would be remedied before the coaches were sold on. Some were extra large and cumbersome, needing at least six horses to pull them, some too lightweight for any but town roads.

'No,' he said, at last. 'You have chosen well, Miss Gilpin. I will negotiate a price with Mr Gilpin.'

'The price to buy is one hundred and nineteen pounds sixteen shillings,' she said firmly. 'We give value for money, Captain, and do not enter into negotiation. If that is too much…?' Her voice faded on a question.

'No, I did not mean I would beat him down,' he said hastily. 'The price seems fair enough. I meant that I would need to arrange for horses and harness and for the coach to be fetched.'

'Let us return to the office and conclude the transaction,' she said. 'The doctor will have gone by now.'

They crossed the yard again and entered the main workshop where several men were using ropes to lower a coach body down the stairs. Joe, supporting himself on two sticks, was standing directing operations.

'What did the doctor say?' Charlotte asked him.

''Tis but a sprain,' he answered. 'I must rest it for a week or two and then all will be well.'

'You will not rest it by standing there. The men can manage without you for a week. Ask

Giles to take you home in the gig, and do not come back until you are recovered. You will lose no pay.'

'Yes, Miss Charlotte. Thank you, miss.'

Charlotte moved on, followed by Alex. 'Do the men usually obey you so promptly, Miss Gilpin?' he queried. He had noticed the adoring look in Joe's eyes as he answered her. The poor fellow was evidently in love with his employer's daughter. He wondered if she knew it.

'Yes, why not? One day the business will be mine and I will have the full running of it, but please God, not for a very long time.'

'Really?' he queried in surprise. 'I had thought a brother or a husband would take over.'

'I have neither brother nor husband.' She was used to people making assumptions like that, but it never failed to raise her hackles and she spoke sharply.

'I beg your pardon,' he said. 'I can see you are a very determined woman.'

A woman, she noted, not a lady. There was a world of difference in the use of the words and reminded her of her conversations with her father on the subject. It simply stiffened her resolve to prove she was as good as any man when it came to business. It was far more important than being a so-called lady. Or a wife, come to that.

They entered the office where her father was

standing looking out of the window on to the busy street, watching the doctor's gig disappearing up the road. 'It's time he changed that vehicle,' he said aloud. 'He's had it three years now and it is beginning to look the worse for wear. I must persuade him to turn it in for a phaeton, much more befitting his status as a physician of the first rank.' He turned from the window to face them. 'Captain Carstairs, did you find something to suit?'

'The captain is going to buy Lord Pymore's travelling chaise,' Charlotte told him, fetching papers from a cupboard and taking her seat at her desk. 'He has agreed our price.'

'Good.' Henry said. 'Captain, do you need embellishments? Heraldry? Additional lines, scrolls perhaps?'

'No, thank you, I cannot wait for such things to be done. It will do me very well as it is, but I do need harness and cattle. Miss Gilpin tells me you can also supply those.'

'Indeed we can. I pride myself on dealing in animals sound in wind and limb. You may safely leave those to me. Do you have a coachman?'

'Yes,' Alex said, thinking of Davy Locke, who had been his servant on board ship and now went by the grand title of valet, though anyone less like a valet was hard to imagine. He was an untidy giant of a man, but a good man to have beside you in a tussle, whether it be confronting law-breakers or struggling to get into a tight-fitting coat. He was, surprisingly for an ex-seaman, very good with horses. He put it down to working on a farm before he was pressed into service with the navy. A man of many talents was Davy Locke.

'I shall have the paperwork drawn up in a few minutes, Captain,' Charlotte put in. 'You are welcome to inspect the premises while you wait.' She gave him what she considered to be a condescending smile. 'You may learn something of coachmaking.'

Alex, recognising the put-down for what it was, smiled, bowed and left the room, followed by Henry Gilpin, who went immediately to inspect the coach body which had been safely brought down to the ground floor and was being set upon a wooden cradle waiting to receive it. It had yet to be set on its undercarriage, painted and decorated and the interior finished, but even so Alex could appreciate the skilful work of the woodworkers.

Henry began explaining some of the processes to him, but Alex was hardly listening. He was thinking about Miss Gilpin. She was certainly very touchy about her gender. Perhaps she wished she had been born a boy. She was undoubtedly handsome with fine eyebrows, a straight nose and a well-defined, determined chin, but he would not describe her as feminine, not in the way he would have used the word. Her gown was decidedly practical, in a heavy grey taffeta, having only the slightest of false hips, and her quilted stomacher was made to match the gown and had no decoration beyond a satin bow on the square neckline. There wasn't an ounce of lace on it anywhere. It was certainly not the height of fashion. She wore her own rich brown hair pulled back into a thick roll on top of her head and fastened with combs. She wore no gloves and her fingers were ink-stained.

And yet...and yet, she had the most expressive grey eyes. There was intelligence behind them, and humour, too, something he could admire. Was she really as competent as she appeared or was there, underneath that façade, a woman as weak and fickle as all her gender? Would she collapse in a flood of tears as soon as her self-sufficiency was put to the test? Did she really know the ins and outs of a coach-building business or was her father simply humouring a spoiled daughter? He found himself wanting to know the answers, to engage her in conversation, to find out what she was really like under that severe exterior. He felt sure such discourse would not be shallow and meaningless. It was a pity he was leaving town so soon, but then, on reflection, perhaps it was not. She was clearly not the sort for mere dalliance and he certainly did not wish for anything deeper, not after what had happened with Letitia. She had soured him for all women.

Why on earth had he suddenly thought of Letitia? He had buried that experience deep inside him where it could not surface, or so he had thought, but standing looking at half-a-dozen workmen manhandling the body of a coach with the aid of pulleys, he was suddenly back in his salad days.

He had met Letitia Cornish on a voyage out to India. Her father was a wealthy nabob and he the mere second lieutenant of an East India-man, plying back and forth between England and Calcutta, carrying European wines, furniture, glassware and even carriages on the outward journey, returning with spices, precious stones, ornaments, carpets and tigerskin rugs. She had been patrolling the deck and had stopped to gaze out over the stern at the wake, as if wishing she were back where she had come from. Hearing his footstep behind her, she had turned to speak to him. 'Lieutenant, I am not in your way, am I?'

'Not at all, Miss Cornish, but there is blow coming up and I advise you to go below. The sea is like to become very rough. Allow me to escort you.' It was couched as a request, but she was expected to obey, which she did reluctantly.

'It is so stuffy in the cabin,' she said. 'I prefer the fresh air.'

'I fear it will become a little more than fresh,' he had said, smiling as he accompanied her to the companionway. 'When the storm is over, I will come and fetch you and you may take the air again.'

He had kept his word and escorted her back on deck as soon as the havoc caused by the storm had been cleared away and they were once more sailing on an even keel. She was looking white-faced, but assured him she had not been sick and would be right as rain as soon as she was up in the fresh air again. Her father had not emerged from his cabin. In spite of being a frequent traveller between England and India, he was not a good sailor and neither was Letitia's maid and she was often left to her own devices. Thus they often met when he was on watch and she was patrolling the deck and they would stop and talk. In his eyes she was perfection with her shining golden hair and clear blue eyes.

He learned she was eighteen, a year younger than he was. Her mother had died years before; she could hardly remember her and Letitia had been brought up by her father with the help of an elderly aunt. Now she was grown up, her father was taking her to India where they expected to stay for several months while Mr Cornish assembled a new cargo to take back to England and after that she was to be brought out in London society. He told her about his life at sea, how he hoped to follow in his father's and uncle's footsteps and become a master mariner for the East India Company. By the time they reached Calcutta they were in love.

Her father would have none of it when Alex had approached him for permission to propose. 'A penniless lieutenant—I should think not!' he had said. 'Whatever gave you the notion I would entertain a scapegrace like you for a son-in-law? After her money, are you? Think to make yourself wealthy at my expense?'

'No, sir, certainly not, sir. I love your daughter and she loves me.'

'Love, bah! What is that but a weak indulgence? Letitia will marry one of the young gentlemen I pick out for her when we return to London. And every one of them will have a title and some standing in society. She is wealthy enough and comely enough to take her pick. You, sir, are beneath her notice.'

Alex had been furious and had to use all his self-control not to lash out at the man, but young though he was, he knew alienating her father would not endear him to Letitia. Instead he turned on his heel and left with the man's derisive laughter echoing in his ears. But he was not yet ready to give up. He knew Letitia liked to ride out very early in the morning before the heat became too intense and so he contrived to be out on horseback at the same time and prevailed upon her to dismount and talk to him. He had been hoping to persuade her to defy her father and run away with him. How foolish that notion was he had not realised at the time. She had tearfully refused to do any such thing. Her dear papa was always right and she would obey him as she always had.

He had not been able to understand her unquestioning acceptance of the fate laid down for her and continued to protest until the time came to part. 'Goodbye, Alex,' she had said and reached up to kiss his cheek and then remounted with the help of her syce and was gone, cantering away, raising the yellow dust.

She had not truly loved him or she would have defied her father, he told himself, she had been having a game with him. It was easier to be angry than admit he had a broken heart and, as his ship was loaded and made ready for the return journey, he left her behind, vowing that no woman, no matter how beautiful or how wealthy, would ever humiliate him like that again. Two years later he heard she had returned to England and married the Earl of Falsham, so her father had had his wish.

He had left the merchant service and had a spell in the cavalry in the hope that such a radical change to his way of life would cure him, but the lure of the sea was still in his blood and he had sold up and joined the navy. In due course he had become captain of a frigate, but with the end of the seven-year-long war with France two years before he had found himself with no ship and on half-pay. It was then he became involved with the Society for the Discovery and Apprehending of Criminals. And now his life was about to change again and he was not at all sure he welcomed it.

Miss Gilpin came out from the office, carrying a sheaf of papers. 'Have you learned anything of coachmaking, Captain?' she asked.

'I have concluded it is a very complicated business,' he answered. 'I have been watching the men put the coach on its cradle. They make it look easy.'

'They are all experienced men, Captain, though we shall miss Joe Smithson until he is well again. I collect I did not thank you properly for your help in getting him up. He is a big strong man, but you lifted him with ease.'

He bowed towards her. 'My pleasure, Miss Gilpin.'

'Your carriage will be ready tomorrow. My father will personally inspect it for defects before he allows it to be delivered, and of course the horses and licence have to be obtained so we cannot do it any sooner. I hope that is convenient for you.'

'Entirely,' he said, bowing. If he had hired a chaise instead of buying one, he might have been on his way before that, but Miss Gilpin had been right; he would need to travel back and forth frequently on society business, so it made sense to buy. 'But I will fetch it from here. I mean to begin my journey immediately. Shall we say noon?'

She looked at her father. 'Will you have the horses and harness by then, Papa?'

Mr Gilpin was only half-listening to their exchange, being more concerned with inspecting the half-finished coach and giving instruction to the carpenters who were to fix the moulding along the edge of its roof. 'Yes, yes, I shall go to Tattersalls this afternoon.'

'How will you pay?' Charlotte turned back to Alex. 'Credit terms can be arranged, if you wish.'

Alex resented the inference that he could not pay for anything he ordered. Just because he elected to dress simply, did not mean he was without funds. Even before inheriting his uncle's estate he had been a wealthy man. He had earned good prize money as a sea captain and his father had left a fortune as a result of his captaincy of an East India merchantman. Each captain was allowed to carry a certain tonnage on their own account, for which privilege they paid five hundred pounds. It was money well spent; both Alex's father and his uncle, the Marquis of Foxlees, had become exceedingly wealthy with this trade. 'There is no need for that,' he said, his tone conveying his annoyance. 'It may be considered eccentric, but it is my strict rule to pay my dues on demand. I shall bring a money order on my bank when I come tomorrow.'

'Thank you, Captain. Then the price is as we agreed.'

He took his leave and went on his way, first to his bank to arrange the draft then to his club where he intended to dine. He had barely sat down and ordered a capon and a couple of pork chops, when he was joined by Jonathan Leinster. 'What, not gone home to the delectable Louise?' he asked him.

'No she has taken the baby and gone to visit her parents. I decided an evening in town would be more congenial than going back to an empty house. I am promised to Lady Milgrove's soirée, later. What about you? I had thought you on your way to Norfolk.'

'I needed a coach to convey me there and decided to buy one, so I have been at Gilpin's.'

'You can't go wrong there. They have a reputation for the best, but not cheap, by no means cheap.'

'That I discovered.'

Jonathan turned to give his order to the waiter before continuing the conversation. 'Did you meet Miss Gilpin?'

'Indeed I did. She seems to think she runs the business.'

Jonathan laughed. 'Not quite, but her father does not disabuse her of the idea. No doubt she will learn the difference when she comes to wed.'

'Is she engaged, then?'

'No, but her papa has been putting it around that he is looking for a title for her.'

'And no doubt she will marry whoever Papa picks out for her.'

Jonathan shrugged. 'Who's to say? I am glad I am married and not in the running. I think she will be a veritable harridan and hard to handle.'

'Do you say so?'

'Yes. You saw her. Do you not agree she is something of an antidote?'

'No, I can't say that I do,' Alex said slowly. 'She could hardly work in the business dressed in the height of fashion with hips a mile wide and coiffeur a foot tall.'

'I don't see why she has to work in the business at all. Gilpin is prodigiously wealthy and can indulge her in whatever she wants.'

'So he intends to buy her a title, does he?'

'So it seems.'

'Then I hope she has the good sense to resist.'

Jonathan looked sharply at his friend, a look that was not lost on Alex, who quickly changed the subject. 'I did not fancy riding to Norfolk by stage and was going to hire a conveyance, but decided to buy one, after all. I shall need it if I am to come up to town for our regular meetings at Trentham House.'

'That's true, and neither can you shut your-self away in the country away from society. You will have to start looking for a wife now you are a marquis.'

'Oh, I shall, shall I?'

'Of course. You will need an heir.'

'There is plenty of time for that.'

'How old are you, Alex?'

'I am thirty-four.'

'Good heavens, there is not a moment to lose! You will be an old man before you know it.' It was said with mock dismay which made Alex laugh. And then, after a pause, 'Come with me to Lady Milgrove's.'

'I will hardly find a wife there,' Alex said, still laughing.

'Perhaps not, but more to the point the evening is in aid of the Foundling Hospital, a charity close to Louise's heart and I promised her I would go. You do not leave town tonight, do you?'

'No, I am to take delivery of the chaise tomorrow at noon, but I shall be on my way directly after that.'

'So, you'll come? I will enjoy it the more if I have company.'

'Very well, I will come.'

Their food arrived and they set to tackling it with hearty appetites.

'No sign of those two escapees, then?' Alex asked.

'No. I am persuaded someone is sheltering them. I sent Sam Roker into the rookeries where they might seek refuge, to see if he could discover any news of them, but so far nothing.'

Sam was the only one of the society who could not be called a gentleman. Officially James's servant, he came and went according to the needs of its members, being a great one for disguise and able to speak the cant of the ruffians who inhabited the seedier parts of the city.

'No doubt they will turn up when you least expect it,' Alex said. 'If you need any help, call on me.'

'I will, if you are not too busy courting.'

'If you do not desist from your nonsense, I shall leave you to go to Lady Milgrove's on your own, my friend.'

Jonathan held up his hands in surrender. 'Not another word. Shall we have a hand of faro to while away the rest of the afternoon?'

Chapter Two

'I've taken on some help for the men,' Henry told his daughter as they rode home in the Gilpins' town coach that evening. 'He arrived in the works this afternoon and said he had heard we were without our overseer and he was looking for employment.'

'How did he know about Joe?'

'I've no idea. I expect one of the other men said something to him. I told him Joe would only be absent a few days and would then be back, but he said he understood that, but he had a wife and little ones and any work of however short duration would be a help. He had good references, so I told him he could start tomorrow, but not as an overseer. He accepted that. His name is Martin Grosswaite.'

'We could have managed.'

'We could, but it would be easier to have another man to help with the bodywork. We are to start a new landaulet tomorrow and we are already short-handed with Colin away sick.' Colin was one of their carpenters and he had gone down with an infection on his lungs, brought about by the wood dust that flew everywhere on the upper floor, which was another good reason for keeping that side of the manufacture away from the painting, varnishing and upholstery.

'Is he a wood worker?'

'He said he could turn his hand to most things.'

'Then I hope you do not come to regret it, Papa.'

He turned to her in surprise. 'Now why should I do that, child?'

'Papa, I am not a child.'

'You are to me. You will be my child however old you grow. Still, I will try to remember not to address you thus. Now why do you think I might regret it?'

'A strange man walked in off the street and you took him on without checking him out. That is unlike you.'

'He had references from Sir Elliott Foster.'

'Did you have them confirmed? They could easily be forgeries.'

'Do you take me for a gull? I have written to Sir Elliott asking him to confirm what he has said about the man. In the meantime, I shall put him to work. I only tell you that you may not be startled when he arrives for work tomorrow. He said he would have to arrange lodgings first so he will not arrive until after noon, but he knows our normal hours of work.'

'You know best, Papa,' she said meekly. She knew her father was letting her know who was in charge, which was undoubtedly because she had taken over the selling of the coach to Captain Carstairs. He prided himself on his own sales-manship and besides, he was not altogether rec-onciled to her working in the business. She knew better than to continue arguing with him. Instead she said, 'Are you going out this evening, Papa?'

'I had a mind to attend the musical recital at Lady Milgrove's. There is a young violinist who is making a name for himself and I believe he is going to play some of Handel's music. At any rate, as one of the Foundling Hospital's trustees, it behoves me to go. Shall you come with me?'

'Yes, Papa, I should like that.' She smiled and added, 'So long as you do not call me child and so long as you do not attempt any matchmaking.'

'Oh, I doubt there will be any eligibles at an occasion like that, fusty old men like me, I shouldn't wonder, and aged dowagers.'

For the most part he was right; the audience seem to have arrived in pairs, married or engaged or widows with companions—all except Viscount Leinster and Captain Alexander Carstairs. The viscount was happily married and the captain ineligible in Mr Gilpin's eyes, so Charlotte felt able to relax and enjoy the music which was very fine.

During the interval when everyone was invited to partake of refreshments, Charlotte found herself standing next to the captain in the line waiting to go to the long table in the dining room, which had been set out for guests to help themselves to a plate of the plentiful food on offer. Her father had disappeared into the library with another of the trustees and had left her to fend for herself, which was typical of him. She smiled up at Alex. 'Good evening, Captain. I had not expected to see you again so soon.'

'Nor I you.' He sketched her a bow. 'Have you enjoyed the concert so far?'

'Indeed, yes. Of course it is not the same without Mr Handel. His loss will be keenly felt by everyone, but especially the poor orphans. He was a great benefactor.'

'So I have heard from my friend, Viscount Leinster. You are acquainted with his lordship, I believe?' He indicated Jonathan with a movement of his hand, which made the lace fall back over the sleeve of his dark-blue evening coat. She wondered if he always wore dark blue when everyone else seemed to favour peacock colours. Viscount Leinster, for instance, was in apricot.

She bent her knee to him. 'Yes, we have met at Long Acre. Good evening, my lord.'

Jonathan acknowledged her with an elegant leg. 'Your servant, Miss Gilpin. I have been telling my friend the M—' He stopped when he saw Alex shaking his head and hastily corrected himself. 'Captain Carstairs, that Mr Handel was a great influence in making the work of the hospital known.'

'Yes, indeed he was. Have you ever visited the hospital, Captain?' she asked.

'I am afraid not. It is a pleasure still to come.'

'You will not have time before you go to Norfolk,' she said. 'But perhaps when you return you will find time for a visit. Mr Hogarth's paintings are particularly fine.' Hogarth was another well-known benefactor of the charity and many of his paintings were on display at the hospital.

'I shall make every effort to do so.'

'I feel so sorry for the motherless children,' she went on. 'They are well looked after and given some training in an occupation when they are old enough and they seem happy, but life in an orphanage must be hard.'

'Do you visit often?'

'When I can. It is the babies I feel most for. Poor little things, being without a mother is so sad. I like to go and help feed them and bathe them and nurse them. I lost my mother when I was a little girl and I know what it's like, even though I have a papa who has tried to be both mother and father to me.'

'You have a soft heart, Miss Gilpin. I am persuaded you will make a splendid mama.' He dug his elbow into Jonathan's ribs when that worthy seemed unable to stifle his laughter and added, as they shuffled forwards, 'Are you here alone?'

'No, my father is here. I believe he has gone into the library with Lord Milgrove and another of the Coram trustees and will join me directly.'

'In the meantime you have no one to serve you. Please allow me to help you. Would you like the chicken, or would you prefer the ham? Some green salad, perhaps? And there are love-apples, too. I wonder how they acquired that name?'

She looked hard at him, wondering whether he was teasing her, but his expression was inscrutable. 'I have no idea.'

'I believe they are supposed to have aphrodisiacal qualities,' Jonathan put in. 'But I have never put them to the test.'

They *were* bamming her. Charlotte felt the colour rising in her cheeks. 'I should like the ham and the green salad,' she said. 'And one of those little tartlets, but I think I will give the tomatoes a miss.'

Alex noted the colour rise in her cheeks and realised suddenly that she was beautiful and for a single heartbeat he was tongue-tied, but gathered himself to put some of the food on a plate for her and helped himself to another plateful, which he carried to one of the little tables arranged about the room. Jonathan, plate piled high, joined them.

While they ate they engaged in a lively conversation about the music they had been hearing, the weather, the terrible state of the roads and the dreadful crime which was becoming more and more prevalent, especially in the capital. Pickpockets abounded, some as young as five or six who had been taught to creep under the skirts of a man's coat and cut away his purse. They were so deft and so slippery, the victim did not know he had been robbed until he went to fetch out his purse to pay for something and by then the culprit was long gone.

'We have to find the gang leaders,' Jonathan said. 'You may depend upon it they are being trained by unscrupulous men. It is not the children's fault. If they are hungry and ragged, who can blame them when someone offers them a way out of their difficulties?'

'Oh, I agree wholeheartedly,' she said. 'Something ought to be done, not to put the children in prison, but to help them keep out of it. That is why the Coram Foundling Hospital is so important—

besides taking in unwanted babies, they house some of these urchins, but unfortunately there are more such children than they have room for.'

'Arresting the men who train them in their pocket picking is equally important,' Jonathan said.

'Lord Leinster is one of the Piccadilly Gentlemen, as am I,' Alex told her by way of explanation.

'I have heard of them,' she said, looking from one to the other. 'I believe they investigate crimes and bring the criminals to justice. I remember reading about some coiners being apprehended through the offices of the Piccadilly Gentlemen. And wasn't there a murderous gang of smugglers rounded up by them recently?'

'We do what we can,' Alex said. 'Unfortunately we are only a small force and cannot be everywhere.'

'Do the Bow Street Runners not work to the same end?'

'They can arrest wrongdoers when they are brought to their notice, but they do not go out investigating crime,' he explained. 'Besides, they do not operate outside London unless they are sent for.'

'There should be runners in every town and on the roads,' Jonathan put in. 'A national force.

It is hardly possible to travel abroad in one's own coach without being held up by highwaymen.'

'I have heard my father say it is the common practice to have two purses,' she said. 'One with little in it to hand over when stopped and the other containing one's real valuables to be well hid.'

'I have heard that, too,' Alex said. 'But so, I think, have the robbers and if they suspect anything has been withheld they rip everything out of the coach to find it and often manhandle the poor travellers when they try to resist. It is sometimes more expedient to hand over one's belongings and hope the criminals will be caught with the booty still on them.'

'Which is a rare event,' Jonathan put in morosely. 'And when they are apprehended and put into prison, they somehow manage to escape.'

'You will surmise from that,' Alex told her, smiling, 'that my friend is even now engaged on tracking down two escaped prisoners. They held up a coach and fatally wounded the coachman who dared to try to defend his passengers.'

'They are dangerous men, then?'

'Very dangerous.'

'Then I hope you will take great care on your journey into Norfolk, Captain.'

He looked hard at her, but there was no irony in her tone and nothing in her expression to suggest she was roasting him and he accepted the advice on face value. 'I shall do that, never fear.'

'My father has devised a secret compartment in some of his coaches,' she said. 'It can only be found and opened if you know the way of it.'

'Is there such a place in the carriage I have bought?' Alex asked.

'Yes, did I not show it to you? How remiss of me. Remind me to do so when you come to take delivery.'

Her father arrived at this point and seated himself at the table to join in the conversation which ranged from ideas for reducing crime to the latest news of John Wilkes's controversial arrest on a charge of seditious libel and his subsequent release on the grounds that the arrest contravened his rights as a Member of Parliament.

'Just because he is a Member of Parliament is not fit reason for him to escape punishment for wrongdoing,' Charlotte said. 'No one, high or low, should be above the law.'

'Oh, I agree,' Alex said, smiling at her vehemence. 'But it is a free country and if a Member of Parliament cannot express an opinion without being arrested, then who can?'

'There is a difference between opinion and sedition,' Henry said.

'Certainly there is.'

'Papa, Lord Leinster and Captain Carstairs are

members of the Piccadilly Gentleman's Club,' Charlotte told her father, changing the subject before the discussion could become heated. 'Did you know that?'

'I have heard the name somewhere, but there are so many clubs nowadays, it is difficult to remember them all. Remind me, my lord.'

He was jovial and wary at the same time and Alex was reminded of Jonathan's assertion he was looking for a titled husband for his daughter. Jonathan was married already and he, as a mere sea captain, would never do. It was strange how that old rejection was still able to hurt, even when the last thing he had on his mind was courtship and marriage.

They were strolling homewards, he and Jonathan, picking their way along the muddy street when his friend mentioned Miss Gilpin again. 'I was wrong and you were right, Alex. Miss Gilpin is not an antidote at all. On closer inspection, her skin has the bloom of good health and her eyes are particularly fine. She looks you straight in the eye when she speaks, almost as if daring you to contradict her. No doubt that is because of the hoydenish way she has been brought up without feminine influence.'

'Is that so? No lady to advise her at all?'

'I believe there was an elderly aunt, but she

died some time ago and since then Miss Gilpin has had only her father for company, which is why she goes to the coachworks every day and he treats her like a son. No self-respecting mother or governess would have left her to fetch her own supper.'

'Then it was as well we were on hand,' Alex said laconically.

Jonathan was not yet ready to give up being a matchmaker and went on, 'But with a little guidance, I am persuaded she would be perfectly acceptable in society.'

'And what, pray, is your interest in the lady, Jon, and you a happily married man?'

'I am thinking of you, my friend. You have all the attributes her father desires and she would make a fine marchioness, not to mention bringing a prodigious fortune with her.'

'Then I wish you would not think of me. I am not looking for a wife. And please note, I do not intend to use my title, certainly not to capture a bride. I am plain Captain Alexander Carstairs and I'll thank you not to forget it.'

Jonathan held up his hand in mock supplication. 'Pax, my friend! I was roasting you. It is not like you to take offence so quickly.'

'I have not taken offence. I simply wanted to make sure you understood.'

'I am not at all sure I do, but never mind, I

will say no more on the subject.' He laughed suddenly. 'I think I prefer the captain to the marquis in any event; the marquis is not so much fun. Do you go home or will you come to White's for a hand or two?'

'I mean to go home. I must be up betimes in the morning if I am to be at Long Acre at noon. I intend to be on my way half an hour later. I think I will take a short detour and call on my mother on the way. She may like to come with me to Norfolk. If the Piccadilly Gentlemen need me, James knows where to find me.'

'Then I will bid you adieu.' Jonathan hailed a chair, which was passing empty, and climbed inside. 'Come back soon. London will be monstrous dull without you.'

And with that the chairmen picked up the handles and trotted off with him. Alex continued on his way, smiling a little, thinking of Jonathan's teasing. He might have the attributes Henry Gilpin insisted upon, but one thing was certain: one spoilt daughter of a widowed father was more than enough. He would never fall into the same humiliating situation again. Neither would he use his title, which in no way altered the man he was.

'It was a pleasant evening,' Henry said as he and Charlotte journeyed home. 'It raised several hundred pounds for the orphans and I was intro-

duced to Sir Bertram Hambleton, who is desirous
of bespeaking a travelling coach. I am assured
by Lord Leinster that he is well able to pay for
it, being heir to Viscount Beresford, who is rich
as Croesus. I am to travel down to his estate in
Oxfordshire to talk about his requirements. There
may be more than one vehicle to manufacture.
Shall you mind being left on your own?'

'Of course not, Papa. You have done it before,
many times, and the work will go on quite well
in your absence. When shall you go?'

'It has not been decided yet. In a week or two.
Sir Bertram has business in town and I must wait
until he is ready to return home. I will see the
work started on the new landaulet for Mr Cor-
ton before I leave.'

'Then it is as well we do have a new man start-
ing tomorrow, if you are to be away.'

'I am quite taken up with Sir Bertram,' Henry
went on, discounting the argument that he never
did any of the practical work and had not done so
for many years. Not that he couldn't if he chose,
he was fond of telling her. 'He is young, twenty-
four, I believe, and besides having good pros-
pects, presents an altogether pleasant demeanour.'

'Papa, are you thinking what I think you are?
You promised not to matchmake.'

'Oh, I am not matchmaking, child, simply
pointing out his good points.'

'And you said you would cease to call me child.'

'I forgot,' he said blandly.

The more her father sang the praises of the various titled bachelors with whom he came into contact, the more determined she was to resist his efforts to marry her off. She was not ready for marriage, was not sure she ever would be if it meant surrendering her independence and giving up her part in running the business. When she fell in love would be time enough to consider that, but not before. *If* she fell in love. Perhaps she never would and a marriage without love was not to be borne. The matter of a title, in her eyes, was entirely irrelevant. Why, Captain Carstairs had no title, but she was convinced that he was every inch a gentleman.

Now, why had she suddenly thought of him? Was it because she had been talking to him only two hours before? Was it because of his masterly handling of the accident earlier that day? Was it his good looks and his easy manner? He had not paid her any particular attention beyond politeness and affability, no more than Viscount Leinster had and his lordship was a happily married man.

Alex rose early, intending to ride in Hyde Park before going to Gilpin's. He would have to leave his mount behind while he was in Norfolk and he would not have the pleasure of a gallop until he returned. Besides, Pegasus needed exercise.

The animal was well named. He carried Alex's weight easily and covered the ground almost as if he were flying. Alex loved the exhilaration and, once in the park, eschewed the usual bridleway and let him have his head. Although early, the day promised to be warm and sunny, a beautiful day for a ride. He was galloping across the rough grass towards a stand of trees when he noticed he was not the only one out early. A lady on a magnificent bay mare was galloping across the grass. She had a wonderful seat, at one with the horse, and was evidently enjoying the ride. He pulled up to watch her, wondering how long she could keep going before the animal decided he had had enough and threw her?

It was not the animal that forced her to pull up, but a horse and tumbril which suddenly appeared out of the trees as she was passing. Alex held his breath, expecting the worst, but she showed herself to be in full control of her mount. She pulled him up with a flurry of hooves and turned angrily on the man who had been driving the vehicle and who had jumped to the ground and taken hold of her bridle. She raised her crop and brought it down sharply on the man's hand, but he did not let go. And then another ruffian appeared and came round to the other side of her and attempted to edge her and her mount towards the cart, making the mare shy. Alex decided it behoved him to intervene.

He was riding without a sword, but he always carried a pistol in a holster on his saddle and he drew it as he approached at a gallop. He dare not fire for fear of hitting her, but the arrival of a man brandishing a gun was enough for the two men; they scrambled into the cart and urged it into a gallop. It was when he turned to go back to the rider that he realised the lady was Miss Gilpin.

He dismounted and ran to where the pale-faced lady still sat on her horse, which was standing perfectly still now.

He reached out to her and she slid from the mare and into his arms. He held her while she regained her breath, which was coming in great gasps. 'You are safe now,' he murmured. He could feel her heart beating hard against his chest, making him realise just how frightened she had been. She wasn't so mannish, after all. Her closeness, the way her body seemed to fit so snuggly into his, the scent of violets on her hair, was enough to send his senses reeling. It was years since he had held a woman like that and she was stirring passions in him which he had forgotten existed.

'Thank you,' she said when her breathing steadied and she drew away from him to look up at him. 'I do not know what I would have done if you had not been on hand.'

He looked down into her face, uplifted to his. Her lips were slightly parted and he was inexplicably tempted to kiss her, but thrust the temptation from him. 'I am glad that I was,' he said, trying to control his ragged breath enough to answer her. 'What did they want?'

'I don't know.' She was calmer now, but still pale, still in his arms. Until she moved, he would not put her from him. 'I have nothing on me worth taking, except my horse, of course. Do you suppose that was what they wanted? Amber is a valuable beast.'

'Perhaps,' he agreed, careful not to wonder aloud why they would bring a cart to steal a horse from someone still riding it, when it would have been easier to take it without a rider on its back. He felt sure it was the rider they were after. 'It was foolish of you to ride out alone. Have you no escort?'

'No. If any of the grooms come with me, they are so fearful for me, they stop me having a good gallop. Besides, at this time of day they are busy with all the other horses. I have never come to any harm.'

'Until now,' he said repressively.

'I am not hurt.'

'You might very well have been if I had not

come along. I have no doubt you could command a fair sum in ransom…'

'Ransom! Good heavens! Is that what you think?'

'It is a possibility—more than a possibility, I should think.' He paused, unwilling to frighten her more than she had been already, though she appeared to have recovered her poise remarkably quickly. 'Do you feel able to ride home?'

'Yes.' She stepped away from him. 'If you would be kind enough to help me mount.'

He fetched her horse and offered his cupped hands to lift her into the saddle and put her foot in the stirrup, and then mounted Pegasus, who had been patiently cropping the dry grass. 'Let us go, then.'

'Captain Carstairs,' she said, gathering up her reins. 'I would be obliged if you did not tell my father of this incident.'

They rode side by side at a gentle walk. 'Naturally I shall say nothing if you do not wish it, but you ought to tell him about those men yourself so that he can take suitable precautions in future. I will not always be on hand to rescue you.'

'No, I do not expect you to be. But if I tell Papa, he will have people guarding me all the time. He might even refuse to allow me to go to the works.'

'And that is important to you?'

'Very important, Captain. It is my life's work.'

'Oh, surely not. You must have other interests.'

'Of course I do. The orphans, for one, and I enjoy gardening and reading.'

'What do you like to read?'

'Everything. Scientific books, books about manufacturing and new ideas…'

'No novels? No poetry?'

She smiled. 'Those, too. I do not think of myself as a blue stocking, Captain.'

'Nevertheless, I want you to promise me you will not go out without an escort again.'

She looked sharply at him. 'Why should I make promises to you, Captain Carstairs? I really cannot think why you expect me to do so.'

'I know it is no business of mine what you do, but I should be sorry to think of you being abducted by the likes of those two. They would not treat you gently, you may be sure.'

'How do you know so much about it?'

'I have twice lately been engaged on kidnap cases for the Society. Desperate men do not hesitate to put an end to their victim's life if their demands are not met, and even sometimes if they are, if they think she can identify them. I should hate that to happen to you.'

'What was the outcome of your investigations, Captain?' she asked. 'Did you restore the victims to their families?'

He smiled, realising she was evading making the promise he asked for. 'One was returned safely to her parents without the ransom being paid because the kidnappers were foiled. The other had not been abducted, but had run away to Gretna Green with a lover. I had the devil's job to persuade her to go back home. The couple had been together for two or three days, so her father felt obliged to allow the marriage to go ahead.'

'A happy ending, then.'

'Who's to know? Her father had his reasons for refusing his consent in the first place and perhaps he was right. Only time will tell.'

'Are you always so cynical?'

'Not cynical, Miss Gilpin, simply a realist.'

'Then you do not think love lasts?'

'I am sure genuine love does, but recognising it when it comes, that is the hard part.'

'Oh, then you are a cynic.'

He was tired of her quizzing him, especially as she was getting very close to the bone, and decided to turn the tables. 'Have you ever been in love, Miss Gilpin?'

'Now that is a very personal question, but as you have been so kind as to rescue me and shown concern for my safety, I will answer you. No, I have never been in love, but I am sure I will recognise it when it comes.'

'But you must have had many suitors.'

'Money-grabbers, Captain, silly young fops who think my fortune will allow them to live in comfort without doing a hand's turn to earn it. I shall not marry one of them. Papa has had to work hard to build up the business and I would not have all that wasted on a ne'er-do-well. Gilpin's is far too important for that.'

He was silenced by this. Her father's business meant more to her than falling in love. Jonathan had been right; she would be hard to live with if that was all she cared about. But at least she was honest. Letitia had not been honest; she had led him on, knowing she was never going to accept him. He shook the memories from him and turned back to Miss Gilpin. She was riding steadily with no sign of the fright she must have had. Foolish and hoydenish she might be, but he found himself admiring her composure, which would have done credit to a duchess. 'Do you go home or to Long Acre?' he asked, as they left the park and rode along Tyburn Lane.

'Home to Piccadilly,' she said. 'I will slip indoors and change before joining my father for breakfast, then we will go to the Long Acre together as usual.'

They turned down beside Green Park and on to Piccadilly and thence to the mews. She pulled up as a groom came out to take her horse. Alex dismounted and held out his hands to help her down. 'Are you recovered?' he murmured, noticing her hands were still shaking a little.

'Yes, thank you. I will bid you good day now, Captain, but remember when you come to collect your carriage, say nothing of what occurred.'

He bowed. 'As you wish. But you must remember what I said about not going out alone. Having failed once, those men might try again.'

'I will remember.'

He remounted and rode back to Mount Street to change and have his own breakfast. He was more than a little worried by the episode with the two men. That they had intended an abduction he was fairly sure and if that were the case he thought they might try again and if Miss Gilpin was foolish enough to ride alone in the park, he could not answer for her safety. He wished wholeheartedly that he did not have to go to Norfolk. Why he was so bothered he did not know; Miss Gilpin was nothing to him and Henry Gilpin had funds enough to pay a dozen ransoms. And perhaps he was seeing trouble where none existed. He left Pegasus with Davy and went indoors.

Charlotte was far more shaken up over the episode that she liked to admit. Had those men really intended to kidnap her? Whatever would she have done if Captain Carstairs had not come along to scare them off? She had been so relieved to see him, she had fallen into his arms. How could she have been so blind to decorum as to let him hold her like that? They had stood so close, toe to toe, his arms encasing her so that she could hear his heartbeat against her ear. No one had ever held her like that before and the strange sensations it had produced in her body had altogether eclipsed the fright she had had. She had looked up into his face and wondered if he would kiss her. But of course, he had not; it would have been the height of impropriety and would certainly have soured their business relationship. That was more important than wondering what he thought about her and whether he knew the effect he had on her. Why did it matter? Because he had held her in his arms and set her heart racing? No doubt he would have rescued any young lady in the same danger. She was not special.

She breakfasted with her father and managed to chat about what the day held for them without saying a word about riding in Hyde Park. She hoped Captain Carstairs would keep his word and not give her away. She could not face any questions about that or any restrictions on her freedom. But she would take care to ask one of the grooms to ride behind her when she went riding in the park again.

* * *

Alex arrived at Long Acre promptly at noon where he found his new carriage had already been harnessed to a splendid pair of matched greys. It was a matter of a moment to transfer his baggage from the handcart he had hired into the boot of the carriage with the aid of the young lad who had pushed it there. He tipped the boy generously and sent him on his way before carefully inspecting the whole equipage, watched by Davy who had been brought along to drive it.

'It meets with your approval?' Henry queried after showing him the secret compartment.

'Most certainly. What say you, Davy?'

'As fine an outfit as ever you could meet, my... Captain,' he amended, catching a warning look from his master.

'Then let us go into the office and complete the transaction,' Henry said.

Alex followed Henry into the office where Charlotte sat at her desk. She was in the plain gown she had worn the day before, her hair was once more dragged back severely into a knot. Miss Gilpin at work was very different from Miss Gilpin at a concert. One was severely dressed in plainspun cloth with the minimum of padding, the other as elegant as any of the ladies of the *ton*, in a wide-skirted dress of heavy blue silk which emphasised a superb figure. It was almost as if she were two different people, three if you counted the hoyden who rode a horse many a man might find hard to handle.

She bade him good morning as if it were the first time they had met that day and he felt obliged to play along with that, asking her how she did and if she had enjoyed the concert the evening before. He was bidden to be seated while she completed the invoice. He watched her as her pen glided over the paper. She seemed composed, the ultimate businesswoman, but he noticed her hand shook a little and realised she was not impervious to him. Why that pleased him he did not know. She was most definitely out of bounds and the episode in Hyde Park was an aberration and he must not continue to dwell on it.

The horses, he discovered, when she handed him the invoice, cost as much as the coach, but he did not doubt they were worth it. Nor did he doubt that Gilpin had made more than a fair profit, but he did not begrudge him that. He was prepared to pay for quality, as so many others were, a fact testified by the man's success. Altogether his bill came to two hundred and forty pounds ten shillings. He filled in the full amount on the bill of exchange and gave it to Miss Gilpin, receiving a neat receipt.

Henry had been to a cupboard and extracted a bottle and two glasses. 'Will you join me in a drink to celebrate?' he said, pouring cognac. The man seemed utterly unaware of the dangerous currents passing between his customer and his daughter.

Alex took a glass of brandy from him and they stood toasting each other, watched by Charlotte, who found herself studying him again. Although he had changed his clothes, he was still wearing dark blue and white, but far from making him look sombre it emphasised his magnificent physique. She felt herself unwittingly remembering how she had stood enveloped in his arms and how warm and comfortable it had been and, afraid her rosy cheeks would betray her, hurriedly looked away.

His glass empty, Alex put it down, bowed to them both and took his leave, having promised to bring the coach back for servicing when it required it.

Davy was already on the box ready to drive off. 'Right, off to Briarcroft,' he told him. 'We will call on my mother first.'

Charlotte watched him go from the window, conscious of a feeling of anticlimax, of wishing she knew more about him. He had an air of aloofness and a cynicism that sat ill with his courtesy and compassion. He had ridden hard to save her from those men, then berated her for riding alone, as if it was any business of his. Just what was his business? She knew he was a seafaring captain and belonged to the Piccadilly Gentlemen, but that was all. He had vouchsafed nothing about his family. For all she knew he was married and had a brood of children. Would a man buying a travelling coach not include a wife in the transaction, if only by mentioning her tastes? He had done nothing like that. And he had arrived at Lady Milgrove's with Viscount Leinster when she would have expected him to bring his wife if he had one. But perhaps the wife lived in Norfolk and did not like town ways. What, she told herself sternly, had it got to do with her? She turned away from the window to answer a knock at the door. In answer to her 'Enter', a man in working garb and clutching a soft felt hat in his hand came in to stand before her.

He bowed his head. 'Miss Gilpin, I am Martin Grosswaite, here as promised. What would you like me to do?' He did not, as she expected, ask to see her father who was in the paint shop, where the artist they employed was about to begin putting a coat of arms on a chaise before it was varnished. She surmised her father had told him to speak to her.

She entered his particulars in the register she kept for employees and then conducted him to the upper floor to be introduced to the head carpenter and set to work. Then she went thoughtfully back to her office. Martin Grosswaite had been perfectly polite and had answered her questions in a straightforward manner, but there was something about him that troubled her. It might have been his craggy face, but she was not one to be disturbed by ill looks, or it might have been his pale eyes, which darted about as he spoke and never once looked directly at her. It made her feel uncomfortable.

She shook her foolish thoughts from her; he had been nervous and anxious to please, that was all, and if he did not please it was easy enough to dismiss him. And with that thought she sat down at her desk and pulled the sales ledger towards her.

Chapter Three

'Alex! I had not expected you.' Mrs Carstairs greeted her son with a huge smile of pleasure and rushed across the drawing room to reach up and put her arms about his broad shoulders. 'I thought you had gone to Norfolk.'

'I shall go tomorrow, Mama. It is only a few miles out of my way to call here first.' He bent to kiss her cheek. 'I wondered if you might like to come with me. I have no notion what to expect when I get to Foxlees, a welcome or otherwise, and should be glad of your advice when it comes to household matters.' Seeing her hesitate, he paused. 'Are you engaged for the next week or so? If so, it is of no consequence, I can go alone.'

'Nothing that cannot be put off. Oh, Alex, I should dearly like to see Foxlees. But how shall we travel? My carriage is not up to so long a journey.'

'I have bought a chaise and a pair of fine horses to pull it. We shall travel very comfortably.'

'Oh, I shall like that above everything.' She clapped her gloved hands in delight. She was a tiny woman, a little plump, made more so by the stuffing she wore on her hips and the flounces on her sleeves. She looked frail, but her looks deceived; she had been used to travelling backwards and forwards to India with her late husband and thought nothing of rough seas and sweltering heat. A carriage ride into Norfolk would certainly not put her in a quake. She hurried away to give instructions for her bags to be packed, Alex's bed to be made up and supper to be served for two.

Over the meal she demanded to know what he had been up to in town.

'Nothing of any note, Mama. I finalised my inheritance with my uncle's lawyer, attended a meeting of the Piccadilly Gentleman's Club and I went to Gilpin's to buy a carriage. Do you know the business is half-run by Gilpin's daughter? I was quite taken aback when she insisted on seeing to my needs herself.'

'I hope you were not gulled.'

'Gulled by a slip of a girl, Mama, how can you think it? I inspected the vehicle very carefully before agreeing to buy it. It was dear, but I think worth it. Gilpin's has an excellent reputation for quality.'

'Did you not go to any dances or routs where you might meet people of the *ton*?'

'I went to a concert with Leinster in aid of the Foundling Hospital.'

'Pah! You will not find a bride doing that.'

'Mama, I am not looking for a bride.'

'How can you say so? Alex, you are a marquis now, not a roving sea captain, and it behoves you to wed and start a family. I should very much like grandchildren.'

'There is plenty of time for that.'

'I do believe you are still pining for that minx, Letitia.'

'No, Mama, I am not.' It was said firmly and brooked no argument.

'There is no point in any case,' she went on, determined to have the last word. 'I had heard that the Earl of Falsham is now a widower and looking for a second wife.'

This was news to Alex and he spent a silent moment or two contemplating it and wondering why he felt nothing more than sorrow that a young life should have been lost. 'I am sorry

for that,' he said. 'Do you know how the Countess died?'

'Giving birth to a daughter, so I heard. The
Earl was said to be very vexed that the child was
not a son. I heard he had gone abroad to escape
his creditors.'

'It is my opinion that there is too much importance put on begetting heirs,' he said, glad that
he would not have to encounter the gentleman. 'I
hope I should not be vexed if my wife produced
a daughter and not a son. I should be happy if
they were both healthy.'

She laughed. 'Just now you insisted you were
not looking for a wife.'

'Nor am I.' He paused. 'How long will it take
you to pack?'

She recognised the deliberate changing of the
subject and smiled. 'Now, Alex, how can you ask
such a question? How many times have I had to
pack to go off to India or the West Indies or the
China seas at a moment's notice? I am an expert
and so is Betty, who is even now putting a few
things in a trunk. I hope the carriage you bought
can accommodate one trunk.'

'It can, Mama, easily. Shall you come out
when we have finished our supper and see for
yourself? There is still enough daylight left.'

Briarcroft was a simple country mansion,
bought with money his father had made on the

first two or three of his cargoes, against the day
when he would give up the sea and retire. Since
his death, his mother had lived there quietly but
happily and Alex often stayed there with her. It
had been his bolt hole when he came back to England after that disastrous affair with Letitia and
it was still the place he came to when he needed
respite. He wondered if Foxlees Manor would
ever take its place.

When he saw it two days later, he doubted it.
Knowing his uncle and cousin had rarely visited
it since his aunt's death and forewarned by the
lawyer, he had expected it to be shabby, but the
extent of the dereliction was shocking. It was
not a large mansion and did not have a park-
land, but extensive gardens which had once been
well cared for, but which were now tangled and
overgrown. The gravel carriage drive was full
of weeds and the house, when they came upon
it, had a neglected air. Ivy clung to its walls and
had invaded the windows. The paint was scuffed,
the door knocker rusty.

'Alex, this is dreadful,' his mother said, as he
helped her down and she stood in the drive to
look up at the façade. 'You could never bring a
bride here. She would die of mortification.'

She was so transparent it made him smile,
but he decided not to comment and went up the

moss-covered stone steps and unlocked the door with the key he had been given.

'Are there no servants?' she asked, preceding him into a dark vestibule that smelled fusty.

'There is a steward and a housekeeper, both of whom live in the village. The lawyer said they would not live here after my uncle died. The rest of the servants moved on long ago.'

'And I, for one, do not blame them.' She was making her way down the hall as she spoke and threw open a door. 'This must be the drawing room.' She strode forwards and flung back the heavy brocade curtains. They fell to pieces in her hands and dust flew everywhere. 'Alex, you surely do not expect me to sleep here tonight?'

'No, Mama, we will go to the village inn, where I will leave you to have some refreshment and a rest while I go in search of the steward.' He laughed suddenly. 'To think my friends in the Piccadilly Gentleman's Club congratulated me on my inheritance. I fear it is like to be a millstone.'

They inspected the rest of the house. It was no better that the drawing room. They returned downstairs and made their way to be kitchen area, where Davy was endeavouring to light a fire in order to boil a kettle. The room was full of smoke.

'Leave it, Davy,' he said. 'The chimneys will have to be swept and all the doors and windows left open to air the place. I am going to take Mrs Carstairs to the local inn and root out the steward. Have you unharnessed the horses?'

'No, sir…my lord. There's no fodder for them, though I've given them a drink.'

'Sir will do very well, Davy, thank you. I will drive my mother to the inn. You stay here and see what needs doing.'

'Everything, sir,' was said with a grin.

'I know. Make a list, most urgent first. I will be back betimes.'

Fortunately the local hostelry was a coaching inn, standing on the cross roads of a substantial village a mile or two inland from Cromer. The coach and horses were led away to be looked after while Alex escorted his mother indoors and requested his best room for her.

'Certainly sir,' the innkeeper said, then turned and flung orders to his employees who were standing around gaping with curiosity. 'I didn't reckon you'd want to stay up at the Manor.'

'How did you know I was bound there?'

'Why, Mr Boniface said the new owner was expected at any time and my son, Arthur, saw the carriage in the village going towards the rise at a spanking pace. We don't get equipages like that hereabouts very often.'

'Where can I find Mr Boniface?'

'He'll have heard you've arrived,' the man said. 'And will no doubt be on his way to the Manor as we speak.'

Alex made sure his mother and her maid were comfortable, then left them to hurry back to the house on foot, which had half the population out of their doors to see him pass. He smiled, bowed this way and that and continued on his way.

He found Davy in the yard in deep conversation with a man in a black coat and black small clothes. He wore a black three-cornered hat over a dark tie wig. He introduced himself as William Boniface, apologising profusely for not being there to greet him on his arrival. If he had been notified of the day and time, he certainly would have been.

'Yes, to be sure,' Alex said. 'It is no matter. But tell me all you can about the house and grounds. It is sadly neglected.'

'It is that, my lord, and sorry I am for it, but the old marquis turned his back on it after his wife died and would not spend a penny to keep it in order. He did not seem to care that it might fall into disrepair, for all he had a son who expected to inherit. The young master seemed of the same mind and now, of course…' He shrugged. 'What do you plan to do, my lord?'

'It can't be left as it is, that is certain. It is hardly habitable.'

'Do you wish to live in it, my lord?'

'I may when I am not in town or I may let it. In either event it will have to be restored. Let us inspect it properly and you may make notes as we go. Davy, you come, too. You may see things I miss.'

All three trooped indoors. Davy had drawn all the blinds back and opened all the windows, which allowed a cool breeze from the German Ocean to blow away some of the stuffiness. They moved from room to room and Mr Boniface covered sheets and sheets of paper with his spidery scrawl. The conclusion they all reached was that it was a solid building and the neglect, though unsightly, was superficial.

'Draw up a proper list of what needs doing and how much it will cost,' Alex told the much-relieved steward. 'I shall stay at the Five Bells for the next few days until it can be made habitable.'

'Very well, sir. Shall I consult her ladyship over the interior decoration and the furnishings?'

'Her ladyship?' Alex queried.

'The marchioness, my lord. I believe she is at the Five Bells.'

Alex laughed. 'There, the gossip has failed you, Mr Boniface. The lady at the Five Bells is

my mother, not my wife. There is no marchioness at present.'

'I beg your pardon, my lord,' he said hastily. 'I
only meant that the house will undoubtedly benefit from the attention of a mistress.'

'You are forgiven.' Alex smiled and the embarrassed man relaxed visibly, before taking his
leave to set about the task he had been given.
Alex went round the house again and found himself imagining what it might be like when it was
restored. There would be new carpets and curtains, new furniture and bed hangings, ornaments
and pictures. It could become a comfortable family home, a fine place to bring up children. He
chuckled to himself, wondering what his mother
would say if he shared that thought with her,
probably something like 'Didn't I tell you so?'
or 'About time, too!'

He left Davy inspecting the wainscoting in the
dining room for woodworm and went out into the
garden, if that tangle of weeds and overgrown
shrubs could be called a garden. A gardener was
another need, probably more than one. He had
a feeling that restoring this house was going to
eat up nearly all his savings. He wandered down
what had once been a terrace and across a stretch
of grass, past a shrubbery and a kitchen garden
to the far boundary. From here he could hear and
smell the sea. He breathed deeply. Yes, it would

do, it would do very well. He turned in the direction of the village to rejoin his mother.

Almost two weeks passed before Charlotte watched her father set off for Oxfordshire, the carriage piled so high with his luggage, drawings, models, samples of wood, cloth, leather and braid, there was hardly room for him to squeeze in. Then she turned and went back to the office to work until it was time to go home. When all the men had gone, she would have to check the building to make sure there were no naked flames or glowing embers anywhere to constitute a hazard. Fire insurance companies would not cover the premises on account of all the flammable materials kept there; her father had exhorted her to be extra careful.

He had also told her not to walk home alone, but to ask one of the men to escort her. She did not like to do that; the men had all done a long day's work and would be anxious to go home to their suppers. Only Martin Grosswaite remained and, for some reason she could not explain, she would not ask him to accompany her. 'If you will not let me escort you,' he said, 'permit me to fetch a chair. At least that way you will be safe from molestation.' She agreed it was the sensible thing to do and while he was gone, had a last look round before locking up. Everything was as it should be.

The chair arrived very quickly so Martin must have found one close at hand. She climbed in and directed the chairmen to take her to Piccadilly. It had been a busy day and what with her father being intent on his journey, she had been left very much to her own devices and that meant walking round the various workshops making sure the men were working as they should, meeting customers who had come to collect their vehicles and keeping her ledgers up to date. She was very tired, but it was a satisfied kind of tiredness and she was looking forward to having a couple of the maids fill a bath in her room so that she could soak the tiredness from her. That it was considered eccentric to bath so frequently did not deter her. Having no company, she might ask Barbara, her maid, to join her for supper afterwards.

It was several minutes before she realised she was not being taken to Piccadilly. The chairmen had turned down a dark alley and were trotting at a pace that was bone-shaking. She put her head outside and commanded them to stop. They ignored her; if anything, their pace increased. She shouted at them again, but it soon became evident that they had no intention of obeying her. Now she was very frightened indeed. Where were they taking her? And why? Captain Carstairs's warning came to her mind. She was being kidnapped!

After several more minutes, they stopped outside a dilapidated tenement and let down the chair. She hurried to open the door to escape, but they had anticipated that and grabbed her arms and dragged her, protesting loudly, into the building, along a corridor which was dark as pitch and into a candle-lit room, where a woman rose from a chair to face them. 'You got her, then?'

'We did, Molly, we did. 'Twas as easy as winking, though she made a deal of noise.' He was a big man with a weatherbeaten face, a moulting bag wig and bad teeth. He was also the man who had grabbed her bridle in Hyde Park. Captain Carstairs had been right in saying they might try again. Oh, how she wished she had listened to him. But he had said nothing about not hiring a chair and how was she to know the kidnappers would use that ruse?

'And I shall continue to do so until you take me home,' Charlotte snapped at him.

His answer was to push her into a chair. His companion, smaller but no less unprepossessing, produced a rope and they proceeded to tie her down. She struggled ineffectually, and when his hand strayed too close to her mouth bit it as hard as she could. He snatched it away and swore.

'And for that, you will pay extra,' he yelled and stuffed a dirty piece of rag into her mouth.

She almost choked and had to force herself to breathe evenly through her nose, but assumed from his words that she had been kidnapped for a ransom. Though the thought of spending a second longer in the company of these three was anathema, it gave her a little hope. Her father, hearing of their demand, would undoubtedly pay to have her safely restored to him. And then she remembered her father was from home. Would Barbara have the good sense to alert someone that she was missing? Or would she be kept here until her kidnappers were able to contact her father? Would he be able to trace her movements through the chair she had taken? Would he think of that? Oh, if only someone would come to her rescue!

'Mama, I am summoned back to town,' Alex said, studying a letter the mail had brought to the Five Bells. It had been marked urgent and the landlord had sent the potboy up to the Manor with it. 'I am needed to solve another kidnapping. It appears Miss Gilpin has disappeared, most likely abducted.'

'Oh, how dreadful for her,' she said. 'But can no one else be asked to look for her?'

They had left the Five Bells to move into a

part of the Manor that had been made habitable and were in the morning room, drinking the tea Davy had made for them. The chimneys had been swept and the house cleaned by an army of women he had hired from the village, supervised by the butler and housekeeper, Mr and Mrs Wharton, who were now back in residence. There was still a great deal to be done. The whole house needed painting, ill-fitting doors needed replacing, rattling windows must be refitted and reglazed and new carpets, curtains, furniture and kitchen utensils purchased. Apart from one or two good quality items of furniture and some pictures and ornaments, the rest would have to go. When all was done, he must decide how many servants he needed, but that could wait until the work was finished and Mrs Wharton would see to the hiring of them.

'Lord Leinster has been making preliminary enquiries,' he answered his mother. 'but I have done this kind of thing before and James thinks I am the best person to undertake the task'

'Do they know who has her?'

'No, that is for me to discover. Mama, do you wish me to leave you here, or shall you go home? I can take you if you do, but you must be ready to leave in an hour.'

'I shall be ready. I do not want to stay here without you. This is your home, not mine, and I miss my little cat, and the church. But can you leave the refurbishment here unattended?'

'It is not urgent. Mr Boniface and Mr and Mrs Wharton will carry the work forward in my absence. I will return as soon as I have Miss Gilpin safely back with her father.'

Mrs Carstairs hurried to tell her maid to pack as quickly as possible and stayed to help her, while Alex sent a man ahead on horseback to bespeak post horses. He had come to Foxlees at a leisurely pace, using the same horses throughout, but he was in too much haste to return the same way. The greys would be sent back to the Manor from their first stop and the new groom would look after them until he returned. After that he went round the house with Mr Wharton, pointing out things that needed to be done in his absence. Within the hour they were on their way.

Alex sat back in the coach, glad that he had purchased a well-built vehicle because Davy was driving at a spanking pace and they were being thrown from side to side over the bumpy roads.

'Mama, is the jolting too much for you?' he asked. 'Shall I have Davy slow down?'

'No, I know you are in a hurry. Do not mind me.'

'Betty?' he queried, addressing the maid.

Betty was looking very white, but she managed a wan smile. 'I wish only for the journey to be over, my lord, so by all means make haste.'

Alex sank back into his seat, contemplating the task ahead of him. The letter had said nothing about how Miss Gilpin had been kidnapped, nor if there had been a ransom letter. It was usually the ransom letter that furnished the first clue about where a kidnapped victim was being held. Without one the case would be doubly difficult.

He found himself wondering how Miss Gilpin had come to be taken. Had she gone out alone after his warning about the dangers? How he wished he had defied her wishes and told Henry Gilpin what had happened in Hyde Park. He felt a surge of guilt that he had not done so, for if he had, her father would have made sure she was always escorted and she might not now be in the hands of abductors.

He found himself imagining all manner of horrors: Miss Gilpin manhandled, struck perhaps, even molested. He shuddered at the thought of that beautiful, proud, self-assured woman being subjected to that. His heart went out to her and he felt the anger bubble inside him, not only anger for her abductors, but anger at Henry Gilpin. The man had more or less abandoned her at Lady Milgrove's concert, which both he and Jonathan had thought was strange. She would have come to no harm there, but was it an example of the off-hand way he had of dealing with his daughter? Did he think she could be treated like a son? Alex smiled inwardly at that; Miss Gilpin herself would undoubtedly accept that as her due, even been glad of it. He would wager she was not feeling glad now. She would be frightened, unless, of course she had manufactured the abduction herself, perhaps to meet a lover who did not meet her father's strict provisos.

Could they have taken themselves off to Gretna Green, where the law requiring three weeks' notice of a marriage at the churches of both bride and groom did not apply? It would not be the first time he had chased after a kidnap victim to discover she had not been kidnapped, but had run away. Somehow he did not think that would apply to Miss Gilpin. He thought she would always face up to her problems. What did apply? His brain went round and round all the possibilities and he wished the coach could take to the air and fly.

'You are very worried about her, are you not?' his mother interrupted his thoughts.

'Yes. I cannot help feeling guilty. I foresaw what might happen and I did nothing to prevent it.'

'How could you have prevented it? You were not even there.'

Alex explained what had happened in Hyde

Park. 'I felt sure they would try again and I begged Miss Gilpin not to go out alone any more.'

'If she did not heed your advice, that is surely not your fault. She is a veritable hoyden by the sound of it.'

'She is opinionated and independent, that is true, but she is still a young woman and deserving of protection.'

'Then it behoves her father to provide it.'

He could not argue against that and fell silent as his imagination painted lurid pictures of what Miss Gilpin might be going through and that was interspersed with memories of the warmth of her body against his when he had rescued her before. He had not thought her a hoyden at that moment.

'You will find her, I am sure,' his mother said.

'I sincerely hope so, but kidnappers are not gentlemen, Mama, and I fear for her.'

'You have told me she is very competent and is in the way of running the Gilpin works. Perhaps she will find a way of effecting her own release?'

'I hope she may not attempt it,' he said. 'The consequences could be fatal.'

'I think perhaps your heart is ruling your head at the moment, Alex.'

He looked sharply at her. 'My heart has nothing to do with it.'

'No?'

'No.'

'If you say so.' It was said with a smile that told him she did not believe him.

Of course his heart was not engaged. He had only met Miss Gilpin four times and two of those had been at the works where their encounter had been strictly businesslike. At Lady Milford's Jonathan had been with him and the conversation had not been personal at all. Even so, he had learned a little of her character and temperament. She was lovely, far more so than he had at first supposed; she had strong views on many subjects and was not afraid of voicing them, but there was a soft side to her which showed in her sympathy with the children at the Foundling Hospital and her wish to do something for them. And the workers at the Gilpin business clearly respected her, even loved her. Joe Smithson worshipped her. Their only other encounter had been in Hyde Park and that meeting had been so dramatic, it hardly signified. Or did it?

The coach slowed and turned into the yard of an inn for their first change of horses. As soon as the wheels stopped turning Davy jumped down and went in search of the ostler and the fresh horses. Alex got out to stretch his cramped legs.

'Mama, do you wish to take a turn about the yard while the horses are changed?'

They had not long had luncheon and no one needed refreshment and so she declined, saying perhaps she would do so at their next stop or the one after that. The horses were changed in double quick time and they were off again, rattling through the countryside at a cracking pace, overtaking everything on the road, much to Davy's delight.

It was very late and quite dark when they arrived back at Briarcroft. Alex would not stay after he had seen his mother and Betty safely indoors, but continued on into the night. With two passengers and their luggage gone, the coach was lighter and they went even faster. Alex was glad he had arranged for the horses to be changed every twelve miles; it meant they were always fresh, though he dreaded to think how much the journey was costing him.

He had arrived back in town just as dawn was breaking and gone straight to the Mount Street house to change from country attire to something more befitting the town and hurriedly eaten some breakfast before making his way to the Gilpin works on foot. Early as it was, Henry was already there and hurried forward to meet him. 'Thank God, you have come,' he said, forgetting to bow or even shake Alex by the hand. 'I am at my wits' end.' He almost dragged Alex into the office where he fetched out the cognac bottle and glasses. 'I was away for a few days visiting a new customer in Oxfordshire and left Charlotte in charge. She has done it before without the least trouble. I came back as soon as I received the message she was missing, but the roads are infernally bad and we were held up by heavy rain and post horses were hard to come by. It took me over two days.'

'Tell me what happened.'

'I don't know what happened, that's the truth of it. The last anyone saw of her was when they bade her goodnight at the end of the day and went home, leaving her to lock up before going home herself.'

'Alone?' Alex asked.

'I told her to make sure one of the men accompanied her.'

'And would she have obeyed you?'

'Naturally she would. She may be outspoken, but she is a dutiful daughter none the less.'

Alex thought of the encounter in the park and doubted it, but kept his thoughts to himself. 'Which of the men was it?'

'I cannot be sure, but I think it was Martin Grosswaite.'

'And what has he to say for himself?'

'I don't know. No one has seen him since.'

'Tell me about him. How long has he been with you? Is he trustworthy?'

By the time Henry had answered, it had become very obvious that Martin Grosswaite had to be found and found quickly. Alex had every employee in the place come to the office one by one and interrogated them about what they knew of Grosswaite, if they had met him before he came to work there, had he said anything about his background, wife, family, where he lived, was he a good craftsman, one that might have been employed in another works—anything to give him a start on his investigation.

He learned very little. The man had once been employed as a servant to an earl, he had boasted, but he had not vouchsafed the earl's name. His carpentry skills were basic; he was certainly not up to anything intricate and they wondered why he had been taken on. On the other hand he was willing and did not mind spending his time sweeping up wood shavings or fetching them ale and a bite for their mid-day meal. He toadied to Miss Gilpin, too, but in their opinion, the young lady was too fly to take any notice of that. They did not know that he had been asked to escort her home. No, they hadn't seen him leave the premises with her. She was just as likely to have sent him home and gone off alone. And, yes, the premises were safely locked up when they came in to work next day and they had to send to Joe Smithson for the spare keys to get in. Alex gained the impression they thought Miss Gilpin too independent by far, though none had said it aloud.

'He did tell me that he had a wife and family when he came to ask for employment,' Henry told him when they were once more alone.

'Did he say where?'

'No, but he might have told Charlotte. She keeps details of all our employees.'

'Then let us see what he told her.'

Henry fetched the register which had Grosswaite's direction clearly written in Charlotte's neat handwriting. 'Southwark,' Alex murmured. 'I think I shall have to pay the family a visit.'

'I've done that,' Henry said, resentful that the Captain had assumed he had been doing nothing to find his daughter. 'No one there has heard of anyone by that name. I have ridden all over town trying to find her and sent men out, too, but as they have no idea where to look it has been a vain exercise. I remembered you and Viscount Leinster talking about the Piccadilly Gentleman's Club and so I went to see his lordship. He asked all the questions you have asked and received the same answers and, as he had to leave town on business, he recommended I should speak to Lord Drymore and his lordship vouchsafed to send for you. I pray you can find her for me. My daughter is the light of my life. I'll pay anything, anything to get her back safe and sound.'

'But there has been no ransom letter?'

'No. If they want money, why have they not asked for it?'

'I think, sir, they are waiting until you are in despair and at your lowest ebb before making demands. It is to make you more amenable.' He paused. 'She could not have gone off willingly, could she? A lover, perhaps.'

'Certainly not!' Henry was outraged. 'She could have no possible reason for such a course of action.'

'She might have thought you would not approve of her choice.'

'There was never any question of that. Charlotte has never shown the least interest in any young man, suitable or otherwise. Only the other day she said she did not think she would marry.'

'So you have discussed it?'

'Naturally we discussed it. She is two-and-twenty years old and it is time she thought about it. I am a wealthy man, she could have the pick of any eligible bachelor she chose.'

Alex smiled wryly. 'But supposing the bachelor disliked the idea of being bought?'

'Then he would be a fool.'

Alex let that go without comment. 'Then if we can discount an elopement, we are left with two possibilities: either Miss Gilpin has met with an accident and is lying in some hospital somewhere or she has been abducted.' He did not mention a third possibility that she might have been murdered. It did not bear thinking about and Alex would not think about it, not until every other avenue had been explored.

'I have been to all the hospitals. I even went round the wards myself in case she was unconscious and could not tell them who she was. It was not a pleasant experience and I wonder anyone ever recovers from the treatment, never mind whatever it was that took them there in the first place. No, I am of the mind that she has been kidnapped. Lord Drymore told me you had experience in that kind of case and would be the best man for the task.'

'I will certainly do my best. I suggest you insert an advertisement in the newspapers, offering a reward for anyone coming forwards with information. It is long odds, but it might flush out the kidnapper's associates. Have you questioned Miss Gilpin's maid? I assume she does have a maid or a companion?'

'Yes, of course she does, but Barbara never accompanied her to the works because I always took her and there would have been nothing for her to do here all day.'

'How trustworthy is she?'

'She has been with the family ever since Charlotte was a baby. They are very fond of each other. She is as distraught as I am.'

'Nevertheless, I should like to question her. Do you give me permission for that?'

'Yes, yes, question whom you like. I'll give you a note for her so that she knows she is to answer all your questions truthfully.' He went to his desk and drew a piece of paper towards him. Alex watched him write, then fold the letter and put the direction on the outside. 'I will be obliged if you will keep me informed of how you are progressing at every stage.'

Alex took the letter. 'I will leave you now and get to work, but if you receive a ransom note, have it brought round to my house immediately. Do not try to deal with it yourself. You might put your daughter in danger of her life if you do.'

'What can I do? Surely I can do something? I am in such a turmoil...'

'I understand. Try to go on as usual, but keep your eyes and ears open and let me know if you hear anything, anything at all, however insignificant it might seem.'

'I will do that.'

Alex had taken his leave and gone to Piccadilly, where he had questioned Barbara and the other servants, learning nothing new, but he was given a miniature of Charlotte, which was a good likeness. He had then headed home to Mount Street, where Davy had unpacked his belongings and instructed the cook to prepare food. He bade Davy join him for the meal in order to acquaint him with developments while they ate. 'If Miss Gilpin was lifted off the streets, then someone must have seen it happen,' he said. 'Long Acre is a busy thoroughfare, people are passing up and down all the time, not only during the day but at night, too.'

'That's just it,' Davy said. 'They are passing by and may not do so again for a month of Sundays. A kidnapper would know that. And she may not have been on foot. Supposing she hired a cab or a chair. Plenty of those about.'

'I had the same thought myself. I want you to check all the chairmen in the area. Ask if someone fitting Miss Gilpin's description hired one of their chairs.'

'What, all of them?' Davy queried.

'All of them. Don't miss any out. I'll go to the cab people. We will meet here again at…' He glanced at the clock on the mantel. '…six o'clock.'

'You need to sleep, my lord. You did not go to bed last night.'

Alex laughed. 'Neither did you. I shall sleep when I know what has happened to Miss Gilpin.' He had until this point been businesslike, treating the case as he would any other, questioning

Gilpin and his employees, searching out the facts, not allowing emotion to come into it at all, but suddenly he let his imagination run away with him and realised she was not like any other, she was someone he knew and admired and finding her was engaging his heart as well as his head. His mother had said as much and he had dismissed it, but it was not so easily dismissed.

Chapter Four

Charlotte had decided that shouting at her captors and struggling would not serve. If she was to free herself, she would have to be more wily than that. On her promise that she would not scream, they removed the filthy gag. She took huge lungfuls of air, though the atmosphere in the room was foetid.

'What are you going to do with me?' she had asked the older of the two men. His name, she learned from Molly, was Hector Ballard. His features were craggy and what teeth he still retained were brown from the tobacco he chewed. His long black hair was lank and looked as though it had not seen a brush or comb for months. He wore fustian breeches and wool stockings and a coat that had once been black, but which now had a green sheen about it. His companion was younger, but no less unprepossessing, and answered to the name of Bert. She did not think for a moment that they were the brains behind her abduction.

They came and went, leaving Molly to be her gaoler. The woman brought her food and small beer which was so unappetising she had, at first, refused it. Molly had simply shrugged and taken it away again and in the end, faint from hunger, Charlotte had accepted the next meal and forced some of it down. She drank the beer because she was so thirsty and it was safer than water, but she did not like the taste.

'All in good time, miss, all in good time.' Hector was the one who did the talking; Bert was the silent one, but she feared him the most.

'My father will be worried to death.'

'All the better.'

'What is this place?'

''Tis Molly's house.'

'Where?'

'Now what d'you want to know that for? Thinking of making a bolt for it, are you? You won't get far if you try that. We'll tie you up even more secure. 'Sides, we don't aim to stay here very long.'

'Then where are you taking me?'

'You'll just hatta wait and see, won't you?'

Four days later they had a visitor. It was Martin Grosswaite. He breezed in, greeted Molly and the two men and sat down to eat with them. Charlotte, who had already decided the man must have played a part in her abduction and was not surprised to see him, was left on some sacking in the corner where a plate of the most unappetising mess was put on the floor beside her. She pretended to eat while straining her ears to hear what they were saying.

'We'll send the note off tonight,' Martin Grosswaite said. 'Have you got the pen and paper?'

'Yes,' Molly told him. 'And you owe me for it and the food she's had.'

'You'll get it when we're all paid.'

'When will that be?'

'When my gaffer pays me.'

'Who's he?'

Martin laughed. 'Do you think I'll tell you that? He won't be named and the less you know the better.'

So Grosswaite was not the man behind her abduction, he was being paid. Charlotte did not doubt that he had wormed his way into the Gilpin works for the sole purpose of kidnapping her. In the two weeks he had been working there, he could have observed her habits and knew she would stay behind to lock up and, in the absence of her father, might be persuaded to take a chair home, which he undoubtedly had waiting close by. Oh, how she wished she had listened to Captain Carstairs and been more cautious. She had never liked Grosswaite and should have obeyed her instinct not to trust him.

After the men had eaten, she was hauled to her feet and dragged to the table where a space had been made among the dirty crockery and the remains of the food for a sheet of paper, pen and ink. 'Now,' Grosswaite said, pushing her down into a chair, 'you write what I tell you. I can read so there's no writing anything else.'

He pushed the pen into her hand. 'Dear Papa,' he began dictating. 'I am in good health as I write and being treated well. If you wish to see me again on this earth, then bring five hundred guineas to…' He paused and looked at Hector.

'The Waterman hard by the Lambeth ferry,' Hector said.

'Write that,' Hector told Charlotte.

'And will I be safely exchanged for the money?' she asked, her brain whirling with the idea of sending her father a coded message, but what could she tell him? She had no idea where she was, though she did not think she had come far in the chair and she could smell the river.

'If you behave yourself. If not…' Grosswaite drew his finger across his throat. 'Bring it at ten in the evening and be sure to come alone. You will be watched.'

She wrote as he dictated. 'This is very impersonal,' she said as she finished it. 'How will he know it has come from me? Anyone could have penned it.'

'Does he not know your writing?'

'To be sure, but my hand is shaking so much, it is not like my writing at all. Ought I not to include something that only he can know about me?'

He stroked the stubble on his chin. She surmised he was growing a beard in order to disguise himself. 'You have a point. Write something so that he knows the letter comes from you, but don't you try any funny business. It won't avail you if you do, for we do not intend to keep you here beyond tomorrow.'

Thinking quickly, she dipped her pen in the ink again and added, 'Give my best regards to Aunt Rivers and tell her not to worry and please send someone for the brooch I left with Mr Bridges to be repaired. It has to be fetched tomorrow for he told me he would not be at home after that. Your affectionate daughter, Charlotte. '

He picked it up and scanned what she had written. 'Who's this Aunt Rivers?'

'She is the lady who brought me up after my mother died,' she told him, hoping he would not know that her aunt had died two years before and her name had not been Rivers.

'And what's so important about this brooch?'

'It is very valuable and I do not wish it to be left on Mr Bridge's premises when he is from home.' She held her breath, praying he would not ask Mr Bridge's direction, but he seemed satisfied and folded the paper before putting it into his pocket.

'Who is Aunt Rivers?' Alex asked Henry Gilpin. Having received a message from Henry requesting him to call on him urgently, he had taken the carriage to the Gilpin works, pretending it needed a small repair. If he was seen coming and going, he wanted a valid reason for it.

'I have no idea.'

'And the brooch?' he asked, putting Charlotte's letter to his nose and sniffing. It smelled of fish and faintly of violets, which reminded him of their encounter in Hyde Park. Why had she not taken to heart his warning that the men might try again?

'I know of no brooch needing repair, though that's not to say there isn't one, but why would she trouble herself to mention it in a ransom letter? Do you think she is trying to tell us something?'

'Oh, undoubtedly,' he said, full of admiration for the lady. To have such a cool head when she must be frightened out of her wits was courageous to say the least. 'I deduce she is not far from the river, probably close to one of the bridges, but she is being moved today if this letter was written yesterday.'

'London Bridge or Westminster?'

'I would not think either. The ferrymen call their landing stages bridges.'

'But there are dozens of those,' Henry said in dismay.

'Yes, but we will start with Lambeth, though I doubt the kidnappers would leave so obvious a clue. I must get to work. If I cannot locate her before tonight, you must have the money ready to take as instructed.'

'I think I would as soon do that anyway. Five hundred guineas is not so very much for a beloved daughter and I would willingly pay it to have her safely back.'

'I can understand that, Mr Gilpin, but we cannot be sure the abductors will play fair with you. Do not attempt to meet them alone. Wait until I can be on hand to watch proceedings and intervene at the appropriate time.' He did not tell the man that it was often the case that kidnappers took the money and murdered their victim anyway, especially if they thought she might be able to identify them and bring retribution down on their heads. He had to protect her from that fate, even if Mr Gilpin lost his money in the process.

'If I can locate her and effect a rescue before that time, so much the better. I will leave you now. When I have news for you, I will come to collect my coach. Please find some little fault with it that you must repair. You never know who is watching and noting if you have sent for help.'

With that he bowed his way out, rejoining Davy who had been left outside to keep watch. 'Did you see anything out of the ordinary?'

'No, my lord, but that's just it. This street is so busy, there's people and vehicles going up and down all the time. It will be worse when the theatres open. Anyone could be watching without us knowing.'

'True. We will proceed on the assumption that Mr Gilpin is being watched.'

'Not you, my lord?'

'No, why would they bother with someone who is naught but a customer? And I will have less of your "my lord", if you please. You always used to address me as "sir" and I wish you to continue to do so. I have done nothing to earn such an illustrious title.'

'Very well—sir. Where next, sir?'

'Home to change into working clothes. We have to go into the stews and I wish to blend in with the other inhabitants.'

'You mean you want us to dress in those horrible rags we wore to flush out that last lot of thieves, is that it?' The clothes had been so ragged and stiff with dirt that even Davy, who was used to the lower end of shipboard life, was repelled. He had wanted to burn them when they finished with them, but Alex had said they might well come in useful again.

'I do indeed. Let us make haste.' He hurried up the steps and in at the front door.

When they emerged into the mews at the back of Mount Street half an hour later, they were unrecognisable. Not only were they ragged and dirty, but Alex's hair had been stuffed up under a scruffy wig which looked as though it had come out of the bargain basket at the peruke makers where customers might take their pick for a few pence. He had also taken the trouble to blacken his fingernails and one of his teeth.

'The things we do for love,' Davy murmured, as they made for the Thames.

'Love?' Alex queried, startled. 'What has love to do with it?'

'Well, you ain't getting paid for it, are you?'

'Oh, I see. No, but if we are successful and I pray we are, I shall expect Mr Gilpin to make a generous donation to the Foundling Hospital.'

'What are we looking for?'

'I do not think we shall look so much as listen.

If anyone boasts of a kidnapping or talks about a bleached covess they've seen, keep on their trail.'

Davy grinned at Alex's use of cant which he had set out to learn with the diligence he applied to everything he did. A bleached covess was a fair-haired lady. 'Right you are, sir.'

'And there's to be no "sir", do you hear? You will give the game away with that. My name is Tom Smith and we are equals. You may address me as Tom.'

'Tom it is.'

'You have the description of the two who stole Mr Wright's chair?' Davy's enquiries about chairs had elicited the information that a Mr Wright had hired out his chair to a couple of men who said they proposed to carry their mistress themselves. He had insisted on a deposit but that hadn't made a bit of difference; they had not returned the chair.

'Yes, but if they used that to kidnap Miss Gilpin it is undoubtedly in the river by now.'

'Perhaps, perhaps not. They might decide it is a good ruse and use it again.'

'Then we are looking for a stolen chair as well.'

'Yes.'

The stink of the river became stronger as they neared it. The river was full of merchant ships at

anchor waiting to load and unload at the Custom
House, lighters, coal barges, the private barges
of the rich, pleasure craft bedecked with bunting
and numerous ferries plying from one bank to the
other. And along the muddy shores barefoot urchins picked over the flotsam and jetsam washed
up there. The two men went up the steps on to
London Bridge. The old houses on it had been
falling down for years before the authorities decided to pull them down and build new piazzas
where the fashionable came to shop for ribbons
and trinkets, hats and gloves and even wallpa-
per. He took no notice of the vendors crying their
wares as he hurried across. He prayed he had in-
terpreted Miss Gilpin's letter correctly and she
was being held near the river. It would be better
to effect her release before the appointed time
for handing over the ransom. And when he did
find her he would have something to say about
young ladies who thought they could travel alone
about town with impunity, however capable they
thought they were. Let this be a salutary lesson
to her. First he had to find her.

Charlotte was indeed near the river, but not at
Lambeth. Early that morning she had been tied
up again, gagged and dumped unceremoniously
into a chair, probably the same one in which she
had been abducted, and taken by her kidnappers

to a new place of concealment, even less savoury than Molly's den. Here they waited out the day. Her gaolers were taking no chances, would not even untie her bonds except to allow her to eat and they stood over her while she did it and replaced gag and ropes the minute she finished. As dusk fell, Grosswaite arrived.

'She's not to be exchanged,' he told the two men. 'I've instructions to take her on board.'

'What about our pay?' Bert demanded. 'You said we'd have a slice of the ransom money.'

'Nothing to stop you,' Martin said. 'We can make sure of that before we do as the gaffer asks.'

Charlotte tried to speak, but could make nothing but grunting noises. Grosswaite laughed and removed the gag. 'You got something to say, me hearty?'

'Who is the gaffer?' she demanded.

'You will find out later. I think you might be pleased to see him.'

'The only person I will be pleased to see is my father.'

'Her pa won't hand over the money without a sight of her,' Hector said.

'Then we'll give him a sight of her. Bring her out.'

She struggled ineffectually as they replaced the gag and carried her down to the water's edge where they dumped her into a rowing boat. The two men climbed in and took up the oars while Grosswaite untied it from the bank and jumped in after them. In a very few minutes they were in the middle of the oily, black, stinking river and the men were rowing upstream, past the anchored ships with their navigation lamps casting a lurid glow, past darkened warehouses and alleys, past waterside taverns which spilled light on to the wet streets that led to the water's edge.

They pulled in to one of the landing stages where Grosswaite left them, then they rowed on. Charlotte had no idea of the time, but felt it was getting close to the hour when her father was supposed to deliver the ransom money. But the men had no intention of handing her back to him. How could she warn him? What could he do if she did?

The men stopped rowing, but did not draw into the bank. They simply sat in midstream and waited, dipping an oar in now and again to steady the boat and keep it on its station.

Half an hour later, a small skiff pushed out from the shore and, as it neared, Charlotte saw, by the light coming from a moored barge, her father sitting in it nursing a rather heavy sack. It drew alongside, rowed by Grosswaite.

'Your daughter, Mr Gilpin,' he said. 'Now we'll have that sack, if you please.'

'Not until my daughter is in this boat with me.'

'It will be more convenient for you to join her, I think,' Grosswaite said. 'There is no room in this for three of us.'

Henry stood up, intending to step from one to the other. Grosswaite grabbed the sack from him and then pushed him backwards into the water. Charlotte uttered a cry muffled by her gag and endeavoured to stand up as Grosswaite jumped across into the bigger craft, leaving the other to float away. What with Grosswaite trying to keep his balance in the dangerously rocking boat and Charlotte on her knees leaning over the side trying to locate her father coming to the surface, it looked as though the boat would capsize and all its occupants would be tipped into the river.

Alex had been searching the riverside all day, but that had produced nothing but false leads. No one in the many taverns and quays along the waterfront had seen the lady or the two men. It had taken a long time to persuade the owners of the warehouses to allow him to search them and some refused altogether, which meant he had to gain entrance by stealth. He found nothing, not so much as a scrap of cloth or a comb. Frustrated, he met Davy, who had been searching the opposite bank, but he had been equally unsuccessful.

There was nothing for it but to go home, discard his disguise and make his way to Long Acre to accompany Henry to the rendezvous in the hope he could effect a rescue, only to be told that Mr Gilpin, too impatient to wait for him, had already left with a heavy canvas bag. He had cursed and set off after him, hoping fervently he would not be too late.

He arrived on the scene just in time to see Henry go overboard. He did not hesitate, but divested himself of his coat, boots and sword and dived in, striking out for the spot where the man had disappeared. Reaching it, he dived again and again, but it was too dark to see anything and he had to rely on feel. Assuming Gilpin would be carried down river, he moved a little way from the spot, but there was nothing to mark where he might be. It was pure luck that his hand made contact with the material of a coat and, grabbing it, he hauled the man to the surface. Towing him, he swam back to the shore and pulled him up out of the water, where he lay exhausted beside him in the mud for several seconds before he had strength enough to sit up. Henry Gilpin was coughing up huge amounts of water, but he was alive and Alex could turn his attention to the rowing boat. It had disappeared into the darkness, taking Charlotte with it.

He cursed roundly. He could not have left Gilpin to drown, but in saving him he had lost his prize. He looked about him. Where was Davy? Had he followed him into the water? But Davy, like so many seamen, could not swim; he would surely not have been so foolish. Had there been more of the gang hidden and keeping watch in case Gilpin tried to doublecross them? They might have taken Davy captive. The loss of Davy and the loss of Miss Gilpin combined to set his temper boiling and he was inclined to take it out on the coachmaker. That worthy was sitting up now and weeping noisily.

'I told you not to go meeting anyone until I was in place to oversee the transaction,' he said. 'I would certainly not have sanctioned getting into a rowing boat. What madness made you do it?'

'I didn't know he would push me in, did I? Now I've lost Charlotte and my money. And I am soaking wet. Where were you when you were needed?'

'Right behind you,' Alex said tersely. 'Otherwise you would have drowned. Did you recognise the man who rowed you out or see who was in the boat with your daughter?'

'It was too dark to see properly and I only had eyes for Charlotte. They had her gagged and tied up, you know. It made me so angry. My poor little girl... We have to rescue her, Captain. I would give anything to see her safely back and those men hanging from Tyburn tree.'

'And so you shall if I have my way. Now we had better get you home so that you may change into dry clothes. And I must do the same.'

'But what about Charlotte?'

'I will come back just as soon as I am in clean linen. I smell like a sewer.'

He stood up and hauled Gilpin to his feet. 'Where is your carriage?'

'I left it in the care of Humphreys, my coachman, behind that warehouse over there.' He jerked his head in the direction he meant.

'Let us hope the both coach and coachman are still there,' Alex said, leading the way.

Henry did not need to be told that the equipage would be a great temptation to the thieves and vagabonds who inhabited the area and that Humphreys would hardly be able to defend it on his own. On the other hand, Gilpin would have been in even greater danger if he had chosen to walk, especially carrying five hundred guineas, which was exceedingly heavy.

They had found the coach and climbed thankfully into it and were soon deposited at Gilpin's Piccadilly mansion. Alex had seen him safely indoors and then had hurried to Mount Street to change. When he had emerged, the gentleman was gone and in his place was a shag bag, once again wearing the filthy clothes Davy so abhorred and a greasy black wig tied into a seaman's tail, on which was perched a seaman's cap. Thus disguised, he had set off again for the waterfront.

There was an urgency in his step, but he refrained from breaking into a run and drawing attention to himself. It would immediately be assumed by anyone who saw him that he was a thief running away from justice and there would be a hue and cry. He would be arrested and having to explain himself to a magistrate would take time he could ill afford. He was doing his best to keep a cool head, but the glimpse he had had of Charlotte in that boat, making it tip dangerously while she searched the inky water for her father, haunted him. One of the men had dragged her in board none too gently and now she was gone again.

He cursed the kidnappers, he cursed Gilpin for being so gullible, he cursed Davy for disappearing just when he needed him and he cursed himself for not being able to locate her sooner. No carefully nurtured young lady, even one as independent and spirited as she was, should have to endure that treatment, and he would be doing his best to rescue her even if he had not met her and admired her. And that was what made it personal. Very personal, he realised with sudden insight.

He went back to the place where she had last been seen and climbed into a ferry which was tied up at one of the landing stages. 'Row where I tell you,' he commanded the ferryman.

'Aye, aye, sir.'

'Davy! Where the devil have you been?'

Davy picked up the oars and pulled out into midstream. 'It occurred to me, my...sir, that I'd do better on the water and not in it.'

'You were undoubtedly right. Did you discover anything?'

'The lady was taken aboard the *Vixen*, moored in the river at Blackwall.'

'That old East Indiaman. I didn't know she was still afloat.'

'Seems she is, though the Company sold her to a private trader. She is only waiting on her full complement of crew and the next tide to set sail. I was on my way to tell you of it.'

'What the devil are they playing at? This is no ordinary kidnap, you can be sure. If they take Miss Gilpin out of the country...' He paused as the outline of the *Vixen* loomed out of the darkness with its mooring lights fore and aft. It was a large merchantman of some nine hundred tons. It had once been gilded and decorated with highly coloured paint, but that had faded to be almost indiscernible. Some of the coloured windows that had graced the stern had been replaced by plain glass. She was lying low in the water, obviously almost ready to sail. There did not seem to be much activity on board, but they could hear the off-duty sailors singing and laughing in the bowels of the ship. The rest of the crew, including the officers, would be enjoying their last hours ashore before returning to the ship. 'We've no time to lose. Davy, make for the shore. It's time we went back to sea. Get yourself taken on the strength, they always need good seamen.'

'And if they don't?'

'Find a crewman who'll let you take his place. Use your best persuasive powers. You know what to do. I will join you as soon as I've been home and dressed appropriately for a second lieutenant and appraised Mr Gilpin of our plans. Once on board, do not reveal that you know me. If we can get Miss Gilpin off before she sails, so much the better, but if not, we will have to sail with her.'

Davy took the ferry back to its landing stage where he left to try and join the crew of the ship and Alex took the boat up river to Whitehall Stairs where he could land nearer Piccadilly and Mount Street. He had to hurry if he was to board the *Vixen* before she sailed. He could have hired a chair, but decided it would be just as quick to use his own feet. Once home, he donned the dark-blue officer's uniform he had worn when a mere lieutenant, packed his sea-going kit in a bag and wrote a report to the Gentlemen, telling them what he proposed, then he hurried to Piccadilly.

Henry Gilpin had changed his clothes, but he had not gone to bed and was distractedly pacing his drawing-room floor when Alex was announced. He swung round. 'Have you found her? Is she safe?'

'She is safe for the moment, Mr Gilpin.' He went on to explain what he had discovered and what he proposed to do. 'I would appreciate the loan of your carriage to take me to Blackwall and a driver to bring it back,' he said. 'There isn't a moment to lose. If you do not see me and your daughter before dawn, you will know we have been obliged to remain on board and sail with her.'

'Oh, my God! My poor, poor Charlotte.'

'As you say, poor Charlotte, but rest assured I will protect her with my life and all might yet be well. Take heart.'

Henry gave orders for the horses to be harnessed and his coach brought to the front door. As Alex climbed in, a bag of money was pressed into his hands. 'You might need this. Use it as you see fit. And, *Captain*,' he added with heavy emphasis, 'remember at all times, my daughter is a lady and treat her as such.'

Before Alex could protest at this cutting and, in his view, unnecessary, admonition, the coach-maker had shut the door and directed Humphreys to take Captain Carstairs to the East India dock.

Alex had known where to find the carousing officers of the *Vixen*, a tavern close to Perry's yard and it was there he had asked the coachman to leave him. He went inside and asked if he might join them, telling them he had a mind to serve on the *Vixen*. He was in luck because the second lieutenant's wife was close to giving birth to her first child and he jumped at the chance to return to her, especially as Alex paid him well and he would not need to seek another berth for some months. When the barge came to row the men to the ship, Alex was with them.

Charlotte sat on the edge of a cot in a tiny cabin, too numb to weep, too numb to take in her surroundings, too numb even to speak, even though that dreadful gag had been removed. Her mind was full of the image of her father disappearing into the blackness of the river and not surfacing. He had almost certainly drowned. The horror of it took away some of the worry about

her own situation. The two men who had rowed
her to the ship and prodded her to climb into
the chair let down for her, had been paid off and
rowed away again. Grosswaite had come aboard
with her and handed her over to the first mate,
who told her his name was Miller. He had not
been rough with her, but made it plain she had no
choice but to do as she was told. 'Behave yourself and you will be well treated,' he had told
her, removing her bonds and the gag from her
mouth. She had soon realised that if she managed
to escape from him, there were others who would
soon stop her and what could she do except jump
overboard to almost certain death? She was not
yet ready for that.

He had helped her down the companionway
to the lower gun deck and down again between
decks to a small cabin where a lantern swung
gently on its hook above a narrow cot. There was
a porthole, but she could see nothing through it
but the flickering lights of other vessels.

'What do you want with me?' She had never
been so frightened in her life and yet she knew
she must not show it. 'Mr Grosswaite pushed my
father into the Thames and drowned him, so how
is anyone to pay a ransom for my return?' Her
words came out thick with misery.

'I don't know anything about drowning and

ransoms,' he said. 'My orders are to look after you and see that you are comfortable.'

Comfortable! How could she be comfortable given the situation she was in? She held herself in check until the door closed on him, then she put her head in her hands and wept. Her tears were for the loss of her father, overriding her own plight. Why did they have to be so cruel to him? He had obeyed their instructions and brought the ransom money, so why push him into the water? He had been her only living relative and without him there was no one who knew of her plight. She had never felt so alone.

The tears dried up with a final sniff and she looked about her. To her left was the door to the cabin, to her right, the porthole. Beneath it was a cupboard. She rose to investigate and discovered it contained a basin, a jug and a chamber pot. At the foot of the cot was a chest intended for clothes, but it was empty.

There was another cot on the opposite bulkhead. How she wished Barbara were with her to share her predicament, but that was a selfish wish; she had to bear it alone. Returning to the cot, she lay back and gazed up at the light, swinging gently with the movement of the ship at anchor. She would have to rely on her own resources to free herself. But how? Ideas followed one another, from bribing a likely sailor into

launching a boat with her in it, jumping overboard and attempting to swim ashore or setting
fire to the ship so that everyone would have to be
taken off. All were discarded as impractical and
in the end she fell asleep from sheer exhaustion.

Charlotte woke when a young midshipman of
about twelve brought her a tray of food, but refused to speak to her. Guessing he had been ordered not to talk to her, she did not press him. She
doubted he knew anything anyway. He doused
the lantern, making her realise the night was at
an end and here was the dawn of a new day.
Could anything be done to get her off this ship
and back on the shore?

There was fresh beef, peas and new-baked
bread, much better than the fare offered by Molly,
and she was hungry enough to eat it with relish.
Above her she could hear orders being given and
feet pounding across the deck. The vessel seemed
to groan and shake and then she saw the other
craft slide away past the porthole and realised
they were moving. She jumped up and tried the
door but it was locked. She hammered on it, but
no one came to her. The crew were all on deck
going about the business of setting sail.

It seemed hours later when the door was unlocked and a seaman entered. 'I'm sent to escort

you up to the quarterdeck,' he said. 'The captain wants a word with you.'

'I want more than a word with him,' she snapped. 'You have drowned my father and taken his money and I want to know why I'm being held prisoner.'

'I know nothing of that,' he said, following her up the companionway. 'And I did not drown your father.'

'No, Mr Grosswaite did. It is all one who actually did the deed.'

'We are not all like Mr Grosswaite,' he said, as they climbed the second ladder and emerged on deck. Above them the sails billowed as they made their way downstream on the ebbing tide. She could just make out the outline of the shore on either side as the Thames widened towards the sea. 'And your father did not drown.'

She turned sharply towards him. 'How do you know that?'

'I saw someone pull him out. He was alive then.'

'Truly? He was saved?' Her spirits rose suddenly and then fell again. 'How could you have seen him? This ship was moored some way from the spot where he went in.'

'I came on board late and was on shore to witness what happened.'

'Thank God for that.' She turned to look more

closely at him. He was dressed as an ordinary seaman, but he was cleaner and smarter than the others she could see working on the deck and among the shrouds. They were all in rough slops and barefoot. 'What is this ship?' she asked.

'It is called the *Vixen*, an old East Indiaman.'

'I'm surely not being taken to India.'

'I have no idea where you are being taken, but I have been ordered to look after you.'

'What is your name?'

'Davy Locke, ma'am.'

'Well, Davy Locke, what do you have to do to look after me? Stop me from throwing myself overboard?'

'I hope you will not do that, ma'am.'

She managed a wry smile. 'No, I am not of a suicidal bent. But neither am I cowed.'

'Good. You will need your courage, methinks.'

They had been walking along the deck towards the captain's cabin when she stopped suddenly at the sight of a tall figure talking to another officer on the quarterdeck. He was dressed in a blue coat, white breeches and wore a white wig topped by a bicorne hat. 'I could have sworn that's…' She shook her head as if to shake away the vision confronting her. 'Surely it can't be.'

'I'm sorry, ma'am, what's bothering you?' Davy asked.

'That man, the tall one. Is he the captain?'

'No, he's the second lieutenant. The other is Captain Brookside.'

'Oh.'

'Why? Know him, do you?'

'I thought for a minute it was Captain Alexander Carstairs, but it couldn't be, could it?'

'Captain Carstairs is a naval man, Miss Gilpin, this is an East Indiaman and in any case, a captain would never sail as a second mate.'

'No, I suppose not, but he's uncommonly like him, even to the shape of his mouth. We are not near enough to see his eyes, but I'll wager they are a mixture of brown and green.'

'As to that, I couldn't say, but perhaps he is a relation of Captain Carstairs. They are a well-known seafaring family.'

'That must be it.' As she spoke the officer turned towards her. He seemed to spend a long time looking her up and down, as if taking in every feature. He was so like Captain Carstairs she found herself holding her breath and only letting it out when he turned away. He spoke to the captain, saluted and then clattered down the steps and hurried along the deck away from her.

She was still puzzling over it when Davy gave her a little push towards the steps and she climbed them to come face to face with the captain, who, in contrast to the long length of his second mate, was short and plump. His stomach strained against the buttons of his waistcoat. She did not wait for him to speak, but went at once into the attack.

'Captain, I wish to know why you have brought me to this? I have done you no wrong and neither has my father. He was prepared to pay the ransom demanded for my release and you reneged on that. It was dishonourable to say the least.'

He lips twitched in a smile at her vehemence. 'I know nothing of a ransom, ma'am. As far as I am concerned you are a passenger on your way to join your betrothed…'

'Betrothed!' she spluttered in disbelief. 'I am not betrothed to anyone. You have the wrong passenger, Captain, and I require you to send me back at once.'

'You are Miss Charlotte Gilpin, are you not?'

'You know I am.'

'Then I do not have the wrong passenger. Your passage has been booked to Calcutta.'

'Calcutta! If you think I am going all that way on the whim of someone who calls himself my betrothed, whoever that might be, then you are wrong…'

'I should not protest too strongly.' The voice came from behind her and she whirled round to find herself confronted by the second lieutenant.

Chapter Five

He was even more like Alex at close quarters. The same upright bearing, the same half-brown, half-green eyes, with the laughter lines on either side, the same strong mouth. She could not see his hair because it was hidden under a white wig. He swept off his hat and bowed to her. 'Lieutenant Duncan Fox, at your service, ma'am.'

She could not help staring at him, hoping he would give himself away, but he returned her gaze coolly and impersonally. 'You really have no choice in the matter,' he added. 'We are at sea and until we make land there is nothing you can do. I advise you to submit and enjoy the voyage.'

'Enjoy it! This is no more than a slave ship and I am being taken into slavery. I can buy my freedom if only I could be put ashore.'

'I am afraid that is not possible,' the captain

put in, although she had been addressing the lieutenant. 'We do not expect to make landfall before Lisbon and then only to take on water and more cargo and another passenger.'

'You could send me ashore if you chose. We are not so very far from land and there are boats.' She indicated a jolly boat suspended on its davit over the stern and the barge now on its cradle amidships.

'Madam, I am being paid to carry you to India and carry you I shall.'

'How long will that take?'

'Sixteen weeks if the weather holds fair.'

'Sixteen weeks!' Her voice rose in indignation. 'I will not endure it.'

'Oh, I think you will. You are well and strong and you will soon find your sea legs.'

'I was not speaking of illness, but my treatment.'

'Have you been ill treated by any of my people? If you have, then tell me who they are and they shall be punished.'

'Then punish yourself, for I consider it ill treatment to take a lady by force and convey her goodness knows where against her will.'

He gave her a twisted smile. 'I was told you had a fiery temper, but to pay it no heed, you would obey your father in the matter of a husband…'

'Obey my father!' she exclaimed. 'Papa has never so much as mentioned a betrothal and he certainly would not try to marry me off against my will. It is all a dastardly trick and I wish I knew the reason for it.'

He shrugged and went to turn away to watch the helmsman. It infuriated her even further. 'And would a loving father and a fiancé leave me without my maid or clean linen? Am I expected to remain in these clothes for sixteen weeks?'

'Miss Gilpin has a point,' Alex said.

'Then find her some clothes,' Captain Brookside snapped.

'Allow me to escort you back to your cabin.' Alex took her arm and guided her towards the companionway, leaving her no choice. He went down first and waited for her at the bottom, watching her come towards him, his hand held out to steady her.

'Do you have such things as ladies' apparel on board?' she asked him, as they went along the lower deck. On either side big guns lay idle at their ports. There were a few off-duty seamen playing cards at the rough tables between them who watched her progress dispassionately.

'I doubt it. Unless gowns are part of the cargo, but we would not be allowed to raid those.'

'You would think if my kidnappers planned

my abduction so carefully, they would have thought of things like that, would you not?'

'You would, but even the best laid plans sometimes go awry.'

'What do you mean, awry?'

'Perhaps they did not intend that you would be on board when the *Vixen* set sail.'

'But you have been paid to take me to India, the captain said so.'

'Not me, Miss Gilpin. I am merely the second mate and obey orders.'

'Whose orders? Those of my so-called betrothed?'

'No, for I do not know him. I obey the captain of the ship. On board his word is law.'

She refrained from speaking again until they reached her cabin and he ushered her inside. 'What game are you playing, Captain Carstairs?' she demanded as soon as they were alone and could not be overheard.

'You are mistaken, ma'am. My name is Lieutenant Fox.'

'And mine is the Queen of Sheba.'

He laughed aloud and for one heartstopping moment she saw Alex Carstairs laughing with her on their ride back from Hyde Park. Of course it was him; it could be no other. 'Forgive me, your Majesty, I did not recognise you.' He gave her a sweeping bow. 'I will leave and go in search of clean raiment for you.' And with that he was gone, leaving her more bemused than ever.

She sat on her cot and contemplated the opposite bulkhead. This was her prison. It would not have been so bad if she knew why she was being held and what they had in store for her. All that talk of a betrothal was nonsense. It was, wasn't it? Who was this mysterious fiancé? And what was Captain Carstairs, alias Lieutenant Fox, doing on board when he was supposed to be in Norfolk? Why buy that expensive coach if he did not intend to use it? Unless it was to get close to her and work out how best to kidnap her? Was he hand in glove with Grosswaite? Was he the gaffer? Was he the mysterious fiancé?

But why the deception? He could have courted her openly; she might even have welcomed it. Had he already spoken to her father and been told he was not eligible on account of not having a title? But when could he have done that? She had been in his company no more than three or four times, not long enough for him to approach her father, although she had to admit she had liked what she had seen of him. She had admired him, felt her heart beat faster when he looked at her, had found comfort in his arms when those two men had accosted her in the park, the same two men who had run off with her in the hired chair. And all the time he was plotting...

She felt betrayed and dismally disappointed. And angry. It was her anger that prevented her from bursting into tears. She had shed them for her father, but, if the seaman, Locke, was to be believed that Papa had been saved, she would not cry for herself. Would Papa have any idea of what had happened to her? What would he, could he, do? It was too late now; she was on a ship bound for distant lands she had only ever read about. Why she could not fathom. It did not seem to be ransom money.

She heard the key in the lock and the door opened to reveal Alex with a bundle of clothing in his arms. 'I am afraid you will have to be a midshipman until your own clothes can be washed and made wearable again,' he said, piling trousers, shirt, stockings and jacket on the bed. 'At least the boy's mother sent him to sea with a clean change of raiment.'

'Thank him for me.'

'I am sorry there is no female servant to help you dress.'

'I can manage,' she said, though she wondered how she was going to untie her stays, which were laced at the back under the bodice of her gown.

'Turn around,' he commanded.

'You can't…'

'I can and unless you intend to spend the

whole voyage without taking off your clothes, someone has to get your laces undone.'

She stood up with her back to him and undid the hooks that fastened her bodice to her stays, so that she could slip it off and reveal the laces. She shut her eyes and held her breath as his fingers moved up and down her back, loosening the stiff garment. His touch sent shivers up and down her whole body. The tingling sensation found its way to her groin and became so overpowering she was hard put not to twist round and throw herself into his arms. As it was she could not suppress a small gasp as the stays fell away and his hands made contact with her body through the thin material of her shift. She had never felt such sensations before. It was exquisite pleasure and torture both together.

The next minute he had untied her petticoat and it dropped to the floor. A second petticoat followed the first and released the frame of the small panniers, which clattered to join the petticoats. She was almost naked, but she did not have the voice or strength to protest. She felt herself sway towards him and his arm come about her, supporting her. She felt his warm breath on her neck and shivered. The sensation in her groin increased until she longed to squirm round and drag his mouth down to hers. She felt reckless, almost outside herself, but a little voice of reason ruined the euphoria by telling her to pull herself together before it was too late. There was nothing for it but to pretend to faint, which she did, letting herself go limp in his arms.

He picked her up and laid her on the cot, where she moaned and pretended to come to her senses. She opened her eyes to find him sitting on the edge of the bed, looking down at her with a gleam of amusement in his eyes as if he knew exactly how he had affected her and why she had pretended to swoon.

'Go away,' she said. It was too late to be angry. 'Leave me be.'

'As you wish,' he said, standing up but, then, unable to resist the opportunity to tease, just to see her flare up like an ember bursting into flame. 'I had hoped to be invited to stay.'

'Never! The sky will fall in before that happens. You took advantage of me and that's not fair when I have no means of defending myself.'

He looked down at her, raking his eyes up and down her body, covered only with her flimsy shift. 'If I had wanted to take advantage of you, madam, you would not be lying there so complacently. Be thankful that I have no wish to do so.'

The tin plate from which she had eaten her breakfast was still on the locker. She picked it up and threw it at him. He dodged and it bounced off the bulkhead and rattled along the floor. Calmly he picked it up and replaced it on the locker. 'Tantrums will not avail you. I suggest you try to keep a cool head. You are going to need it.' Then he picked up her clothes and left her to fume. But he did not lock the door again; there was really no point to it—she had nowhere to go.

Alex could not have stayed a moment longer. She had been so pliable, so lovely, so desirable, her perfect body barely covered by the shift, which had done nothing to hide the round shape of her breasts with their dark nipples. It had taken all his self-control not to throw himself on top of her and rain kisses all over her body and the only answer he had to that was to be brusque and pretend indifference.

He had heard the story of the fiancé and was puzzled by it. Did she have any idea who that might be? Was it a disappointed suitor unable to take no for an answer? Or was it all a sham on her part to be with a lover? It would not be the first time he had had to deal with something like that on the Society's business. Because she was the sort of person she was, he found that hard to credit. But how did he know what sort of person she was? He had been wrong before.

He was reminded of Jonathon Leinster's assertion that Mr Gilpin was looking for a title for his daughter and that gentleman's warning as he sent him after her, for a warning it certainly was. That, together with Captain Brookside saying she would obey her father in the matter of a husband, had sent him hurtling back to another voyage and another young lady. He remembered that miserable voyage home from India when life hardly seemed worth living and he had wished every storm they encountered would put an end to his existence. But he had been young and strong and the feeling passed, leaving him older and wiser. Females were fine for a little dalliance, for an hour or two of amusement, but not for a lifelong commitment. So he had resolved and so he must remind himself when Miss Gilpin tantalised him. If he was to succeed in fulfilling his mission to rescue her, then he must take his own advice and keep a cool head.

He took Charlotte's garments to the sailor responsible for the officers' laundry and then returned to the deck where the barefoot men were climbing the ratlines to set more sail. He watched them working high above him, calling out an order now and again until the ship was under a billowing canopy of white and the men returned to the deck. Davy jumped down beside him, but gave no sign of recognition. Alex took a step towards him and murmured, 'Have you discovered anything?'

'No, sir, but I reckon the captain don' know

any more than he said.' The answer was given in a whisper.

'I thought not. Are any of the kidnappers on board?'

'Only one, name of Grosswaite, but he's sick as a dog and won't leave his bed.'

Alex saw Lieutenant Miller approaching them. 'Get back to work,' he said loudly for the lieutenant's benefit. 'And be a little quicker next time or you'll find yourself on extra duties.'

Davy knuckled his fist to his forehead and hurried away.

'You're too soft with them,' Miller told him. 'They'll take advantage.'

'I don't believe in driving the men too hard, Lieutenant. Fit, contented men will work with a will when they are needed in a crisis.'

'You can put those theories into practice when you become a captain, if you ever do. You're a mite old still to be a lieutenant.'

'I am content as I am.'

'Then go about your business.'

'Am I to be responsible for Miss Gilpin?'

'If you feel like acting the lady's maid, then do so. It's not a task I'd want.'

Alex smiled at that. The man could not know what had just transpired in Charlotte's cabin and it was as well he did not. 'Why hasn't she come on board with a maid? Seems strange to me. She's obviously a lady.'

'How should I know? I only obey orders.' He grinned suddenly. 'You might as well begin now for there she is. She don't make much of a midshipman, I must say.'

Alex swung round to see Charlotte dressed in trousers, shirt and short jacket emerging from the companionway on to the deck. He caught his breath at the sight of her. The loose clothes seemed somehow to emphasise her femininity, not detract from it, especially as she had been unable to dress her hair and it fell about her face in a tangle of curls.

Alex started towards her with the first lieutenant's laughter in his ears. 'You make sure and keep the lads away from her. We don't want to deliver damaged goods.'

Alex bowed to Charlotte, which she acknowledged with a slight bending of her head, both determined to be formal and put the episode in the cabin behind them, she because she was dreadfully embarrassed about it, he because he had been unnerved by it. And that puzzled him. He was breaking his own rules about how he treated the female of the species, but she was not simply another female, she was special. The realisation took him by surprise.

'Is it permissible to come on deck, Lieutenant?' she asked him. 'I feel the need of fresh air.'

'Of course, but I think you should be accompanied. The men are a rough lot.' He turned to walk beside her.

'How far have we come? Are we out of the Thames? I cannot see land any more.'

'We are in the mouth of the estuary, but will soon be out into the German Ocean and turning south towards the Channel.'

'Is there any chance at all I shall be put ashore before we leave England behind?'

'I doubt it.'

'What do you want with me?'

'Me?' he queried. 'I want nothing from you, Miss Gilpin. I am simply here to obey my orders.'

'Oh, so you are not my mysterious fiancé?'

'Whatever gave you that idea?' He was genuinely astonished.

She gave a cracked laugh. 'I don't know. Something about the way you treat me perhaps…'

He knew she was referring to the episode in the cabin. 'That won't happen again,' he said softly. 'Not through me or anyone else on board this ship, you have my word on it.'

'What I cannot understand is why I had to be abducted,' she went on, unwilling to talk about that. 'It is hardly the accepted manner of courtship.'

'No, it is not and certainly not one I would have chosen.'

'Oh. Are you married?'

He smiled. 'No. Sailors make poor husbands. They are never at home.'

'I was not thinking of you, but the mystery man who claims to be betrothed to me,' she said quickly.

They were on safer ground now. 'You truly do not know who it might be?'

'I have no idea. I thought at first it might be Martin Grosswaite, but he is not subtle enough to dream up such a scheme. And he talked about the gaffer as if he were answering to a higher authority.'

'Martin Grosswaite. I believe we have another passenger of that name.'

'He is the man who paid my two kidnappers and brought me on board. He also pushed my father into the river. I thought Papa had drowned, but I have been assured he was rescued.'

'Who told you that?'

'One of the seamen. He seemed more sympathetic than most. He said he'd seen someone pull him out. I wondered if he had made the rescue himself.'

'Perhaps he had,' he said laconically. 'Did he tell you his name?'

'He said it was Davy Locke.'

'I know him. You may trust him.'

'But may I trust you, Lieutenant?'

'You must make up your own mind about that.'

'Ah, I am not sure that I do. Davy Locke told me a naval captain would never sign on as a mate on a merchant ship, so why are you on board?'

He wanted to tell her the reason, but decided it would be unwise. While she was unsure of him, she would behave as was expected of her and not arouse suspicion. It would be time enough to tell her the truth when they were both safely out of danger. 'I am a second mate, nothing more. A man has to earn a living somehow.'

She decided not to challenge that. 'Have you been detailed to be my protector?'

'Yes.'

'But does that stretch to helping me to escape?'

He laughed. 'How can you escape from a ship under full sail? A dolphin, are you? Or a mermaid? You would make a very fetching mermaid, I think.'

Her lips twitched in spite of the seriousness of the conversation. 'No, I am a midshipman. Are midshipmen allowed ashore when the ship puts in for supplies?'

'It depends on the captain. This one is not inclined to leniency and in any case it will not be for several weeks. You had best make the best of it until then, but for heaven's sake don't think up any harebrained schemes to free yourself. You will not succeed and will find yourself locked in your cabin until we reach Calcutta.'

'I see. You are my jailer as well as my protector.'

He bowed. 'As you say.'

They had reached the stern and stood silently looking out over the wake being left behind. He noticed the tears lying on her lashes, though she brushed them away. 'Do not despair,' he said softly.

'I am not despairing, I am angry.'

'With me?'

'Yes, you are as bad as all the others, pretending to be Lieutenant Fox when I know perfectly well you are Captain Carstairs. Or perhaps Carstairs is the false name and you are really called Fox. If you are, you are well named, for a more sly character I have yet to meet. Even those two who kidnapped me did not pretend to be other than they were.'

He let the insult go unanswered. When he had come aboard and the captain had asked him his name, he had caught sight of the ship's figurehead and said the first thing that came into his head. It was particularly apt when he remembered he was the Marquis of Foxlees, something he had been inclined to forget this last two days. How long it would be before he returned to take up his responsibilities there? he wondered. A very long time, as things stood. 'Who were they? Did you discover their names?'

'Hector Ballard was one. The other was called Bert. I never heard his family name. They were the two who accosted me in Hyde Park and they were paid by Martin Grosswaite, who had been working at Gilpin's for the previous two weeks.'

He did not pick up on her mention of Hyde Park, though he was tempted to say, *I told you so.* 'And he was paid by someone he called "the gaffer", is that right?'

'Yes.'

'And you have no idea who the gaffer is?'

'No. Have you?'

'No, I have not.' He made up his mind to question Grosswaite as soon as an opportunity arose. 'Have you turned down any suitors recently who took the rejection badly?'

'No. I have always tried to let them down gently, even when I knew their motives were purely greed.' She sighed. 'It is not always agreeable being rich.'

'There are many who would not agree with you: the starving, orphans, desperate mothers, out-of-work sailors.'

'I know. Including penniless gentlemen who live beyond their means and expect marriage to be the answer to their predicament.'

'Have you come across many of those?'

'Too many. Enough to put me off marriage for good.'

'Really?'

'Yes, really,' she said firmly. 'And do not say I will change my mind when I meet the right man. I have heard it all before.'

'Then I won't. Do you think your mystery fiancé is one of those fortune hunters?'

'I don't know. He had money enough to pay the kidnappers and pay my fare to India, it seems.'

'Perhaps he did not. Perhaps he simply promised to pay them when they delivered you and you had agreed to marry him.'

'That I will never do, you can be sure of that, Captain. Or Lieutenant. Which is it to be?'

'Lieutenant, if you please.' He was full of admiration for her pluck. Instead of going into hysterics or passions of weeping and wailing, she was calmly trying to rationalise her predicament.

'Lieutenant, then. I will die rather than submit. I like my life as it is, or rather as it was, and somehow or other, I mean to return to it.'

'Then I hope you do,' he said.

'I keep thinking of my father and wondering if he is well after his ducking; the Thames is full of all manner of noisome debris. I keep seeing images of him going under the water and not coming up. Do you think Mr Locke was right and he was rescued unhurt?'

'Davy is usually right,' he said.

'I worry about him. Papa is an old man and I am his only child. I keep imagining how my disappearance must be affecting him. We have always been so close, especially since my mother and then my aunt died. If only there was a way to let him know I am alive and well.'

'Perhaps when we make land you will be allowed to write to him.'

'If you could arrange that, I would be most grateful.'

'It will be up to the captain, but I will ask for you if you like.'

'Thank you.'

'In the meantime I believe it is time for dinner. Allow me to escort you to the mess.'

They turned and began walking again, back towards the bow on the windward side. The sea was rougher now and he took her hand and tucked it beneath his arm to steady her. His touch was almost enough to overset her, just when she was congratulating herself on her steady nerve. If she had not already been convinced that he was Captain Carstairs, that touch would have made her sure of it. It was enough to send shivers all down her body to the tips of her toes. What she could not understand was what he was doing on board. Did it have anything to do with her abduction? Was he part of the plot? She did not want to believe that, but what other reason could there be? She did not believe it was simply to earn a living. Humble lieutenants did not buy expensive carriages, especially if they had no intention of using them.

The third mate and a couple of midshipmen, who were already in the mess, jumped to their feet on seeing her. She bade them be seated again and took her own seat. Alex left her to be served with pork chops and green beans by a steward and returned to the quarterdeck. He had not intended to deceive her over his identity; the false name had been adopted simply because Carstairs was too well known in the maritime world and he would never have been taken on as a second lieutenant. She knew who he really was, but not that he was there to rescue her and return her to her father. There was nothing he could do about that until they made land and in the meantime it was back to his duties as second mate.

It was the beginning of the routine of life aboard an East Indiaman. Charlotte's own clothes were returned to her cabin cleaned and neatly folded, but she could not lace her stays without help and would not ask Alex to do it for her. She could not risk losing her self-control all over again. Besides, the midshipman's clothes were comfortable and far more practical than her own when she was walking about the deck. If Alex noticed what she was wearing, he did not comment. Whenever he was free of shipboard duties, he would accompany her on her perambulation. He gave her a tour of the ship and explained about masts, shrouds and ratlines, topsails, gallants and jibs, and told her about the hierarchy of the crew and the part played by each member.

'But if it is a merchant ship, why does it have so many guns?' she asked.

'Because of pirates, Miss Gilpin. The cargo is more often than not very valuable and includes gold coin with which to do business. We have to be able to defend ourselves. Besides, until recently, we were at war with France and they would think nothing of seizing an unarmed vessel. They still would, notwithstanding the cessation of hostilities.'

He went on to speak of the East India Company and the vast trade it did not only with India, but China, too, and the rivalry of other countries, like France and Holland, which resulted in battles, both on land and on the ocean. He talked about his childhhod at Briarcroft and his parents, his time in the navy and his part in the war with the French. Not once did he deviate from his insistence on being Lieutenant Fox and though she did not know the reason for it, she always addressed him as Lieutenant. In turn she told him about her beloved aunt who had brought her up, about the broad education her father had provided for her and his hopes for her future, and about the coachmaking business and her plans for it.

'I think building a ship must be something like building a carriage,' she said, looking round at the vessel. 'On a much larger scale, of course. It uses the same materials, wood and cloth, glass, paint and varnish, and the same skills are needed to construct it.'

'Yes, I suppose you are right. I have never thought of it. Do you think you could build a ship?'

She laughed. 'No, of course not, I would not be so presumptuous as to claim that.'

'But you could build a coach?'

'I could direct its manufacture and I can do some of the processes, like the decoration and the needlework. Papa…' She choked on his name as her situation was borne home to her. 'Papa let me practise on the smaller vehicles. I keep thinking of all the jobs we had on hand and wondering how he is managing without me and if Joe Smithson has recovered from his fall and is back at work. Papa will need all hands if I am not there.'

'No doubt he can hire help, but I imagine the

business is the last thing on his mind while you are lost to him.'

'But I hope he does not neglect it on account of me. He worked so hard to build it up. When I was growing up he would be down at the Long Acre premises long into the night working after all the men had gone home to their beds. My aunt was never sure if he would be home for his supper or not. I think he missed my mother and being busy helped. I spent many hours there myself when my aunt wanted a rest from my childish pranks.'

'You a prankster?' He laughed. 'I do not believe it.'

'Oh, I managed to get into as much mischief as any boy,' she told him. 'I think Papa was sorry I was not a boy and indulged me to my aunt's despair.'

'I can imagine that,' he said. 'Whatever the rights and wrongs of that, it has made you brave as a lion.'

'Until now I have never had anything to be afraid of.'

'You are afraid now?'

'A little because this is all so strange to me and the further we go, the further I am from all I hold dear, and I do not know how it will end.'

'We none of us know that,' he said softly.

'No.' If she had been free and going on this voyage of her own will and Papa had condoned it, she would have enjoyed it. If Alex had really been her fiancé and not her jailer, she would have delighted in his company. He was knowledgeable and entertaining and, like her, had a wry sense of humour. He also had a fine singing voice, she discovered, when the off-duty sailors sang and played pipes and violins to entertain themselves. She was only too aware that, but for him, her situation would have been a hundred times worse. She had seen some of the crew eyeing her up and down appreciatively and was grateful for his escort. When he was on watch and unable to be with her he made sure Davy Locke was close at hand.

The passage round the south-east coast of England and into the Channel was choppy, but she was not sick until, several days later, they reached the Atlantic Ocean and turned south into the Bay of Biscay. It lived up to its reputation with gales and mountainous seas and every man on board was needed to man the ship. Charlotte, who had been boasting she was never sick, succumbed and took to her cot where she lay in misery, her stomach heaving while the ship bucked and tossed like an infuriated horse. She could calm a horse, but this creaking wooden prison was at the mercy of an untameable sea. She did not care what happened to her, if only it would stop. Someone came and bathed her face, took away the stinking chamber pot and brought fresh water for her to drink, holding her head up and putting the cup to her lips, but she was only half-aware of these ministrations and thought it was Barbara.

After three days, she came out of her semi-comatose state to find the lamp had stopped its wild gyrations above her head and the sea no longer pounded at the porthole. And Alex was sitting on the opposite cot, watching her with a smile of infinite tenderness. He had discarded his wig and revealed his own dark hair, somewhat tousled, and he had three days' stubble on his chin and upper lip.

'Ah, you are back with us again,' he said. 'How do you feel?'

'A little weak,' she said. 'And hungry.'

'Good, I will have food sent down to you.'

'It was you, wasn't it?'

'Me?'

'You have been looking after me.'

He smiled. 'As you so succinctly put it, I am your protector and your jailer...'

'And my nurse.' She was mortified to think of what he had had to do. It was far beyond the duties required of a jailer. She looked down at herself and discovered she was in a strange nightshirt. She had been undressed and there was only one person who could have done it. 'Oh, that you should have had to…' She stopped, unable to go on for picturing the scene. His eyes on her naked body, his hands touching her, pulling the garment down about her, tucking her into bed. It was not revulsion she felt, but a strange sensation of wishing she could remember it.

He inclined his head in a little bow. 'I could not leave you to lie in soiled garments. It was my privilege and pleasure to make you comfortable.'

She laughed, still a little weak. 'A pleasure I do not believe.'

'Then let us say Captain Brookside was afraid you might die and he would be delivering a dead body to your betrothed and in that event would not be paid,' he said. 'Someone had to make sure you lived.'

'I wish I might know who that mysterious man might be. I have been having such dreadful nightmares about him and they were so real.'

'I know. You tossed and turned so much I was afraid you would fall out of your cot and hurt yourself.'

'Do you still maintain you are not he?'

'I am not he, though he is to be envied.'

'I should not envy him,' she said, as some of her spirit returned. 'He is in for a dreadful shock when I do come face to face with him.'

'It might be sooner than you think. I am told he is expected to come aboard at Lisbon.'

This was news. It seemed she was not to wait until they reached Calcutta before meeting him. 'Then what?'

He shrugged. 'We shall have to wait and see.'

'And then you will be freed of your duty as protector and jailer and I will be in even worse straits. I have to escape, Lieutenant. If you won't help me, then I must try alone.'

'I do not think that will serve. Even if you managed to get off the ship and on to dry land, you will be in a foreign country without money, clothes or escort. It cannot be done.'

She managed the ghost of a smile. 'Cannot is not a word I recognise, Lieutenant.'

'If you attempt it, I shall be obliged to prevent it, for your own safety, you understand. Why not wait until the gentleman comes aboard? He might be persuaded to change his mind and take you home.'

'I wish that could be so, but if he took so much trouble to kidnap me, it is unlikely, don't you think?'

He was inclined to agree. 'You can but try. Time enough to think of escape if he refuses.' He stood up. 'I will go and arrange for food to be sent down.'

'I would rather dress and go to the dining room. This cabin stinks.'

He laughed. 'So it does.' He pushed open the

porthole. A fresh sea breeze drifted in. The sea outside was calm as a mill-pond. It was diffi-cult to believe that only a few hours previously it had been hammering at that same porthole like a demon from hell, which she, in her nightmare, had thought was where she was. 'I will have it cleaned and aired while you are away. Shall I help you dress?' This last was said with a quirky smile.

'No, thank you,' she said quickly. 'I can dress in the midshipman's clothes. I like them and per-haps they will put off my mysterious courtier.'

'I doubt it,' he said laconically and reluctantly took his leave. He had discovered, in the last few days, just how sweetly feminine she was, just how vulnerable and just how desirable. He had wondered, as he washed her, and changed the nightshirt several times a day, just how much she knew what was happening. Her naked body, with is rounded breasts and flat stomach, its pearly whiteness had churned his insides into knots. It had needed all his self-control only to do what was necessary to minister to her needs. And he would allow no one to help him. The whole three days he had hardly left her side. Now she was well again, everything would go back to what it was before. But how could it?

He had watched over her as she tossed and turned and held her when she seemed as though she would fling herself out of her cot, speaking softly to soothe her. And as he did so, a great tenderness had welled up inside him and he knew he would do anything to help her, whatever it cost him personally. His vow never to let another woman into his heart was fading fast. It was more frightening than being in a battle. The only way he could deal with it was to banish that thought and concentrate instead on trying to make plans to fulfil his mission. But that was made doubly difficult because he did not know what he was up against.

He made his way to his own quarters where he changed his clothes and shaved off his stubble and, once more presentable, found a seaman to clean Charlotte's cabin, then made his way to the upper deck. There was little wind and every sail was set in order to make up for lost time. The storm had done extensive damage and the crew were busy mending sails and repairing shrouds. A carpenter was hammering at some damaged superstructure and others were swabbing the decks. He maintained a cool exterior though he was aware of the sniggers behind his back. Lady's maid and nursemaid were the least of the names they were calling him, but he was also aware there was a certain amount of envy attached to the murmurings. None would dare say anything openly so he ignored them and returned to the duties of a second lieutenant.

The ship was hardly seaworthy which was why the Company had sold it to a private trader. Captain Brookside was barely competent and had kept all the sails at full stretch when it would have been prudent to shorten sail. It had been touch and go whether they foundered in the storm. Alex had tried politely to suggest taking in sail, but had been dismissed curtly. 'You may sail a ship as you think fit when you have one of your own to command,' he had been told. 'I suggest you go and look after our passenger. Her fiancé will not thank us for delivering a pale ghost of the woman he left behind.'

He turned to see a strange man emerging from the lower deck. He was thin as a stick, his face white as paper. This, Alex decided, must be Grosswaite. He walked over to him. 'Mr Grosswaite, I presume.'

'Yes, who are you?'

'Lieutenant Fox, at your service, sir. I hope you are fully recovered.'

'No, I am not,' the man snapped. 'But I can't stay in that stinking hole any longer.'

'I will have your cabin cleaned, sir. Would you like to take a turn about the deck while it is done?' He turned to order a seaman to do it.

Grosswaite, whose legs were decidedly unsteady, walked gingerly, hanging on to the ship's rail, while Alex walked beside him. 'I cannot think why anyone would ever put to sea,' he said. 'It is nothing short of hell.'

'Why did you put to sea, sir, if you find it so unpleasant?'

'Britain is an island, Lieutenant, you cannot go abroad without going to sea, can you?'

'True, but the shortest crossing is from Dover to Calais—could you not have gone that way?'

'I did suggest it, but my employer would not hear of it.'

'Your employer?'

'Yes.' He shut his mouth firmly on disclosing any more and Alex changed tack.

'You came on board with Miss Gilpin, I believe.'

'Yes. Unfortunately I have been too sick to attend to her.'

'No matter. She has been well looked after. I am curious to know why she is not attended by a maid.'

'Her maid refused to accompany her.' He gave a hoarse laugh. 'She obviously has more sense than to trust herself to the ocean, more sense than her mistress.'

'What do you mean, more sense than her mistress?'

'Why, the lady is so anxious to be with her

lover, she would not wait for me to find her another maid.'

'Is that so? There is no accounting for ladies' whims, is there? Why did she have to run away to be with him? Was he not acceptable to her family?'

Grosswaite turned to look hard at him. 'You are asking too many questions, Lieutenant. I do not know the ins and outs of it and have more sense than to ask.'

Alex laughed. 'I meant no harm. I was simply making conversation and curious about the identity of the fiancé she denies any knowledge of.'

'That is not your business, Lieutenant. I suggest you keep your curiosity to yourself.'

'I beg your pardon. We will talk of other things. The weather is set fair now and I spy land on our starboard. We will, I think, reach Lisbon on schedule.'

Charlotte came on deck to see Alex deep in conversation with the hated Grosswaite, and he was laughing. She turned abruptly and went back to her cabin. How could she have been so foolish as to trust him? He was probably even now telling Grosswaite that she was planning to escape when the ship dropped anchor in Lisbon harbour. The snake! He had pretended to be sympathetic to her plight, though she was honest enough with herself to realise he had never said he would help her. She was furious and disappointed and more miserable than she had ever been in her whole life.

She found a seaman with a bucket of water and a mop swabbing out her cabin. The bedding, including the thin mattress, had been removed and the lanyards which fastened the cot to the bulkhead had been let down, so that it hung flat against the wall to allow him to clean under it. She stood uncertainly in the doorway, her only refuge denied to her.

'Sorry, miss, I will be finished in the shake of a lamb's tail.' He was polite, but she could see he was looking her up and down, taking in her appearance with an appreciative eye. 'Would you like to wait in the passengers' saloon until I have finished?'

As far as she knew there was only one other passenger and he was on deck talking to Captain Carstairs, so she made her way to the small saloon below the captain's cabin. There were one or two books on a shelf and she took one down and began leafing through it, but her mind was not on what she was reading. She lifted her eyes to the ornate window with its coloured glass and saw land on the horizon. It was some way off, but close enough for her to know that in a day or two at the most, they would be turning into the Tagus and making their way upriver to Lisbon.

And then she might know what her captors had in store for her.

Supposing she could get ashore and evade them, what then? How did one go from Lisbon back to England? She would need to hide until the *Vixen* had sailed on without her and then find a ship going in the opposite direction, but without money how was she to pay for that? And in spite of everything that had happened, she was curious about the man who claimed to be betrothed to her. Who was he? Could he be persuaded to take her back to England? Would he demand a huge ransom for returning her, far more than the five hundred guineas originally asked? Grosswaite had that and she did not think for a moment he would share it. That was her answer. She must steal it back!

Was Grosswaite still on deck talking to Captain Carstairs? How long would he be there? She crept out of the cabin and made her way to a cabin further along the corridor from her own, guessing it belonged to her abductor. Thankfully there was no one about. She crept in and bent to open the chest at the foot of the cot. She had hardly lifted the lid when she heard the door behind her open and whirled round to be confronted by Davy with an armful of clean linen. Because he was wearing rope sandals she had had no warning of his approach.

'What are you doing in here, Miss Gilpin?' he demanded.

'I mistook it for my own cabin. It looks exactly like it.'

'You will forgive me if I do not believe you, ma'am. If you are up to mischief, it could go ill for you.'

Alex had told her she could trust Davy, so dare she? Would he help her? She took a deep breath. 'Mr Grosswaite has money belonging to me and I would have it back.'

'Did you think to persuade him to hand it over?'

'No. He would never do that. I propose to find out where he keeps it and steal it.'

'Miss Gilpin, begging your pardon, but that's madness. He will report the loss to the captain and every man jack on board will be questioned and flogged. You would not want that, would you?'

'No,' she said hesitantly as her plan floundered at the first hurdle. 'Would the captain really do that?'

'You may depend upon it.'

'What am I to do, then? I must have money if I am to escape.'

'Why not ask Ca…Lieutenant Fox?'

'He'll not give it to me. He said if I attempted to escape he would prevent me.'

'And he would be in the right.'

'Everyone is against me,' she said, with a sigh.

'The second lieutenant ain't against you, ma'am. Neither am I, but you must consider the consequences of what you do, not only for yourself but the lieutenant and all the crew. Please go back to your own cabin. The cot is freshly made up and there is clean water. I will not tell the captain or Mr Grosswaite about finding you here.'

She slipped past him and returned to her cabin utterly dejected. It seemed she was fated to meet her mysterious fiancé, after all...

Chapter Six

Davy had promised not to tell Captain Brookside or Mr Grosswaite, but he had made no such undertaking in respect of Lieutenant Fox, and he lost no time in recounting what had happened to Alex.

'You did right, Davy,' Alex said. 'We can't have her wandering all over the ship taking matters into her own hands. She will have to be watched more closely.'

'How can we do that, sir, when we are expected to carry out our proper duties?'

Alex was thoughtful for a moment. 'I will tell Captain Brookside that she has threatened to take her own life. He will not want that to happen. I fancy he is not being paid until she is safely delivered to this unknown fiancé. Captain Brookside has no great confidence in my seamanship and he knows I looked after her when she was ill. It is a subject that seems to amuse him, so he is bound to delegate the task of watching her to me and I shall ask for you to help me. We must endeavour to keep her happy and entertained until we anchor in Lisbon harbour.'

'And then?'

'Much depends on how events unfold. If necessary, we shall have to smuggle her off the ship. There will undoubtedly be a hue and cry when she is missed, so it would be best done just as the ship is preparing to sail again.' It sounded a simple task as he told it, but he knew it would be far from easy. He smiled suddenly. 'And I think Miss Gilpin was right. We do not want to leave Grosswaite in possession of his ill-gotten gains, do we?'

Davy grinned. 'No, sir, the devil we don't. When you give me leave, I'll see to it.'

'Not a word to Miss Gilpin, mind. When our plans are complete I will tell her of them, not before. She is a valiant young lady, but headstrong with it, and is like to scupper them with some ill-considered action.'

'Aye, aye, sir.'

Charlotte had become aware of her new situation that evening. Everywhere she had gone her footsteps were dogged by Davy Locke. He had even stationed himself outside her door when she retired for the night and he was still there in the morning, curled up on the floor with his head against the bulkhead. She had to step over him to get out and that instantly woke him. He scrambled to his feet. 'Good morning, ma'am.'

'Good morning, Davy. Do you usually sleep in the corridor? What is the matter with your hammock?'

'It's too crowded and airless below decks,' he said. 'And I wanted to be sure you were safe.'

'Safe?' She laughed. 'You mean you wanted to be sure I did not go looking for my money again.'

He had the grace to look ashamed. 'Orders,' he said.

'Yes, and I know whose orders.'

She left him and went in search of Carstairs. He was having breakfast in the mess prior to going on watch. He saw her outside the door when the steward left it open and immediately excused himself and joined her. 'Miss Gilpin, were you looking for me?'

'Yes. Why am I being watched?'

'It is the captain's orders.'

'Why?'

'It is not done to question the mind of the captain, Miss Gilpin.'

Furious with him, she marched away and made her way on to the quarter deck and the captain's cabin. She was stopped outside by a sailor who tried to prevent her entering, but she pushed past him and opened the door.

Captain Brookside was sitting at a large table studying the charts spread about him. There was a half-empty glass of rum holding down one corner and an inkstand holding down another. He appeared not to notice her.

'Captain, I would have a word with you, if you please,' she said.

He looked up, but did not rise. 'I am afraid I am too busy to speak to you now, Miss Gilpin. Join me for dinner, we will talk then.' He called out to the sailor to come and escort Miss Gilpin back to her cabin.

Charlotte flung out of the cabin and, ignoring the sailor, made her way to the rail and stared down at the sea. It was crystal clear and she could see rocks with colourful fish darting in and out of them and wondered how far down they were. For a moment she wondered if the ship might run against them and founder. Would that be a good thing or a bad thing for her? She was never called upon to decide because the leadsman was calling out the depth to the first lieutenant on the bridge who gave his orders to the helmsman and they passed the danger without coming to grief.

She looked up. The coast seemed very close, but she had been aboard long enough to know distances could be deceptive at sea and the long rocky coastline with its sandy coves was probably more than a mile away. Could she swim that far?

'Thinking of going for a dip, Miss Gilpin?'

She whirled round to face Alex. 'Oh, it is you again. Can a body not move on this ship without being tormented by unwanted bodyguards?'

'I beg your pardon. I am thinking only of your safety.' His voice was cold and impersonal and she realised that any rapport she thought had grown between them had been a sham meant to disarm her. He had nursed her only to be sure she did not die on him. The knowledge tasted bitter in her mouth.

'Yes, of course, my safety. You have to deliver me safely to my betrothed, you and Mr Grosswaite. I have never been so deceived in anyone until I met you, Mr Fox.' And having delivered that in as haughty a voice as she could manage, she turned and left him.

He smiled grimly, but did not follow her. She had undoubtedly seen him talking to Grosswaite and come to the wrong conclusion. That was a pity because she now considered him her enemy along with everyone else on board the ship. So be it. It meant that now he did not have to fight a growing desire for her which threatened his ability to do the job he had been asked to do.

They were closer in shore now and the hands were aloft, taking in the topsails and wearing the ship to enter the mouth of the Tagus. On either side were sandy beaches and fertile plains. A few sheep and a couple of men on donkeys watched their progress uninterestedly. Alex knew the harbour of Lisbon well; in the recent conflict, it had been a welcome haven after a run in with a French man o'war when they needed to make repairs and restock. He had spent some time ashore while waiting for this to be done and explored the wide, open squares and avenues being rebuilt after the dreadful earthquake and tidal wave of ten years before.

The old part of town with its narrow alleys and close-packed houses, which was on the steep hills surrounding the city, had escaped the worst of the devastation. Here he might find a hiding place for Charlotte until they could board a ship going back to England. He had given the lieutenant whose place he had taken on the *Vixen* some of the money Henry Gilpin had given him, but he had ample left to pay for lodgings and a return fare. There was also the not-so-small matter of leaving the ship himself with Davy. They had both signed on as part of the crew and jumping ship was a serious crime.

They made their way slowly upriver and dropped anchor in the harbour. It was crowded with shipping of all kinds, from merchantmen to men o' war, fishing smacks with red-and-brown sails to rowing boats, barges and cutters which plied between the larger ships, carrying men and supplies. He wondered how long Captain Brookside intended to stay and how long he had to put a plan into action.

He noticed a boat being rowed out from the shore. Besides two oarsmen it carried a passenger and it was making straight for the *Vixen*. He made his way to the starboard entry port and waited with curiosity for the man to come aboard.

He was tall and thin and vastly overdressed in a mock uniform of red coat and white breeches, black tricorne and shiny black Hessians. The coat was highly decorated with gold epaulettes, gold frogging and silver buttons. Beneath it was a long white waistcoat with buttons from neck to hem, though only the middle two were fastened.

Captain Brookside went forwards to meet him and offered his hand as the man's head and shoulders appeared above the deck. 'My lord, welcome aboard.'

He hauled himself inboard. 'You were a deuced long time getting here, Brookside.'

'We encountered a severe storm and could not

make way. I crowded on all the sail I dare. And after that we were nigh on becalmed.'

'Well, you are here now. Have you brought her?'

'Yes, my lord. Come to my cabin while she is fetched. I have a particularly good cognac I should like you to try.' He turned and, seeing Alex, snapped, 'Mr Fox, fetch Miss Gilpin, if you please.' Alex turned to obey. He did not like the newcomer one bit and the thought of Charlotte in the man's arms sickened him.

He went in search of Charlotte and found her in her cabin gazing out of the porthole at the busy harbour and no doubt thinking of escape. She turned to face him and he saw evidence of tears. She was undoubtedly feeling very low. He longed to comfort her, but dared not. If he showed any sign of sympathy, she might give him away and then he could do nothing to help her. 'Miss Gilpin, the captain's compliments and will you please join him in his cabin.'

'Very well.'

He escorted her back to the upper deck and ushered her into the captain's cabin. She gave a startled cry at the sight of the man who stood drinking a glass of cognac with Captain Brookside. 'Lord Falsham, what are you doing here?'

Alex was as startled as she was. Of all the men who could have been her abductor, it had to be Gerard Foster, Earl of Falsham. His mind whirled back to his last interview with Letitia. She had said she would marry the man her father had chosen for her, leaving him angry and humiliated. Had Gilpin also chosen Falsham? He was, after all, an earl. Would Charlotte react in the same way as Letitia had?

'Why, my dear, I am come to join you,' Falsham said.

'Join me? I do not understand. Has Papa sent you?'

'In a manner of speaking, yes,' he said.

Brookside turned and noticed Alex still standing just inside the door, listening. 'Mr Fox, go about your business, if you please.'

Reluctantly he withdrew, unsure what was going on and unable to hear the rest of the conversation. Had Gilpin really sent Falsham? And why had the Piccadilly Gentlemen been contacted if Gilpin condoned what was happening? Why would a father do that? The only ray of reassurance he had was that Charlotte had seemed surprised by the man's appearance and hardly overjoyed. Who was acting a part and who was genuine? He wished with all his heart that he had not taken on Gilpin's commission; it had embroiled him in far more than the simple kidnapping of a wealthy heiress, it had involved his own feelings and made him confront his past. But he had taken it on and he must see it through.

What he did not understand was why, if the Earl was the abductor, he had come to Portugal ahead of his prize. Why not travel on the *Vixen* with her? Alex remembered his mother telling him Falsham was in debt and forced to leave the country ahead of his dunners. Had he run through all of Letitia's money?

He went in search of Davy to find him manning the barge taking the officers ashore for some respite while the ship was re-provisioned and repairs made to the damage caused by the storm and he decided to go ashore with them. Miller and the other officers were intent on conviviality and whoring, but he had other things on his mind, to find accommodation ready for Miss Gilpin when the time came to take her under his protection.

'Are you come to take me home, my lord?' Charlotte asked.

'All in good time, my dear. There are certain matters to be decided before that happens.' He looked her up and down, taking in the boy's clothing and his lip curled. 'You look like the worst kind of fly-by-night in that rig. Have you no lady's clothes?'

'Only those I was wearing when I was kidnapped. I had no change of raiment and could hardly wear the same gown for the whole voyage.'

'Dear me, that won't do. We must go shopping at once. Go and put on your gown.'

'I have no maid to help me into it.'

'Where is your maid?'

'At home in London, I expect.'

'You mean she has not accompanied you?'

'How could she, my lord? She was not with me when I was kidnapped. I am alone.'

'That was never intended.' He laughed suddenly. 'No matter. Captain Brookside will excuse us, I know. I will act the maid.'

'Certainly not!' she snapped, remembering how she had felt when Alex unlaced her and knowing it would be very different if this man touched her. She shuddered at the thought.

'Come, my dear, do not be so coy. As your future husband I am sure it is permissible for me to help you dress. Why, there are ladies in London who make a show of having gallants watch them being dressed.'

'I am not one of them.'

'No, I am thankful to say. I should not like to share your delights with others.' He was looking her up and down as he spoke, making her curl up inside with revulsion. 'But you must have new clothes, you must surely agree to that, and I cannot take you ashore in those clothes. Why, we would be the laughing stock of the populace.'

Now they were in the river, away from the

ocean and not moving, the heat was oppressive and she felt the midshipman's clothes sticking to her back. It would be so much cooler if she had a light gown to wear and she really did want to go ashore, for it was easier to think of escape once on dry land. 'I can manage, my lord, if you wait here,' she said, as an idea came to her. Without waiting for a reply she returned to her cabin, leaving him to continue drinking with Captain Brookside.

In her cabin she put on her petticoats and skirt over the midshipman's shirt, put her bodice over that as if it were a short jacket.

Half an hour later, respectably covered, she presented herself back in the Captain's cabin.

'My God, what urchin have we here?' Lord Falsham exclaimed. 'Is that the best you can do? The sooner we get you properly rigged out the better.' And with that he took her arm and guided her to the starboard entry where Davy and the other oarsman had brought the barge back to the ship. Captain Brookside ordered them to take the earl and Miss Gilpin ashore. She was helped into a chair and winched down where one of the oarsman helped her into the boat. Lord Falsham followed in like manner.

It was only a short row to the wide marble steps of a great open square surrounded on three sides by new pink-and-green buildings. The fourth was open to the river. The boat pulled in and they disembarked. On dry land again Charlotte felt strange, not at all sure of her balance, and almost stumbled, but Lord Falsham's hand under her elbow steadied her. She shook him off and made her way up the steps ahead of him.

She looked about her. Steep hills rose in a semi-circle about the lower part of the town and these were covered in narrow roads and pastel-coloured buildings. There were still gaps left by the great earthquake and some building work was still going on, but the city had been rebuilt in magnificent style. The streets in the new part of the town were geometrically laid out—their buildings all had dormer windows and iron balustrades from which colourful flowers tumbled. Charlotte was in no mood to appreciate it, being too caught up with thinking of ways to obtain her freedom. Alex had been right—in a strange country whose language she did not understand, without money or clothes, escape would be nigh on impossible. She decided it behoved her to pretend to be submissive and then perhaps her escort might relax his guard. Besides, running off without a plan about how she was to proceed would not serve; she would be hauled back and put under guard and that would end any hope she had of escape.

'Where are we going?'

'To buy clothes befitting your rank, though unfortunately we will have to be a little careful of our resources until more money can be sent out to us by your father.' He was beckoning to a cab driver as he spoke.

'What makes you think he will send you money?'

'Oh, I do not doubt it. He will not allow his daughter to be in want, will he?' He opened the door of the cab and helped her into it and, after directing the driver to the Rossio, climbed in beside her. 'I have already let him know I have you safe in my protection and he will be only too thankful to supply all we need.'

She felt obliged to acknowledge the truth of this. Leaving the harbour behind them they entered a great square tiled in black-and-white mosaic. It was teeming with the life of the city. There were pedlars selling everything from dried cod and fresh sardines, to figs and oranges and wine. Black-clad women waited their turn to fill their pitchers at the fountain. The air was redolent with a thousand different smells. Here the cab stopped and she was hustled into the cool interior of a shop where Lord Falsham, who seemed able to communicate in Portuguese, negotiated the supply of everything she might need for a prolonged stay, watching as she was decked out in one outfit after another and commenting upon each.

The old gown and the midshipman's shirt were discarded and she left the shop in a light blue silk, trimmed with pink-and-white flowers. New stockings and shoes and a fetching straw hat tied with blue ribbon finished the ensemble. She scooped up the borrowed shirt as she left. 'We must send this back to the ship,' she said. 'The young man lent it to me in good faith and in good faith I must return it.'

'If you must,' he said, leaving an address where everything was to be delivered and escorting her out of the shop. The cab was still waiting. It took them away from the river and up a very steep, narrow road with pastel-coloured houses on either side, their balconies tumbling with flowers. These had evidently escaped the earthquake for they were older and more widely spaced with colourful tiles on the walls and luxurious gardens, which could be glimpsed through iron gates.

'Where are we going?' she asked.

'I have taken a villa, so that we may wait in comfort for the money to come from your father.' He gave a low chuckle and then added, 'Together with his wholehearted agreement to our wedding.'

'Wedding?' she echoed. 'What makes you think he will do that?'

'There are several reasons, my dear,' he said, infuriating her with his complacency. 'He has made no secret of the fact he has been looking for a title for you and countess is as good as he is likely to get, considering you have no breeding. And you have been missing for weeks and that must have caused some gossip.'

'I was kidnapped.'

He smiled. 'There is no evidence of that. You left the Gilpin premises freely and never arrived home, but that could just as easily have been because you had plans to join me.'

'I was forced to write a ransom note and I know my father brought the money because I saw him. Mr Grosswaite took it from him and pushed him into the river.'

'He did what?' He was obviously taken aback by this.

'He grabbed the bag of money and pushed Papa backwards into the Thames.'

'You mean he drowned?' His face, in spite of the heat, had gone very white.

'No. I have been assured he was pulled out alive.'

'Thank God for that. For a moment I thought my plans had been thwarted. It would not do for you to inherit before I have you as my wife.

Grosswaite and his associates will be punished severely, I promise you.'

'Was five hundred guineas not enough?'

'Nowhere near enough, my dear. I thought at first it might be enough to pay my immediate debts and it tickled my fancy to think that Gilpin himself would be paying my debt to him, but then I realised that to continue living in the style to which I was accustomed, I would need a great deal more. It occurred to me that with the Gilpin coachmaking business, together with the money lending which I am persuaded is hugely profitable, I could manage quite well. So, my dear, the voyage to India is to be our honeymoon.'

'Papa will never agree to that.'

'Oh, I am sure he will, if only to save your honour. You must realise that to return home without a husband after being so long away will damn you in the eyes of society. Not only will you never be received in any decent drawing room again, but it will reflect on your father's business. He will find his customers disappearing like puffs of wind. I advise to you reflect on that.'

She was silenced. Her whole being cried out that she would not submit, that nothing on earth would persuade her to marry this objectionable man, but a warning voice inside her head told her that he was right about the consequences of not doing so. He had laid his plans diabolically well.

'No answer to that?' he queried mildly. 'No furious denial?'

'You suggested I should reflect on it and that is what I shall do,' she said as coolly as she could manage.

'Good. I was sure you would be sensible.'

The cab stopped outside a large pink single-storey villa. He jumped out and helped her down. She stood on the rough road, looking about her while he paid the cab driver. The house had a garden of exotic plants she had never seen in England outside a conservatory. Here were jacaranda and acacia, palm trees, fig, orange and olive trees loaded with fruit, and colourful flowers lining the gravel paths.

He took her arm and led her to a great oak door, which opened as they reached it. In its frame stood a young woman who eyed Charlotte suspiciously. 'Madeleine, this is your new mistress,' he said, ushering Charlotte before him into a wide hall with a blue-and-white tiled floor. 'You are to look after her and when I am not present you are to accompany her wherever she goes. We will have dinner now.'

Madeleine bobbed a curtsy without speaking and went off into the back regions of the house.

'While we are waiting I will show you round your new home,' he said.

It was a substantial building, its thick walls

and tiled floors making it cooler than the sun-drenched garden outside. There was a drawing room and dining room and several bedrooms, though she only saw inside one, which she was told would be hers. It was minimally furnished with a huge bed, a couple of cupboards, a chest of drawers and a washstand upon which stood a jug of water and a bowl. There was a single colourful rug beside the bed and thin gauze curtains stirred faintly in the slight breeze coming off the sea. Charlotte's biggest concern at that moment was finding a way of preventing the earl from coming to her bed that night.

'Now, I do believe dinner is ready,' he said, as Madeleine appeared in the doorway.

While they were eating a dish of salt cod, a chicken and crusty bread, served by Madeleine who seemed to be the only other occupant of the house, her clothes arrived.

Once the meal was over, she returned to the bedchamber where Madeleine unpacked them for her and tidied them away into the cupboards and drawers, all without uttering a sound. Charlotte presumed she was Portuguese and did not speak English. Nevertheless she tried out her French in an effort to obtain information. If she could make an ally of the girl, it might help. Madeleine seemed to understand her, but her answers were monosyllabic.

They returned to the drawing room to find the earl lounging in a chair, a cigar in one hand and a glass of wine in the other. Opposite him stood Martin Grosswaite. They had evidently been arguing, for Grosswaite looked sullen and the earl angry. 'Martin has been severely reprimanded for his ill treatment of your father and is ready to apologise,' the earl told her. He looked hard at Grosswaite, who shifted uncomfortably from one foot to the other.

'My apologies, Miss Gilpin,' he mumbled.

'It is not me you should be apologising to, but my father.'

'He will do so,' the earl went on. 'Just as soon as we are married and reunited with that worthy gentleman.'

'How long will that take?'

'Impatient, my dear?' he queried, his lip curling in a strange smile.

'Yes, for I think my father will come out himself to rescue me.'

'All the better, for then he can witness the wedding. In the meantime we will be comfortable enough here until we hear from him.' He turned to Grosswaite. 'I'll have that five hundred guineas, if you please.'

'My lord, I haven't got it. It's been took.'

'Took—what do you mean, took?'

'Stolen, my lord, from my locker on the ship.'

'You are lying.'

'No, my lord, I am not lying. It is the truth. I went to fetch it this morning before coming ashore and it had gone. You can't trust anyone these days.'

Charlotte had a good idea who had taken it and was about to say so, when she decided against it. She could use that money herself. All she had to do was find Davy and make him give it to her. How that was to be done occupied her for some minutes and she did not pay attention to the rest of the conversation, until she heard the earl order Grosswaite back on board the *Vixen*. 'You will report the loss to Captain Brookside and make sure he knows that he will pay dearly if he does not discover the culprit and have the money returned.'

'Most of the crew have been allowed ashore,' the miserable Grosswaite said. 'It'll be half spent by now.'

'No doubt by you.'

'No, my lord. I haven't touched a groat. There was nothing to spend it on while we were on the high seas. I was going to bring it to you intact.'

'Hmm.' His lordship's tone was one of doubt. 'Go back and tell Captain Brookside that he will be held responsible. Not a farthing will he have

from me for his services until that money is in
my hands.'

'Yes, my lord.' He backed his way out.

Charlotte watched him go and then turned
back to the earl. 'Am I to be confined to the
house, my lord?'

'Not at all, but you will not venture out alone.
For your own safety, you understand.'

'It is cooler now, I should like to walk in the
garden.'

'Then we will do it together.' He put down his
empty glass and ground out the last of the cigar
under his heel before standing up and offering
her his arm. She ignored it and walked out into
the garden. The villa was high on the hill and
from the viewpoint at the end of the garden, she
could see the roofs of the lower town, the steeples
of the churches and the harbour crowded with
shipping. The river itself wound its way west-
wards, broadening out towards the sea.

She did not feel disposed to make conversation with him and would have preferred to ignore
his presence at her side, but she wanted to learn
all she could and had decided that, until she was
ready to make her dash for freedom, she would
pretend to fall in with his plans. 'Do you know
Lisbon well, my lord?'

'Tolerably.' He pointed. 'The square by the
river where we landed is the Terreiro do Paco

and the big square where we did our shopping is the Rossio, the centre of the newest part of the town. Up there...' His arm moved to the hillside on his left. 'Are the ancient quarters of Alfama and Mouraria and the castle you can see on the heights is St George's.' He turned to his right. 'Over there are the Bairro Alto and Madragoa Districts. The higher parts of the town escaped the worst of the earthquake and remain picturesque. We will explore together, if you are good.'

She consigned all this to her memory for future use. 'Where have all the ships come from and where are they bound?' she asked.

'All over the globe,' he said. 'India, China, the Cape of Good Hope, the New World, the Mediterranean.'

'England?'

'Yes, undoubtedly some, like the *Vixen*, come from England.'

'Are there any going home?'

'I have no idea, but you can forget that idea. I will take you home when we are married and have had our honeymoon. By that time the gossip over your disappearance will have died down and we will be received with tears of joy by all our friends and relations. You will take you rightful place in society as the Countess of Falsham and I shall be able to live my life as I see fit.'

'You have forgotten one thing, my lord. You

have not ascertained whether I wish to become the Countess of Falsham.'

'That goes without saying,' he said, then laughed. 'Many young ladies would give their right arm to have that title.'

'And I would give my right arm not to,' she snapped.

'Dear me, and I thought we had reached agreement on the subject. I see I shall have to be more persuasive.'

She knew what he meant and her heart sank.

Alex returned to the *Vixen* to discover that the earl had taken Charlotte into Lisbon and the captain had no idea when they would be back. The repairs to the ship would take two weeks and he supposed they would return to continue the voyage when the ship was ready to sail again. Apart from those who had to stand watch, the officers had been given leave until it was time to prepare to sail and that included Alex.

He knew he must act before then; the further they went, the harder it would be to effect a rescue and return to England. The trouble was that he was not at all sure Charlotte wanted to be rescued. For two pins he would give the whole mission up and go home, but the memory of Charlotte in his arms, Charlotte sick and clinging to him, Charlotte standing in the stern in her midshipman's outfit, Charlotte defiant, Charlotte laughing, Charlotte unhappy, would not let him do that. She might pretend to be strong and in control, but that was only bluff. She was young and frightened and still weak from her *mal de mer*. Besides, he had been commissioned by Mr Gilpin to bring his daughter safely home and he had never yet allowed himself to be beaten by anything he attempted to do. Except once. He was not so green now, not so easily intimidated, but it behoved him to be cautious.

While in Lisbon he had taken two rooms in a respectable boarding house in a quaint old street just below the Castle, and intended to hire a girl to serve Charlotte as a maid and companion when the time came. He wanted to observe the proprieties, though he wondered if it might not already be too late. Had she gone willingly with Lord Falsham? If she had, there was nothing he could do for her.

He went in search of Davy, calling him up from the lower deck where those of the crew still on board were carousing. 'Have you discovered anything?' he asked him.

'No, we rowed them ashore and they got into a hackney and were driven off. Last I saw of it was when it went into the Rossio. I tried following, but I lost it in the crowds.'

'How did she seem?'

'Calm. They talked. There was no animosity that I could see. I reckon she was glad to see him.' He chuckled. 'She maybe thinks he will rescue her from us.'

'Maybe she does.'

'Are we going home, Captain? I don't like this ship above half. It's like to break up if we get another tempest like we had coming here.'

'We cannot go with a job half-done, Davy. Besides, we signed on for the voyage.'

'So we did, but that don't signify.'

'It does, you know. Jumping ship is a crime and you would be hounded by the pressmen and on to another ship before you could take breath.' He laughed at his servant's dismay. 'I got you into this, Davy, and I shall get you out, never fear. But not yet, not until we know what's afoot between Miss Gilpin and the noble earl. I must go back ashore and endeavour to find out.' He leaned over the side of the ship and hailed a local boat, containing two men selling fruit to the sailors.

'You want melon?' the man in the stern said, holding up a large yellow fruit. 'Or oranges, very juicy, very sweet.'

'I'll buy all you've got if you carry me ashore,' Alex said.

They came alongside at once and the one who had spoken grabbed the ladder. Alex scrambled down into the flimsy craft and was soon being rowed strongly for the steps, where he disembarked. Money changed hands though he did not take the fruit. The men rowed off again well satisfied.

Chapter Seven

~~~~~~~~~~

Everything had conspired against her and Charlotte felt as low as anyone could go, but not so low as to allow the earl into her bed. When supper was finished and she could no longer keep the conversation going, she made her excuses and retired to her room. Having made sure the window was secured, she heaved a chest across the door and lay on the bed without undressing. It was unbearably hot and she longed to open the window, but dare not.

An hour after retiring she heard footsteps outside her room. Someone lifted the latch and, finding the door firmly barricaded, laughed softly. 'Never mind, my dear, there is plenty of time.'

This was followed by a female giggle and the footsteps retreated. A door shut along the corridor and then there was silence. Charlotte breathed a huge sigh of relief and got up to open the window and let in what little air there was. The sky was clear and a full moon lit the scene in a silvery glow. The pale stucco of the nearest buildings stood out starkly throwing long shadows. Somewhere, out of her sight, the river wound its way to the sea. Somewhere down there the *Vixen* lay at anchor. On board would be the men she had come to know, those who were courteous because it was their nature and those who were polite because they feared the wrath of the captain. Was Captain Alexander Carstairs on board? Why hadn't she exposed his deception to Captain Brookside? Why had she carried on with the pretence that he was Lieutenant Fox? Why couldn't she get him out of her head?

She turned and went back to her bed where she lay awake, determined to be gone from there before anyone else was up the next morning. She would go to the British Consul and tell him her story; he was the obvious one to help her.

As soon as it was light enough to see, she tidied her clothes and, listening carefully for sounds of anyone moving about, dragged the chest away from the door and crept from the room. She made her way through the silent house, pausing outside the earl's bedroom door. All was quiet. Heart in mouth, she opened the door from the kitchen and made her way to the iron gates. They were locked. Almost crying with frustration, she ran round the wall until she came to a section that had been damaged, probably by the earthquake. Even so it was a struggle to climb up and over and her gown was torn and both knees grazed by the time she found herself on a rough track on the other side.

'Such an undignified way for a lady to behave.'

She looked up from shaking out her skirt to find herself looking up into the amused eyes of the Earl of Falsham. He was leading a saddled horse and was evidently returning from a ride. She cursed her ill luck. A minute sooner or a minute later and she would not have encountered him.

He took her arm and turned her about to walk alongside him. 'Where were you off to?'

'To see the British Consul.'

'Do you know who he is?'

'No, but I can find out.'

'I doubt you would be admitted without an appointment, especially looking like that.' He looked at her torn clothing. 'Only a day's wear out of it and now it's ruined. I seem to recall telling you that we had to be careful of our resources, but I do not suppose a little thing like the cost of a silk gown has ever troubled you. What it is to be rich beyond avarice.' He smiled suddenly. 'However, if you are good, I will take you to meet His Majesty's Minister Plenipotentiary to Portugal, which is Mr Edward Hay's correct title. He is holding a ball at the Residency tonight and I have no doubt I can secure us an invitation. Yes, now I think of it, it is a very good idea for you to be seen in the society of Lisbon. It will give credence to our story.'

'Your story, not mine,' she snapped.

'Oh, dear, how often must I remind you of the consequences of crossing me? A tarnished reputation will not help you and I am prepared to lay odds your father will encourage you to accept my suit, so why not relax and enjoy your time in Lisbon?'

The only thing that prevented her from lashing out at him with tooth and claw was the prospect of meeting and speaking to the Minister. She returned silently to the villa with him, entering by a back gate which led directly to the outbuilding that served as a stable. After he had handed the horse over to the garden boy, who seemed also to act as a groom, he escorted her into the house where she went to her room to change out of the torn gown into a light sack dress. She was inclined to stay there, rather than rejoin the earl, but she was hungry and starving herself would not serve, so she made her way to the dining room for breakfast, which was served by Madeleine. The earl was jovial and talkative, ignoring the fact that Charlotte had little to say. Afterwards they walked in the garden until the sun became too hot and then retreated into the house which was cooler.

Grosswaite arrived in the afternoon and bewailed the fact that the captain had ordered all the men's belongings to be searched and the money had not turned up. 'He has given them twenty-four hours to come forwards with the culprit and the guineas or he will have the whole lot flogged,' he said.

'Surely he cannot flog the whole crew?' Charlotte said, reminded of Davy's assertion that he would do so.

'He can do as he likes,' Grosswaite said, looking closely at her. 'I wonder if you know what has become of that money?'

'I know nothing of it. I wish I did. If I had it, do you suppose I would be here, depending on Lord Falsham for my existence?'

'Now, now, my dear,' his lordship soothed. 'We have established that you are happy to be under my protection, so let us have no more tantrums. I suggest you go and lie down to rest in your room until it is time for Madeleine to help you into your prettiest gown and dress your hair. We must not let ourselves down in front of the Minister and his guests.'

Defeated for the time being, Charlotte went to her room and sat on the bed, furious and helpless and planning what she would say to the Consul when she met him.

Early in the evening, Madeleine came to her with hot water, brushes, combs and powder to prepare her for the reception, at the end of which ministrations a butterfly emerged from its chrysalis. She was dressed in a wide-skirted open robe of cream brocade with wide panniers. Its stomacher was held to the bodice with rows of satin bows, one above the other from the pointed waist to a low neckline. The sleeves were double flounced with lace just below the elbow. Her hair had been piled with false curls and powdered within an inch of its life. Dotted about this creation were several more satin bows.

Even the earl was impressed. 'Why, my dear,' he said, looking her up and down, 'I had no idea you were so comely. I shall be the envy of every man there.' He was dressed in an ostentatious coat of pea-green satin decorated with white embroidery and silver buttons. He had white breeches and stockings and silver buckled shoes with high heels. On his head reposed a white wig of huge proportions, high at the front, with three stuffed curls on either side and a tail curled and held in place by a wide satin ribbon. He looked a veritable macaroni.

He held out his hand to her. 'Come, let us go. I have hired a carriage for the duration of our stay.'

She ignored the proffered hand and preceded him out to the carriage. It was a ramshackle affair, scuffed and dusty, and would have disgusted her father had he seen it. 'Where did you find that?' she asked in disdain

'Oh, I know it is not up to Gilpin's standards, but you can hardly expect that, can you?' he said, helping her in and taking his place beside her.

The carriage was so narrow she found herself squashed up against him and tried to shift away. He noticed it and smiled. 'For appearances' sake, I expect you to behave with dignity,' he went on. 'You are my affianced bride, so remember that and act accordingly. At the moment you are being treated with every consideration and respect, but I can make life very uncomfortable for you, if you cross me.'

She did not answer and they were soon at the British Minister's residence where a glittering assembly of the Lisbon elite was gathering: government officials, British merchants and travellers, local businessmen and senior officers of both navies, many with their ladies. They joined the line waiting to be greeted by their host and hostess. Charlotte realised Mr Hay would not listen to her while he was thus occupied, so she smiled and curtsied and followed the earl into the ballroom.

Alex spotted Charlotte entering the ballroom on the arm of the earl. She was splendidly attired and did not appear to be in any distress. In fact, she smiled and curtsied on being introduced to the Minister and his wife and though he was too far away to hear what was said, she seemed in good spirits. It made him angry to see her preening herself like that. She was no different from Letitia, selling herself for an extravagant gown and the title of countess.

Edward Hay's father had been a friend of his own father's and though a few years older than Alex, was well known to him. He had called on him as a matter of courtesy earlier that day. On being asked what had brought him to Portugal, he had confided his mission and the dilemma of being unsure if Miss Gilpin had truly been kidnapped or had come out of her own accord in which case, was he justified in interfering?

'I cannot advise you on that score,' Edward had told him. 'You had best wait and see. The *Vixen* will not move from here for at least two weeks and if you should need longer, I may be able to arrange with the port authorities to delay it with some trifling concern over her cargo.'

'Thank you, sir.'

'In the meantime, come to my ball this evening. I believe the Earl of Falsham has asked for an invitation for himself and his affianced bride, which I have no reason to refuse. You may be able to judge matters then. Have you lodgings or are you sleeping on board the *Vixen*? You are welcome to stay here, if you wish.'

'Thank you, sir. I have taken lodgings in order to have somewhere for Miss Gilpin to stay should she wish to leave the earl, but until she is under my protection and needs it, I shall stay there myself.'

'Very well, but let me caution you against acting hastily. The earl has powerful friends and if Miss Gilpin is set upon staying with him, you might make enemies by removing her, besides having the trouble of holding on to her once you have her, should she kick up a dust.'

'I am aware of that, sir. I have a letter to go to Miss Gilpin's father, one to Lord Drymore and another to my mother. Would you allow them to go in the diplomatic bag?'

'Certainly. Bring them with you tonight. There is a ship leaving for England on the morning tide.'

Alex had thanked him and taken his leave

and then gone into town to buy himself a suit of clothes in which to go to the ball, having brought nothing on board the *Vixen* but a spare uniform, and that for a lieutenant. Now here he was in his finery of dark-amber satin, standing beside a potted palm in the reception room of the elegant Residency, which had replaced the Embassy destroyed in the earthquake ten years before, watching Miss Gilpin being introduced to others of the assembly by Mrs Hay.

Having gone halfway round the room, they came to Alex. 'Lieutenant Fox of the *Vixen*, madam,' he said before Mrs Hay could conjure up his real name.

She looked startled, then, smiling, turned to the earl. 'Lord Falsham, this is Lieutenant Fox of the *Vixen*.'

'We met on board,' the earl said. 'I believe you are acquainted with my fiancée, Lieutenant.'

'It has been my privilege to serve Miss Gilpin.' Alex bowed to her. 'I trust I find you well, ma'am?'

'I am very well,' she said.

Her looks belied that statement. Underneath the rouge her complexion was pale and her grey eyes lacked their customary brilliance. 'Do you intend to continue your voyage to India?'

'We do,' the earl put in before she could answer. 'It is to be our wedding tour.'

'Then I shall have the felicity of seeing you once more aboard the *Vixen*.'

'Come, my dear.' The earl took her arm. 'There are others we must meet. Good evening to you, Fox.' And with that he drew her away.

Alex watched her go. What had seemed good spirits when seen from a distance had been shown to be a pretence at close quarters. She was not happy. He resolved to ask her to dance.

The earl was keeping a close watch on her and though he had taken her into a set himself, he was obviously not allowing her to dance with anyone else. Alex waited until Falsham was deep in conversation with Captain Brookside, no doubt about continuing the voyage, and then approached Charlotte, who was sitting alone with a fixed smile on her face.

'Miss Gilpin, may I crave the honour of a dance with you?'

She looked startled as if he had dragged her back from some deep contemplation and looked at the hand he held out to her. She took it and rose to her feet.

'You are looking very fine this evening,' he murmured, as they paraded down the line of dancers, her hand held tightly in his. 'The midshipman has been transformed into a lovely young lady, the envy of every other lady here. Lord Falsham is to be congratulated.'

'On what, sir?'

'His good luck. Or should I say his cleverness?'

'Both,' she said dully.

They separated at the end on the line and turned to other partners and it was a minute or two before they were once more facing each other. 'I cannot believe you are happy with the situation in which you find yourself,' he said, as they came together.

'And I cannot think why you interest yourself in my affairs, Lieutenant.' She executed some steps, sideways and back.

'Because I would hate to think of anything ill befalling you.'

'It is too late for those sentiments, Lieutenant Fox. The ill befell me the day I was abducted, taken by force away from my father, my home and my business and everything I hold dear.'

'Were you taken by force?'

'You know I was.'

'Do I? It could all have been a ruse on your part to join your lover.'

'My lover? Who can that be? Tell me, for I should like to know his name.'

'The Earl of Falsham?'

She gave a brittle laugh. 'He did not need to kidnap me. He could have courted me openly in London.'

'Why didn't he?'

They separated again. 'Why didn't he court you in London?' he repeated when they returned to each other. It was a very unsatisfactory way to conduct a conversation, but he could hardly drag her away to talk to her, which is what he would have liked to do. And kiss her until she cried for mercy.

'I do not know. Perhaps he was afraid of rejection and wanted to make sure of my compliance.'

'He would only have needed to speak to your father and obtained his consent. You would have obeyed Mr Gilpin, would you not?'

'Naturally I would, but Papa would let me choose my husband for myself.'

'So long as he has a title.'

'He never stipulated that.'

'No? I heard he was looking for a title for you.'

She looked sharply at him. 'Who told you that?'

'Does it matter? The earl has a title.'

'Lieutenant, I cannot see that this is any of your business, but I will say that titles are of far less importance than proficiency in business. Papa would not want to see all he has worked for dissipated by a profligate husband, title or no.'

'And is the earl profligate?' he asked, wondering if she really did put the business before her own happiness.

'I do not know, except he owed for his last two carriages, but then gentlemen of rank rarely pay their bills if they can get away with not doing so. It hardly signifies.'

The dance came to an end. He bowed, she curtsied and he escorted her back to her seat

'Now I begin to see Falsham's thinking,' he murmured in her ear. 'You were right; he wanted to make sure of your compliance. Does he have that now?'

'Ah, there you are, my dear.' Alex turned to see Lord Falsham bearing down on them. 'It is time to go in for supper.' He took her arm and led her away.

Alex watched them go and he still did not know whether he ought to interfere. He had written to Henry Gilpin, asking for instructions, and another letter to James to keep him abreast of what had happened and asking his advice, but it would be weeks before he could expect replies to either and by then they would be on the high seas again and Charlotte's position would be even more compromised. In the eyes of the world it already was, unless she could be returned to her father still unmolested and the Earl of Falsham be seen by society as the villain he was. He admitted there was more to it than the pursuit of justice. It might have started out that way, but his own feelings for Charlotte had grown with every day until his head and heart were in torment and that, in itself, formed a barrier to his disinterestedness. Was his determination to separate her from the earl for her sake or his own?

Charlotte was still unsure of Captain Carstairs's position and still troubled by her physical reaction to him. The mere sight of him started her heart racing and the touch of his hand was enough to set her body on fire. She had to hold herself aloof in order to control the aching in her limbs and in her heart, which she suspected might be love, though she was too inexperienced to know for certain. If only she could be sure of him, not as a lover, because she was convinced he did not see himself in that light, and under the circumstances it was hardly appropriate, but as an ally to whom she could confide, someone she could turn to for help. She wished heartily that the earl had not interrupted them when he had—she might have been able to make up her mind whether to unburden herself. But even if the captain could be persuaded to help her to escape from the earl, she would only be exchanging one so-called protector for another. Her reputation would still be tarnished. She would be labelled a Cyprian, one of the demi-reps on the fringe of society, the target of gossip. Even if she did not care for herself, she cared very much on behalf of her father and the future of Gilpin's. Unfortunately the earl had been right about that.

She ate a little of the good food provided, not because she was hungry, but because she needed to keep up her strength. The Earl was full of *bonhomie*, laughing and joking with others about them, telling everyone they were waiting for her father to join them. He had been booked to travel with them, he said, but an unexpected matter of business had meant he had to stay behind and travel at a later date. 'I had business in Lisbon which could not be postponed and could not delay my own departure, and my dearest Lottie would not let me go without her,' he said, putting his arm about her shoulders and squeezing her towards him. The action repelled her, but she smiled her fixed smile and submitted, but of one thing she was certain, somehow or other she would get away from him before the night was done. If she never dared return to England, she would have to find some way of living in a foreign country.

They returned to the dancing after supper, but though she looked for him, there was no sign of Captain Carstairs. His absence made her feel more alone than ever. 'I am feeling exceedingly hot,' she told the earl. 'I must go out into the air.'

He looked hard at her, as if deciding whether

this was some ruse of hers. 'You do look some-what flushed. I hope you are not sickening for anything.'

'No, no, it is the heat in this room,' she said. 'I will recover in the cool air.'

'Then by all mean, let us take a stroll in the garden.'

She knew it would be no good suggesting she go alone and made no protest when he accompanied her. After several minutes walking silently up and down the paths that dissected the lawns and flower beds, they returned indoors and he sent for the carriage to be brought round to take them back to the villa and they took their leave of Mrs Hay. The Minister himself was engaged in conversation in another room, she told them, but she hoped Miss Gilpin would soon feel better and invited her to call the following afternoon if she felt up to it. They left without Charlotte being able to put her dilemma to the Minster. In any case, she was suddenly unsure whether she could trust him any more than anyone else; the Earl of Falsham was just too plausible. It seemed her de-liverance would be entirely up to her own efforts.

As soon as Madeleine had helped her out of her finery and left her that night, she had pulled the chest against the door again and lain awake waiting for daylight, then she dressed hurriedly in the midshipman's shirt which she had not yet been able to return and put a plain muslin skirt on top of this, leaving off the padded hips because she was planning on riding. She climbed out of the window, telling herself that by leaving the chest against the door, it would be assumed she was still asleep and they would delay rousing her. The window was further from the ground than she realised and she fell on landing and twisted her foot. Picking herself up, she shut the window behind her and hobbled across the garden to the rough hut that housed both the horses and the garden boy. He was fast asleep on a heap of straw, his jacket and trousers folded on a stool nearby. She saddled the carriage horse, not the earl's mount, then turned towards the boy, who still slept. She had not come with the intention of taking his clothes, but the opportunity was too good to miss. She bundled them in her arms and led the horse out on to the road. Once clear of the villa, she found a low wall and climbed into the saddle. The next minute she was galloping away across the scrub that grew on the hillside above the town.

Once she was sure she had not been followed she stopped and scrambled into the boy's clothing and then sat on a hillock to survey the city lying in the dawn below her. The view was beautiful with the early morning sun lighting up the pastel-coloured buildings, the pink roofs, the church spires and the castle atop the opposite hill, but she was in no mood to admire it. She was free, but where was she going next? She had no idea of the geography of the country and could not speak the language, though she had discovered that Spanish and French sometimes sufficed. She mounted up again and turned her horse down the steep terrain towards the centre of Lisbon. It would be easier to hide in the city than in the countryside, she decided, and she needed to find some way of earning enough money to take her home.

She rode down into the great square of the Rossio, crowded and noisy even so early in the morning, and set about exploring the roads leading off it, past houses with wrought-iron balconies and blue-and-white tiles around their doors and colourful plants spilling from their balconies. At any other time she would have been fascinated by it all, but her only thought at that moment was on wondering what job she was fit for. All she knew anything about was running a coachmaking business. The thought made her smile and she set off to find one.

She had been walking the horse for nearly an hour, up and down the narrow alleys that wound their way upwards from the lower city streets when it was sometimes necessary to pull to one side and hug the walls to allow a carriage or a cart to pass. It made her realise why the carriages were so narrow; any wider and they would not have been able to negotiate the alleys.

Coachmakers needed space to do their work, so she rode down to the river level and began exploring the new part of the town. There was much rebuilding still being done, but the new city was impressive with its fine buildings and regular roads. It was here, close to the river, she watched coaches coming and going through a large archway. If they were not constructed here, they were being hired out. She dismounted, tied up the horse and found her way to an office where she knocked and entered. Two men were working at tables covered with ledgers and plans. The elder looked up, but he did not stand and she suddenly remembered she was dressed as a boy and not a smart one either. He addressed her in Portuguese, which she did not understand. How was she going to make herself understood if no one spoke English? It could be a real obstacle to employment.

'Do you speak English?' she asked, remembering to lower the tone of her voice.

'I speak it a little.' This came from the younger of the two men.

'Good. I am seeking employment and you look

as if you could do with some help.' She nodded towards the piles of papers.

The young man translated for the benefit of the older one, who laughed and went into voluble Portuguese.

'My father asks what do you know of coaches and coachmaking?'

She took a deep breath. 'I worked for Mr Gilpin, coachmaker, in London for a time. You have heard of him?'

'I have,' the young man said. 'I was in London after the earthquake destroyed our home and went to find work to earn enough to start again. That is where I learned to speak the language.'

'Did you work for Mr Gilpin?' She was fairly sure he had not; she had a good memory for all her father's employees and their families. It was one of the things that made her so popular with them.

'No, Mr Godsal. They were business rivals.'

Their conversation was interrupted by the older man demanding to know what they were talking about. His son translated for him and listened to his reply.

'He wants to know what work you did for Mr Gilpin?'

'I was a clerk.'

'That is no good to us if you cannot write and understand Portuguese.'

She had thought of that and while she was familiar with all the processes of coachmaking, some of it was hard physical work and most of it skilled and they would soon realise she was not up to it. 'I know, but I can do other jobs, particularly the varnishing and painting. I can draw a fine line, scrolls and coats of arms by way of decoration.'

'You know the secret of Gilpin's varnish?' he asked.

'I do.'

He told his father this and there followed an argument between father and son at the end of which the son turned to her. 'My father wishes to know why you are in Portugal and looking for work.' He looked her up and down. 'Your clothes, I think, are locally made.'

This was the difficult part. She took a deep breath. 'I was in the area of the London docks and was pressed into service by the navy. I am not a sailor, sir, and I found life at sea most uncomfortable. I am afraid I jumped ship when we docked here and I bought the clothes on the market. I must earn enough money to go home.'

The young man laughed. 'So, we are to hide you as well as employ you?'

'If you would be so kind.' She gave him one of her most endearing smiles and realised her mistake when he looked startled. Captain Carstairs had been right; acting the boy would not be as easy as she had thought.

'How old are you?'

She dare not hesitate over this, though her brain was whirring. 'Seventeen, sir.' Being so young might account for her apparent femininity and only half-broken voice.

'And your name?'

'Charles Manley.' Charles because it sounded like Charlotte. Manley because it was the first that came into her head and she was amused by the irony of it.

'I am Manuel Rodrigues and my father is Joachim.'

She executed a wonderful leg and was suddenly reminded of the games she used to play with her friends at the school she attended. For some reason she was always cast as the boy, but this was no time for dreaming of times past, which could never come again.

There followed another lengthy discussion between father and son, while she waited, hardly daring to breathe. At last the young man turned to her. 'We are prepared to give you a trial. There is a coach almost finished. It has been painted, but we would like you to decorate according to our customer's specification and then varnish it in the Gilpin way.'

'And my wages?'

'My father says we will decide on your reward at the end of the day. You will eat your dinner with us.'

'Thank you. I must also find somewhere to sleep.'

'We will also decide that when business is done for the day.'

It was too good an opportunity to quibble over the conditions. Even if they paid her nothing at the end of the day it was a day of freedom, one step nearer going home. 'Thank you.' She bowed her head in acquiescence.

'Come, I will take you to the workshop.' He gathered up the design of a coach and led her from the office, across a yard and into another large building. The scene that met her eyes was so familiar, it made her gulp with homesickness. Although it was nothing like as big a concern as Gilpins, there were men working on every aspect of coachmaking, from woodworkers and metal workers to upholsterers and painters. They looked up in curiosity until Manuel explained who she was and what she had come to do. One or two smirked, but she ignored them and looked about her, sizing up the operation.

'This is the carriage,' Manuel said, indicating a coach painted in bright yellow. 'It has been ordered for a count, a man great in government.'

He spread the drawing out on a bench. 'Can you make it look like that?'

'I can,' she said firmly, though she was far from sure. She had watched Gilpin's painters many and many a time and had even practised on a dog cart, but never a full-sized vehicle. He pointed to brushes and pots of paint and left her to work.

Remembering she had left the horse tied up, she hurried outside, untied it and slapped its rump to set it free. If it was seen and recognised, the earl would know where she was. It ran off towards the Rossio and she went back to begin work.

She could not converse with the other employees and so she worked in silence, studying the drawing now and then as she painted a thin black line all round the body of the coach, finishing with a scroll on either side of the front and beneath the box at the back. There was another line round the circumference of each of the four wheels and again round each hub. She was slow and careful and it took most of the day. By the middle of the afternoon she was ready to begin on the coat of arms. This was going to test her artistic ability to the limit, and though she had always been good at drawing and had often been praised by her drawing master, this was different. She mixed her colours and fetched a stool so that she could sit at the task. Before long she realised she had an audience; the men had stopped work to watch her, jabbering to each other in Portuguese. She knew they were waiting for her to make a mistake and that made her nervous. She was extra careful and had only half-finished the first one when the men suddenly disappeared and Manuel came to tell her that was the end of work for the day.

'Tomorrow you will finish the design and apply the first coat of varnish,' he said, after carefully inspecting what she had done.

'You mean I may stay?' she queried with a beaming smile.

'Yes.'

'Thank you, thank you. I must find accommodation.'

'I will take you to Madame Felix. She has a boarding house nearby. With luck she will have a vacancy.'

Charlotte was lucky, she realised that. She could so easily have failed in her mission and been forced to throw herself back on the mercy of the earl. Instead she had work which provided her with a small wage and a room which, though simple, was clean and adequate for her purpose. She refused to dwell on the memory of her large bedroom at home, her wardrobe full of elegant clothes, her maid, Barbara, who looked after her and was more friend than servant, and the comparatively easy work she had at Gilpin's. She was free and mistress of her own destiny. No one knew where she was, not the Earl of Falsham, not Captain Carstairs, not even her father. Perhaps when she was more settled she might write to him. For the first time in weeks she fell asleep as soon as her head touched her pillow.

And then she dreamed. She dreamed she was on board a ship in a storm and the vessel was being pounded on rocks and breaking up. And then she heard Alex Carstairs calling her name above the roar and crash of the waves, calling more and more urgently, as the sea engulfed her. She woke with a start and sat up to find herself in bed, warm and dry. And there was no Alex.

It took her several minutes to calm herself and try to understand the dream. Was it something yet to come or simply a memory of the storm in the Bay of Biscay when he had looked after her so tenderly? She had been half in love with him then, but it had been spoiled when she found him deep in conversation with Martin Grosswaite. He was two men in one: Captain Alexander Carstairs, the refined and elegant man about town and Lieutenant Duncan Fox, second mate of the *Vixen*, and she had no idea which was the true man and he would not tell her. How could you be in love with a man like that? But, oh, how she longed for his touch, the feeling of safety he gave her when she was in his arms. Was that love?

Chapter Eight

Alex could not rest. His head was full of images of Charlotte. Was she content with her situation and waiting only to hear from her father to accept his decision that she should marry the Earl of Falsham? Gilpin, who made no secret of the fact that he wanted a title for his daughter, might very well, under the circumstances, condone what the earl had done and urge her to accept. And whatever she said to the contrary, the prospect of becoming a countess must be a big enticement. If only he could find out how she really felt. To do that he must contrive to see her alone.

Where was Falsham keeping her? He and Davy had spent the whole of the day after the ball combing the city for her to no avail. 'This chasing about to no purpose will not serve,' he told Davy the following morning as they sat over breakfast in the lodgings he had taken. When they were alone, Davy always took his meals with him, although he was alive to his position when they were in company. 'We must put our thinking caps on. Someone in this city must know the earl's direction.'

'Captain Brookside,' Davy answered. 'He would have to know so that he could tell him when the *Vixen* is sailing.'

'That's true, but Brookside will not tell me anything unless I confide why I want to know, and I am not sure if I can trust him not to tell Lord Falsham.'

'Would that matter?'

'Of course it would matter. I do not want to alert his lordship of my true intent. He will take Miss Gilpin further from our reach.'

'He can't go far if he intends to sail with the *Vixen*.'

'We cannot be sure of that. I heard him say he was waiting for Mr Gilpin to join them and the *Vixen* will have sailed long before then.'

'If that happens, all your troubles will be over.' He was taken aback when Alex laughed.

His troubles over? It might mean the mission he had been sent on was over, but that was not the whole of it. There was the little matter of his pride, his feelings and the overwhelming desire to know what Charlotte herself felt, not to mention his antipathy towards the Earl of Falsham. Perhaps the man could not be blamed for his losing Letitia, but he acknowledged, with surprise, that no long seemed to matter. What did matter was Charlotte. He could not, would not, believe she would acquiesce to anything arranged for her if she did not wish it, so did she wish it? She was more mature than Letitia, more independent, more resourceful, altogether more desirable. And stubborn.

'I am going out,' he said suddenly, rising from the table.

'Do you want me to come with you?'

'No. You go and see how matters stand with the *Vixen*. See if you can find out when she is sailing.'

'Aye, aye, sir.'

Alex left him and made his way to the Rossio. Falsham had bought clothes for Charlotte and the shop would have delivered them. All he had to do was wheedle the direction out of the proprietor. Why had he not thought of that before?

There were several shops to choose from and he went from one to the other, telling them he had come to pay the Earl of Falsham's account. The first two denied all knowledge of an account, but the third was delighted to take his money, for which he insisted on a receipt which included the direction of the earl. Armed with this information, he lost no time putting it to use.

Outside the villa, he stopped to consider his strategy. First he had to establish that Charlotte was there. He walked all round the property and found a way in at the rear. There was a boy working in the garden, but he took little notice as Alex passed and made his way to the house. At the kitchen door he encountered a plump young woman, who spoke to him in Portuguese.

'*Não entendo*,' he said, using one of the few phrases he had learned.

'English. You are English?' she answered. 'I speak a little. Tell me what you want.'

'The Earl of Falsham, is he at home?'

'No. He is gone riding. Come back later.'

'Perhaps Miss Gilpin is in. I should like to speak to her.'

'She is not here.'

'Where is she?'

She shrugged. 'I do not know.'

He wondered how true that was. Had Falsham found another hiding place for her? Was she being close confined? Did that mean he was not as sure of her as he would have liked? The morning was far advanced and the sun climbing in the sky and he did not think the earl would ride in the heat of the day. 'Then I will wait to see his lordship.'

'As you wish.' She conducted him to the drawing room and left him to go about her work. He took the opportunity while the servant was outside talking to the garden boy, to go round the house. Charlotte was certainly not in any of the rooms. Where was she?

Falsham arrived half an hour later to find Alex at ease in one of the chairs in the parlour. 'Fox, what the devil are you doing here?' he asked, as Alex rose to his feet.

'A courtesy call, my lord,' he said. 'I am planning a picnic into the hills and came to invite you and Miss Gilpin. I expect Captain Brookside, Mr Miller and Mr and Mrs Hay to join us. It will be a pleasant change from the heat of the city and set Miss Gilpin up for her voyage to India.' He paused. 'I assume we shall see you and Miss Gilpin on board the *Vixen* when we sail?'

'Do you know when the *Vixen* sails? Brookside told me he has been delayed by some interfering harbour clerk finding fault with the bill of lading.'

'But perhaps the delay is fortuitous. It will allow more time for Mr Gilpin to arrive.' They were skirting round each other like a pair of fighting cocks. 'And you can give Miss Gilpin the treat of a picnic. Could we not ask her if she would like it?'

'Not today.'

'That is a pity, I need to know in order to make the arrangements. Miss Gilpin is not ill, is she?'

'You are uncommonly interested in my fiancée, Lieutenant. Why is that, I wonder?'

'I would not like to think the lady was unwell. She appeared pale when I spoke to her at the ball.'

'No doubt the sea voyage tired her.'

'Then she is resting?' The words were couched as a question.

'Yes. I will speak to her about the picnic when she joins me. Now, I beg you to excuse me, I see Mr Grosswaite has arrived and wishes to speak to me.'

Alex, far from satisfied, took his leave. Charlotte was not at the villa, so where had the man hidden her? He waited outside to see if the earl came out, intent on following him, but the only person who put in an appearance was Grosswaite. He was torn between waiting about for the earl and following Grosswaite. He decided on the latter, but the man simply went back to the harbour to wait for the barge from the *Vixen* to take him to the ship. Alex walked over to stand beside him.

'Are you living on board, Mr Grosswaite?' he asked pleasantly.

'It is cheaper than lodgings, Lieutenant.'

'Is Miss Gilpin already on board?'

'Why would she be on board, when she has his lordship to look after her on dry land?'

'But the *Vixen* will sail as soon as the repairs are done and wind and tide are favourable.'

'Then no doubt his lordship will be informed and he will board at his convenience.'

'With Miss Gilpin?'

'Naturally with Miss Gilpin, though I expect her to be the Countess of Falsham by then.'

'Do you know where the lady is?'

Grosswaite turned and looked hard at Alex. 'What business is it of yours where she is, Lieutenant? Fancy your chances, do you?'

'Not at all, but if she is being held against her will, then, as a gentleman of honour, it behoves me to rescue her.'

The man laughed. 'If you can find her, you may ask her that question.' The barge had arrived at the steps and he walked away to board it.

Defeated for the moment, Alex turned to go back to his lodgings. He met Davy on the way and recounted what had happened. 'We have to watch the earl night and day,' he said. 'Sooner or later he will lead us to Miss Gilpin.'

'We might have to wait until the *Vixen* sails.'

'That might be too late. According to Grosswaite he expects her to be married by then. I am going back to have another look round the villa and keep an eye on the earl. If I haven't located her by eight this evening, you can take the night watch.'

'If you have located her, what then?'

'I will decide that when I come face to face with her.'

They spent three days on watch day and night. The Earl was out and about, riding in the hills surrounding the city, going to clubs frequented by Englishmen and gambling heavily, attending a soirée where he excused the absence of Miss Gilpin by saying she was indisposed. The difficulty was not knowing where the earl was going to be next. Alex would hurry to a place he had been told of, only to be too late; the earl had gone, or he would arrive just in time to see his coach disappearing up the road or, if he was on foot, would lose him in the crowd. Had they been in England, it would have been easier; there would be no language and customs to contend with and he would have been able to call on the assistance of the rest of the Gentlemen. With only Davy to help him, their surveillance was patchy.

Every day increased his anxiety. He did not think she could have married the earl, because the man would have made a noise about it, invited half the elite of Lisbon to witness it, but that did not mean he had refrained from taking her virginity. The thought of that did not improve Alex's temper. There was nothing for it, but to challenge the earl outright.

He called on the gentleman again, this time determined not to prevaricate. If he saw Charlotte and she sent him away, then that would be the end of it. He could only tell Henry Gilpin he had done all he could, but the lady herself was content with the situation.

'You again,' the earl said. Alex had arrived early in the morning and the man was at his breakfast and was alone. 'I am afraid we will not be able to attend your picnic.'

'Forget the picnic. There will not be time to arrange it before the *Vixen* sails. It is not about the picnic I have come. I want to know what you have done with Miss Gilpin. She has not been seen by anyone since the Minister's ball. If you have harmed her...'

'Harm her? Why should I do that? I intend to make her my wife.'

'So you say, but I wonder if the lady agrees. Let me see her and hear from her own lips that she has accepted you.'

'She is not here.'

'Where is she?'

'Staying with friends until the wedding can be arranged. It would not do for her to be living under this roof before the knot was tied, would it?

Now, please leave. I have much to do and cannot be wasting time pandering to a lovesick sailor.'

That was too much for Alex. He grabbed the man by his satin coat and hauled him to his feet. 'You will tell me where Miss Gilpin is or I will beat it out of you.' As he spoke he shook the man until his teeth rattled. 'Speak or...'

Falsham, who was no hero, suddenly realised Alex meant what he said. 'She left after the ball and I do not know where she is.'

'Is that the truth?' Another shake.

'Yes, I would like to know where she is myself. Gilpin will not thank me for losing her.'

'No, I do not suppose he will.'

'She stole my horse.'

'Your horse?' How far could she have gone on that? he asked himself. She might not be in Lisbon at all.

'Yes, but it found its way back to the stables where I hired it.' He gave a harsh laugh. 'Pity it can't talk.'

Alex let go of the man, who sank back into his chair. It had been an unsatisfactory interview in one respect, he still did not know where Charlotte was, but neither did the earl. She had run away! Oh, brave, brave Charlotte. But where was she? 'I am going to find her.'

He turned to leave and the earl, recovering a little, called after him, 'I would demand satisfaction for that outrage, Lieutenant Fox, if you were a gentleman.'

Alex laughed, setting aside the temptation to tell the earl he outranked him, and went on his way. He would save the satisfaction of that for another day.

He went back to his lodgings to find Davy waiting for him with a huge grin on his face. 'You want to know where Miss Gilpin is?' he asked.

'You know very well I do. She is no longer with the earl.'

'No, for she is dressed as a lad and working down by the harbour. I couldn't believe my eyes at first, so I waited and watched. It was her all right.'

'Working? What was she doing?'

'She is employed by a coachmaker called Rodrigues.'

'A coachmaker!' Alex's first reaction was to laugh, the second was to dash down there and demand to speak to her; he had turned and reached the door before he hesitated. He needed to be more subtle than that. 'I will go and hire a horse and carriage,' he said. 'We are going to need one when we find Miss Gilpin. You will follow the earl wherever he goes. Don't let him out of your sight because I know he is as anxious to locate Miss Gilpin as I am and I have to find her first.'

* * *

Charlotte had completed the decorative painting on the carriage to the elder Senhor Rodrigues's satisfaction on her second day there and one of the other workers had come to help her varnish it. Unable to communicate except by signs, they had worked silently together and, by the end of that day, the first coat was finished. Her father would have applied seven coats of varnish to any prestigious coach he made and each had to harden before applying the next, but Manuel had said three was enough. She had persuaded him to a fourth.

She was in the course of warming the varnish for the last coat to make it cover more smoothly, when she heard a voice she recognised and looked up to see Alex in conversation with Manuel. It was too late to run and hide for he was looking at her with that familiar half-smile, which made her hackles rise at the same time as it set her heart beating almost in her throat. How she longed to throw herself into his arms, to feel cherished and protected. But that would make him and everyone else laugh, besides mortifying her. She was, after all, meant to be a boy. She turned from him to stir the varnish and take it from the fire to cool.

'That has a most unpleasant smell,' he said, approaching her. 'Do you not find it so?'

'I am used to it,' she mumbled in her youth's voice, though she did not, for a moment, think she had deceived him.

'No doubt you are. I have encountered it before myself, at the coachworks of Mr Henry Gilpin in London. There is no mistaking it.' He dropped his voice. 'Nor you neither.'

'Sir, I must not waste time talking, or the varnish will go off before I am ready.'

'As you wish.'

He turned back to Manuel and concluded the hiring of a landaulet and a horse to pull it and then left without speaking to her again. Charlotte looked up to see his tall back disappearing through the door and longed to call him back. She felt tears welling in her eyes and dashed them away with her sleeve. Young men did not cry. Neither did independent ladies who prided themselves on their strength of character.

She cleaned her brushes and her hands and prepared to leave the premises and go to her lodgings. As always, she looked carefully about her before venturing outside, but she wondered if the caution was necessary, considering Captain Carstairs knew where she was. Would she have to run away again, just when she felt she had fallen on her feet? It was so unfair.

She had crossed the square and turned into the

narrow road where Madame Felix had her boarding house, unaware that she was being followed.
A few yards further on Alex caught up with her.
'What game are you playing now, Miss Gilpin?'
he asked quietly, falling into step beside her

There was no point in denying her identity. 'I
am playing no game.'

'No, for it is deadly serious. Do you know
what you are about?'

'Yes.'

'Forgive me if I doubt that. You could be in
danger.'

'From Manuel Rodrigues and his father? They
will not harm me.'

'How do you know that?'

'They have been very good to me and I trust
them. And they like my work.'

'What about the other workers? If they have
not tumbled to the fact that you are a young lady,
they very soon will. I remember saying you did
not make a very good midshipman, you are far
too shapely. As for working as a coachmaker...'

'I *am* a coachmaker,' she said angrily, wishing he had not said that she was shapely. It reminded her how he had looked after her when she
was ill and she did not want to be reminded. His
behaviour then and since had been at odds and
confused her. When she was in his company, his
physical presence held her in thrall. She wanted

to melt into him, to feel his strong arms about her, to be held as he had held her in her cabin, nothing between their two bodies but thin cotton. In his presence she was weak as water. When he was absent she made her head take over from her heart and convinced herself he was no more to be trusted than anyone else. Head or heart? She did not know which was right. 'I know as much, if not more, about building coaches than any of them in there.' She jerked her head back towards the coachworks.

He smiled. 'Have you visions of taking over and making the business your own?'

'Do not be so silly.'

'It is not I who am silly,' he said. 'What are you calling yourself?'

'Charles Manley and I will thank you to remember that.'

'And what story have you told them?'

'That I was pressed into the navy and forced to serve, that I jumped ship and want to earn enough to take me back to England.'

'Very droll,' he said, trying not to smile. 'And they believed you?'

'Yes. Why not?'

'You cannot possibly keep it up.'

'What else do you suppose I should do? I have to earn a living.'

'You do not have to. You know the Earl of

Falsham is anxious to have you back? He is hiding the fact that you are missing for the moment because it would make him look very foolish, but it will not be long before he tells the world you have been kidnapped and then the coachmaker will not protect you. The workers will give you up for a reward.'

She felt her newly won independence slipping away from her. Was nowhere safe? She refused to acknowledge he was probably right and marched on, her back stiff and head held high. He remained glued to her side.

'Will you go back to Lord Falsham?'

She stopped walking and turned angrily towards him. 'So this is what you are about, trying to persuade me to go back to that…that…' Words failed her. 'You have been hand in glove with him all along. I cannot think which is worse, a man who makes no secret of who he is and what he wants, however bad, and another who hides behind a veneer of friendliness and concern.'

He was angry, too. 'You do me a great disservice, madam. I do not hide what I am from you or anyone.'

'No? Then what is Captain Carstairs doing posing as Lieutenant Fox? If that is not hiding, I do not know what is.'

'One day I will tell you, when you have learned to trust me.'

'Why should I trust you any more than I trust Manuel and Joachim Rodrigues? Or the earl himself?'

'Ah, now there's a question. Come with me and I will tell you.'

'Certainly not!' She resumed walking, but he had no difficulty in keeping pace with her.

'Charlotte, you are not safe on the loose, the earl will find you in the end, just as I have.'

Charlotte. He had called her Charlotte. 'I wish…' she began slowly.

'What do you wish?' he asked gently.

She could not tell him, it would diminish her to admit she needed him, needed him for all manner of reasons: to protect her, to defend her, to stand beside her against a hostile world, to make her feel loved and cared for, to make a woman of her. Her determination not to be lured into marriage, was crumbling. The pity of it was that he was not trying to lure her. 'Nothing you can do.'

'Try me. Do you wish to go home to England?'

'Yes and that is exactly what I intend to do, just as soon as I have money enough to pay for a passage.' She had begged writing materials from Madame Felix and had written to her father, begging him to come and fetch her home, but she had no idea how long the letter would take to reach him and then he had to find a berth on a ship. And perhaps he would not come, perhaps he would write to the Earl of Falsham and agree to the marriage. Oh, she prayed not. She had always been a dutiful daughter, but if that happened she would have to defy him. Learning to make a living might serve her well in the future.

'I admire your spirit, madam, but it will take an age and in that time—' He broke off, letting her imagine the earl coming for her and making sure she did not escape again.

'What choice do I have?'

'Let me take you.'

'What is the difference between you taking me and the Earl of Falsham doing so? My reputation would still be in tatters.'

'Not if you were married.'

'I know that and so does Lord Falsham.' She gave a brittle laugh. 'He is counting on it.'

'Do you want to marry him?'

'No.'

'What if your father advises it?'

'He will not make me.'

'Are you certain of that? It would silence the gossips and would, in the eyes of society, be a perfect match.'

'I do not care two pins for society.'

'But your papa does. For the sake of your reputation and his credibility, he might insist.' He paused while she digested this, though he did not doubt she had already thought of it. 'There is an answer.'

She stopped and turned towards him again, wanting to trust him, to hear him out. Everything he had said was true, whether she wanted to admit it or not. Dare she trust him? The more he talked, the more inclined she was to put her faith in him. 'Go on. I am listening.'

'I need to be sure you are set against Lord Falsham, no matter what arguments are put forward in his favour.'

'I am set against him. I cannot imagine anything worse than spending the rest of my life with him.'

'Has he…?' He paused, trying to frame his question. 'Has he forced himself upon you?'

She turned to face him, her face suffused with colour. 'Has he ravished me, you mean?'

'Has he?'

'No. I think he is afraid such a deed would not stand him in good stead with my father and he is counting on Papa agreeing to the wedding and making me accept.'

'Would you?'

'I have already told you I would not.'

'Then marry me.'

She stared at him open-mouthed. 'What did you say?'

'Marry me. Here and now. That would put an end to his lordship's plans, would it not?'

She started to laugh, but it was not a laugh of merriment, but near hysteria.

'I am glad you find that amusing,' he said stiffly.

Her laughter turned to tears and she could not stop them. They rained down her cheeks in a flood. He pulled her into an alley away from the curiosity of the people in the street and held her in his arms while she sobbed. 'I'm sorry,' she managed to say when the tears dried up. 'I cannot believe you are in earnest.'

'Oh, I am in earnest.'

'But why? Why interest yourself in my affairs unless it is to usurp Lord Falsham? He wants me for my wealth and makes no secret of it. Is the same true of you?'

Her sharp response squashed any idea he might have had to tell her he loved her. Instead he said, 'No, I have no interest in your wealth. It seems to me to be a stumbling block to true happiness.'

'How right you are, but at this present moment I have no wealth, I do not have a feather to fly with.'

'All the more reason to accept my offer. Once safely back where you belong in London with your father, we will have the marriage annulled. I give you my word.'

'Oh,' she said thoughtfully. 'You mean it is to be a temporary marriage of convenience?'

'Yes. Did you think I meant anything else?'

Her tears had stopped, but her heart was near to breaking. He didn't want her. For all her wealth, he disdained her. If he had said he loved her, asked her in the approved manner, she would have been very tempted, more than tempted, to say yes, but not like this, not even to escape from the earl and be taken home. Her life would be purgatory, loving him and knowing he did not love her. 'I thank you, Captain Carstairs, but, no. Please do not ask me again.'

'You can be sure I will not do that, Miss Gilpin. I am a man and I have my pride.'

They had arrived at her lodgings. She ran from him and went inside, slamming the door behind her. She, too, had her pride.

Alex turned and walked back down the hill, wondering what had made him offer for her on the spur of the moment like that. It had been unbelievably clumsy and invited a rejection. He should have thought about it more carefully, waited until she was more receptive, not only to the idea of marrying, but to a declaration of love. Angrily to tell her he would not ask her again was the height of folly because he was a man of his word. Now, once again, they were at loggerheads. He felt tempted to kidnap her, but that was exactly what Falsham had done and he would not lower himself to follow in the footsteps of that gentleman.

He must tell her the truth of why he was in Lisbon, put everything back on a business footing and make arrangements for her to stay in a safe place with ladies to look after her until a ship arrived going to England. His feelings for her and his antipathy for the Earl of Falsham had conspired to cloud his judgement and make him forget his duty. He set off for the British Minister's Residency. Mr and Mrs Hay would surely take her in and keep her safely away from Falsham.

'I am reluctant to intervene without some assurance that Falsham does not have the right of it,' Edward said when, after a wait of two hours while the Minister dealt with state matters, Alex had been shown into his office and made his request. 'A betrothal is as binding as a wedding.'

'But there is no betrothal, certainly not one Miss Gilpin has agreed.'

'Perhaps she is simply a disobedient daughter. If I could be sure Miss Gilpin's father is against the marriage, it would be another matter entirely. I would invite her to stay under my protection.'

'Then I hope Gilpin considers his daughter's happiness more important than his coachmaking and comes out to Portugal to fetch her home. In the meantime, could you suggest she stays with you until her father comes, just for appearances' sake? I am concerned that she is exposed to all manner of danger where she is, and not only from Lord Falsham.'

'I will suggest it to his lordship.'

'To do that, you will have to divulge where she is.'

'That is true but, as you say, she cannot stay where she is; the idea of a gently nurtured young lady earning a living as a boy is appalling. I suggest you explain to her what I have suggested and persuade her to come here. I shall not keep her hidden away, but I shall make sure she is chaperoned at all times. No doubt Lord Falsham will allow her clothes to be brought here.'

Alex was not sure he liked the idea of the earl being consulted, but it was the best arrangement he could make. He thanked his friend and left to go back to Charlotte's lodgings.

Charlotte had only picked at the supper her landlady had prepared for her and then excused herself and gone to her room, to lie on the bed staring up at the ceiling, wishing she was back at home in London and everything was as it had been before the appearance of Captain Carstairs. Being in love was supposed to be a wonderful feeling, but this was not wonderful, it was making her miserable. Her situation in a strange country where she did not speak the language, being sought by two men, one of whom she held in aversion and the other... She was not sure of the other at all. Having to disguise herself in order to earn a living was bad enough without the anguish of unrequited love.

She did not hear the knock at the door at first, but it was repeated and Madame Felix called out to her that there was a gentleman downstairs wishing to speak to Senhor Manley. 'Tell him to go away,' she called, without opening the door. 'I have no wish to speak to him.'

She heard Madame go back downstairs and a murmur of voices as she relayed the message and then the street door was opened and shut again. Charlotte rose from the bed and went to the window to see the back of Captain Carstairs, in his lieutenant's uniform, disappearing down the hill. Falling back on the bed, she allowed herself the luxury of tears.

The next morning she rose bleary-eyed, knowing she had no choice but to go on with the life she had made for herself, but she would be doubly watchful. Alex had been right; the earl could find her as easily and he had. It might mean she would have to disappear again and where would she find work and lodgings as congenial as those she had?

She looked about her as she left the house to go to work. The road was crowded with people coming and going in carts, carriages and on foot, but she saw no one she recognised. Joining the throng, she made her way down the hill. And then he was beside her again and her heart did a strange flip and gave her an intense feeling of pleasure and pain. She could not control her emotions and that made her angry with herself. She refused to acknowledge his presence until he spoke.

'Why would you not see me last night?' he asked.

'I had already retired and there was nothing you could say that would change matters.'

'Not even an apology?'

'For what?'

'For my clumsiness in making an offer which, if I had stopped to consider, I should have known you were bound to reject. All I was trying to do was to help you. I still want to do that.'

'Why?' she asked again. 'I do not understand.'

He took a deep breath. 'Because, Miss Gilpin, you are in need of help, that you cannot deny, and because I had the felicity of knowing you and your father in London and when you disappeared, he asked me to find you and bring you back in my capacity as a member of the Piccadilly Gentleman's Club, and that is what I am trying to do.'

'Oh.' She digested this extraordinary piece of information for a moment. He was not interested in her as a person, she was simply another of his cases. It was not flattering. On the other hand, it did mean he was not in league with the earl. 'Is that why you pretend to be Lieutenant Fox?'

'Yes. I could not obtain a berth on the *Vixen* as Captain Carstairs.'

'Why did you not tell me this before?'

'It was better for you not to know. That way you would not inadvertently let the cat out of the bag. I was not sure who your kidnapper was and it might very well have been Captain Brookside. And remember, Grosswaite was on board and he would have noticed at once if you had been well disposed towards me. As soon as we reached Lisbon Falsham claimed you. When I saw you at the ball you did not seem unhappy with your situation. Until I saw you yesterday, I was not sure if that were the case or not.'

'And now?'

'You have assured me you do not wish to marry the Earl of Falsham, nor me, and so I have spoken to the British Minister and he has agreed to have you to stay with him and his wife as his guest and ensure you are chaperoned at all times. He expects Lord Falsham to agree to this and have your clothes sent to the Residency. You will live more comfortably there without the need to disguise yourself or go to work.'

'I see. But it will mean Lord Falsham knows where I am.'

'To be sure. The Minister is reluctant to upset the earl more than he can help and he needs to be diplomatic at all times, so the need for a chaperon until your father arrives will be put to the earl. Mrs Hay has agreed to perform that role.'

'Supposing Papa does not come, relying on you to fulfil your mission, what then?'

He smiled wryly. 'Then, Miss Gilpin, that is what I shall have to do. Let us resolve one thing at a time. The most important at the present time is your safety.'

He was so businesslike, so impersonal, so detached from any emotion while she was seething with conflicting emotions, most of which centred around the way his physical presence affected her. He managed to make her heart beat so fast she was sure he could hear it, to turn her legs to rubber and make her hands shake. She wanted to touch him, to feel his warmth, to bask in his love and protection, but that was not possible. Instead she resorted to prevarication.

'You have a job to do, Captain,' she said, as they reached the archway leading to the coach-works. 'And so have I. I do not leave work unfinished, especially when someone has put his trust in me to complete it.'

'You cannot mean you want to stay here where you will be prey to any unscrupulous man who sees through that flimsy disguise and wants to have some sport with you, besides the risk of being found by the earl and abducted all over again? If you do not go to the Minister of your own free will, he will not be able to help you. I will come in with you and explain to Senhor Rodrigues why you cannot continue in his employ.'

'I do not need you to explain, I am perfectly able to do so myself. Manuel understands English.'

'You call him by his given name, I notice.'

'To distinguish him from his father.' She looked at him and laughed. 'If I did not know differently, I would surmise you were jealous, Captain Carstairs.'

He did not grace that with an answer. Instead he said, 'Go in. I shall go and fetch my carriage and bring it here to wait for you.' He looked down at her garden boy's clothes. 'It would be better not to be seen near the Residency in that rig.'

'Very well.' She disappeared inside the building. He went down to the waterfront where he

had left the landaulet. A French merchantman
had dropped anchor in the river and the crew
had just been rowed ashore. It was unfortunate
that it coincided with a group of English seaman returning to the *Vixen* and a ribald comment
from one had resulted in a fight between the two
groups, which was acrimonious and violent. He
was obliged to wade in and restore the peace
which took some time but in the end he sent the
English tars back to the *Vixen* and apologised to
the Frenchmen, something he was loathe to do
when his inclination was to pitch in on the side of
his compatriots. The French matelots were angry
and not prepared to be appeased, but a handful
of escudos soothed their tempers and he was able
to find the landaulet, put the hood up and drive
back for Charlotte.

He sat outside the coachmakers for over half
an hour, becoming more and more impatient,
concluding the stubborn girl was finishing the
work she had been given before leaving. He left
the carriage and went in to fetch her out. She was
nowhere to be seen in the workshop or the office. 'The young English lad,' he said, addressing the younger Rodrigues who was working at
his desk. 'Is he here?'

'No, he left just over half an hour ago.'

'Do you know where he went?'

'No. He said he was going to stay with a friend until he could find a way of going back to England.'

'I thought I was that friend.'

'Then mayhap his shipmates have found him. He'll not like that, he said being a sailor did not suit him.' Manuel looked hard at him. 'But you are a sailor, sir.'

'I am and anxious to find the lad before he falls into more trouble.'

'I am afraid I cannot help you.'

'I do not mean him any harm. He will not be in trouble if I take him back to the ship at once before she sails.'

'I still cannot help you. I would if I could. I liked the lad, he was a good worker, but I doubt he made a good sailor.'

'No, he did not. That is why I want to protect him. If he comes back, tell him his friend is still waiting.' He picked up one of the pens on the desk, dipped it in ink and drew a blank piece of paper toward him. 'This is where I can be found. Tell him that.'

Having written the direction, he put the pen down and left. Charlotte was obviously sticking to her disguise. What had got into her now? Why could she not have waited for him? This was turning out to be the hardest assignment of all those he had done for the Piccadilly Gentlemen and he never felt more frustrated. The foolish girl still did not trust him.

Chapter Nine

Charlotte struggled against her bonds, but they were tied so tightly the effort hurt her wrists. And the gag they had stuffed in her mouth was choking her. The carriage had drawn up right beside her and she had innocently opened the door, believing Alex was inside it. Instead she found herself being hauled in to sit beside Madeleine and a young man who had swiftly tied her up and gagged her. What a fool she had been to go out onto the road to wait for Alex and an even bigger fool for not realising the earl did not do his own dirty work and was bound to send someone else. When it was too late, she realised the carriage was not the one Alex had bought from Rodrigues.

She had been so relieved and happy that Alex had found her first, especially after he had explained about the Piccadilly Gentlemen and suggested a solution to her immediate problems. It had not meant he reciprocated the love she had for him, but at least she would be able to see him and speak to him if he called on the Minister and she would be protected from the earl. Papa would come and they would go home to England, back to their cosy existence, moving daily between Piccadilly and Long Acre, building up the business, supporting their favourite charities and attending social gatherings. And Captain Carstairs would move on to his next case. She told herself, not very convincingly, she would be content with that.

But even that hope had been dashed the moment Madeleine and the strange man seized hold of her and bundled her in the anonymous coach, tied her up and gagged her. What was Alex doing? What had he thought when he came back to fetch her and found she had gone? Had anyone seen her being pulled into the carriage? Had anyone heard her cries before they were cut off by that suffocating gag?

When the coach turned away from the road leading to the earl's villa, she realised he would not risk taking her back there since Alex knew where it was. They started to climb through narrow streets that were so steep the horse was struggling. On each side rose the walls of close-packed houses which shut out the sun. The alley gave way to a small square and an imposing steepled church. They passed this and went into an even narrower alley and here they stopped. The carriage could go no further.

They forced her out on to the rough dirt road and pushed her along in front of them and in at the door of one of the houses. The room she found herself in was cool after the heat outside. It was furnished with a table and half-a-dozen wooden chairs, a heavy sideboard in a dark wood and several potted plants.

'Sit down,' Madeleine commanded, removing the gag.

Charlotte sat in one of the chairs and took huge lungfuls of air and it was a moment before she could speak. 'Water,' she murmured. 'Give me water, please.'

Madeleine disappeared through a door into another room, leaving the man to watch over her. Charlotte heard her speaking to someone and then she reappeared with a glass of water, nodding to the man to untie her hands so that she could take it.

She gulped the liquid down and immediately felt better. 'Where am I?' she demanded. 'What do you want with me?'

'You are in my mother's house,' Madeleine said. 'You will be looked after here.'

'On the earl's orders?'

'No. It was my own idea.'

'Why?'

'I mean to help you and myself as well.'

'I do not understand.'

The girl laughed. 'I do not want you coming between me and my lord. He is determined to marry you, but it is me he loves. I want us to be as we were before you came.'

Charlotte remembered the giggles outside her bedroom door, and the way the girl looked at the earl and managed to touch him now and again as if by accident. 'How was it before I came?' she asked, trying hard to remain calm.

'For two years we have been close, for two years so happy, but then he went back to England and when he returned he told me his bride was going to join him. I was angry.'

'I imagine you were,' Charlotte said. 'But you have nothing to fear from me. I have no wish to marry Lord Falsham.'

'So you say, but my lord says you will. He says you dare not go back to England unwed.'

'Then I shall stay here unwed. Lieutenant Fox has arranged for me to stay with the British Minister in Portugal. He was gone to fetch a carriage to convey me to the Residency just before you arrived.'

'That will not help me. My lord would know you were there and he will not give up. He says there is too much at stake, though I do not know what he means by that.'

'He is talking about money, Madeleine. He is in great need of it, I think.'

'Pah! That cannot be. He can buy anything he wants. No one questions how much money he has. He is a most generous man.'

'He can afford to be, seeing he exists on credit. When his creditors start to demand payment, he will be hard put to come about. That is why he wants to marry me, for the money I will bring to the marriage. I have seen it all before with other young gentlemen and I have always resisted and I shall go on doing so. Take me back where you found me, or better still, to the British Minister's residence. I will pay you well.'

The girl laughed. 'What with?'

'I can arrange for money to be transferred from London to a bank in Lisbon.'

'No. That will not help me to keep my lord, will it? He will be angry.'

'What do you propose to do with me then?'

'My mother and Carlos will look after you.'

'Who is Carlos?'

The young man who stood watching them suddenly launched into torrents of Portuguese, to which Madeleine answered, none of which Charlotte could follow. 'This is Carlos,' she said indicating the young man. 'He is my brother.'

'I see, but this is all so unnecessary. I will not marry Lord Falsham, whatever he says, you may be sure of that.'

'He will make you.'

'He most certainly will not! You cannot hide me here for ever. Someone will come looking for me.'

'They will never find you.'

Charlotte feared that might be true. How could anyone penetrate the warren of close-packed houses and know which door she might be hidden behind? She had got away from the earl's villa; she would have to do the same from this place.

'If you tell the truth and will not marry my lord, I will let you go.'

Charlotte breathed with relief and stood up. 'Thank you.'

'Not now. When my lord gives up looking for you and is good to me again, then I will.'

'Oh.' She sat down again.

Carlos began arguing with his sister, but in the end he shrugged his shoulders and left the room. 'Come,' Madeleine said. 'We will eat.'

She led the way into the adjoining kitchen where an elderly lady in a plain black gown was stirring something in a pot over the fire. 'My mother, Senhora Salvador,' Madeleine said. 'Sit down.' She indicated a chair at the table.

The old lady ladled a thick stew into a bowl

and put it on the table in front of Charlotte without speaking, but she looked Charlotte up and
down, taking in her boy's attire and clicking her
teeth in disapproval.

'Thank you,' Charlotte said. *'Obrigada.'*

Carlos came back into the room and mother,
daughter and son sat down with Charlotte to eat.

The food was surprisingly good, a mixture of
different fish, Charlotte thought.

Afterwards she was conducted up two flights
of stairs to a small bedroom. 'You stay here,'
Madeleine said. 'Got to sleep.' She left the room
and locked the door behind her.

There was a narrow bed with a mattress, a
pillow and a thin sheet. There was also a tiny
window which looked out on to a back yard and
beyond that the backs of other houses. This was a
densely populated area and there would be no escape in that direction, even if she could get downstairs and find her way out there. It would have
to be by the front door. But how? And when?

She wondered what Alex was doing. Was he
searching for her? Would he have any idea where
to look? Would he simply shrug his shoulders and
forget all about her? After all, he had offered her
marriage and she had laughed in his face and he
had frostily said he would not ask her again. Oh,
Alex, she thought, don't give up on me, please

don't give up. I need you so desperately. She was tired of trying to be brave, she wanted someone to hold her, take the worry from her shoulders and that someone, she admitted, had to be Alex Carstairs.

She pictured him hammering on the door, pushing aside anyone who obstructed him and bounding up the stairs to her. She imagined sinking into his arms and being held and comforted and told how much he loved her and could not live without her. She savoured it for a minute and then pulled herself together. It was only a daydream and not to be indulged in for fear of making her weaker. She had to be strong, had to draw on her own resources to extricate herself.

Alex was frantic. What had happened between the time he had left Charlotte and his returning? She had seemed perfectly amenable, even relieved, by his suggestion she should go to the British Minister's Residency. Had that been a front to cover her intention to disappear a second time? One of Rodrigues's workers had told him he had seen her getting into a carriage which was not one of theirs. So where had she gone? He had told her why he was in Portugal and she had seemed relieved and ready to trust him. She had no reason to flee from him and he did not believe she had.

It had to be Lord Falsham who had found her and abducted her yet again. He knew it would do no good to confront the earl again, much as he would have liked to beat the truth out of him. And he doubted Falsham would have taken her back to the villa, knowing it was the first place anyone would look for her. Besides, she had escaped from there once and his lordship would not risk her doing it again. Falsham had told him she was with friends. Who and where were they?

His frustration and anger were consuming him. Not since he had lost Letitia at the green age of nineteen had he felt so helpless. In war he had always been decisive, forming a plan of action and making sure it was carried out. Even in peace, with the management of his affairs, he was self-assured. And the work he had been given for the Society for the Discovery and Apprehending of Criminals held no terrors. He went about it with a cool head. What was different now?

Oh, he knew what was different. He was in love—that was the difference. It was clouding his judgement and making it difficult for him to think clearly. James had told him when he first joined the Piccadilly Gentlemen's Club that they should not become emotionally involved with the subject of their investigations and that had made him laugh. Every single one of them had married as a result of meeting the love of their lives while working for the Gentlemen. And he had said he was immune!

After leaving the coachworks he had gone to explain to the Minister why Miss Gilpin was not with him and what he thought had happened.

'My dear fellow,' Edward had said. 'Unless we can prove that Lord Falsham has broken the law, the Portuguese authorities cannot, and will not, arrest him. Indeed, we cannot even accuse him of abduction unless we know without a shadow of doubt that he is holding Miss Gilpin against her will. That did not appear to be the case when he brought her to the ball.'

'She was hoping to speak to you and ask you to help her, but she could not escape the earl's attention long enough to seek you out.'

'That may be so, but my wife invited her to call the following day and she did not.'

'No, because she had run away and found work and lodgings disguised as a boy, which goes to show how desperate she was.'

'She may have done so again.'

'I do not believe it. She was lucky the first time, but it is unlikely she would be so fortunate a second time, even if it were her intention, which I doubt. The last time I spoke to her and told her of your invitation she was happy to accept. I intend to find her and bring her to you and you shall hear that from her own lips.'

'Very well, but take care. Do not break the law yourself or you will be the one in trouble and not his lordship. He has powerful friends in Lisbon.'

'You will do nothing to help?'

'There is nothing I can do, except perhaps invite his lordship and Miss Gilpin to any social activities we may be arranging. If he brings her, then I will take the opportunity to have a private word with her. I can do no more.'

Alex thanked him and left. It was late in the day and he had eaten nothing since breakfast. Perhaps a meal would stimulate his brain. He went in search of Davy and they went to an eating house not far from the lodgings he had taken.

'I am at an impasse,' he told Davy, after learning from him that the earl had not left the villa all day and the only people he had seen had been the maidservant, the gardener and Mr Grosswaite who had arrived in the middle of the afternoon. 'I want to hit out at something, preferably the Earl of Falsham, but I am afraid if I do he will move her again. And it is not an action that would be approved by the Gentlemen.'

'I'll do it for you, if you like,' Davy said.

'No, certainly not. He will have you clapped into prison for assault and I wouldn't be able to help you. I must think. What is his weakest point?'

'His gambling and his shortage of blunt, I should say.'

'You are undoubtedly right, but I could not raise Miss Gilpin's fortune and that is what it would take, though if I had it, I would certainly pay up and not mind.' He noted Davy's smile at that, but decided not to comment. He had never been inclined to wear his heart on his sleeve, not since Letitia had disappointed him and he was not going to start now.

'You play a good hand of cards,' Davy said. 'Better than his lordship, I'll wager.'

'You are surely not suggesting I should engage in gambling with the earl? For what stakes? Miss Gilpin herself?'

'Why not?'

'He wouldn't do it and I could not be sure of winning.'

'Yes, you could. I learned a thing or two when I was in the service. I could show you.'

'Cheat, you mean? I have never done such a thing in my life. It is dishonourable.'

Davy shrugged. 'You could call him out, demand satisfaction.'

'He will not duel with me. He thinks I am not a gentleman.'

'Tell him you are. There ain't a man in the kingdom can best you with a sword.'

'I haven't used my sword in anger for two years. It is almost rusty with disuse.'

'No, it ain't. I keep it sharp and shiny, like I do everything of yours.'

'I know, Davy, I know.' He sighed. 'But he would have the choice of weapons and he might choose pistols. I do not think I could deliberately shoot one of my own countrymen and supposing he kills me—how will that benefit Miss Gilpin?'

Davy conceded it would not.

'There is nothing for it but to kidnap Miss Gilpin and hold her fast until a ship arrives going to England.'

'You said you would not do that.'

'I know I did, but desperate ills demand desperate medicine. I am done with prevaricating. I have been commissioned by Henry Gilpin to bring his daughter home and, by hook or by crook, that is what I intend to do.'

'We have to find her first.'

'You do not have to do anything, Davy. If I fall foul of Portuguese law, then so be it, but I won't involve you.'

'Begging your pardon, my lord, you cannot manage on your own and I won't be cast aside. You need me.'

Alex laughed. 'Very well. It will have to be done before the *Vixen* sails because he'll have her on board in the shake of a lamb's tail as soon as tide and wind are favourable and I do not intend for her or either of us to be carried all the way to India.'

'I am much relieved to hear it, my lord. I have no fancy to go there again either, hot, disease-ridden place that it is. I near died of a fever the last time I was there.'

'I have no wish to go myself,' Alex said and was thoughtful for a moment. 'He might have taken her on board already. Resourceful as she is, it would be impossible for her to escape from there without help. I am going to see Captain Brookside. I shall tell him the truth and he will have to make up his mind whose side he is on. You go back to watching the earl.'

They parted and Alex walked down to the harbour and hailed a boat to take him out to the *Vixen*.

There was a skeleton crew on board, most of whom were below decks, but a couple of sailors were on watch. They touched their forelocks as he climbed aboard. 'Where is Captain Brookside?' he asked, hoping the captain was on board and not ashore.

'In his cabin, Lieutenant.'

Alex made his way to the cabin, knocked and entered. Brookside was sitting at his desk surrounded by charts. He was in his shirt sleeves and without stock or cravat.

'Lieutenant Fox,' he said, refilling his glass from the brandy bottle which was half-empty. 'You might as well go away again. The damned port authorities have found something else wrong with the cargo. We shall miss the next tide.'

Alex allowed himself a secret smile. Edward was doing all he dared to help him. 'I am sorry to hear that,' he said. 'Have the passengers come aboard?'

'No, they will come when I send word we are about to sail, though God knows when that will be. Why do you interest yourself in their affairs, Lieutenant?'

'Not Lieutenant,' he said. 'You have addressed me incorrectly. I am Captain Alexander Carstairs.' He watched the man's mouth drop open and smiled. 'I am also the Marquis of Foxlees. If you require proof, then no doubt the British Minister will supply it.'

'Then what in hell are you doing aboard my ship?'

'I have been commissioned by Mr Henry Gilpin to rescue his daughter from the clutches of the Earl of Falsham, who had her kidnapped in London and brought unwillingly on board your ship.'

'Kidnapped,' he echoed. 'Be damned to that for a tale.'

'You have heard Miss Gilpin say more than once that she had been brought aboard against her will, but you chose to ignore her. That makes you an accessory to a criminal offence, Captain Brookside.'

'It has nothing to do with me, Lieutenant. I do only what I am paid to do.'

'Captain Carstairs, if you please. I believe I am your senior.' Alex was not too sure of that, but it did no harm for Brookside to think it. 'Have you been paid?

'Captain Carstairs, then. The arrangements made between me and his lordship are nothing to do with you.'

'Ah, then I assume you have not been paid. You are acting on a promise.' Alex gave him a disarming smile. 'I do not envy you trying to get blood from a stone. The Earl of Falsham is counting on Miss Gilpin's father coming up trumps. He is going to be vastly disappointed, if I have my way.' He paused to look at the captain, who had emptied the glass of brandy down his throat and was reaching for the bottle. 'If you wish to redeem yourself in the eyes of the law, you will co-operate with me. The consequences of not doing so...' He stopped to allow the Captain to think about it.

'What would you have me do?' he asked after a long pause.

'Do you know where Lord Falsham is holding Miss Gilpin?'

'That I do not. I have not seen either of them since the night of the Minister's ball.'

'If you do hear where she is, you will appraise me of it immediately. And you will not sail with Miss Gilpin on board.'

'I must take advantage of wind and tide as soon as these dammed harbour clerks admit there is nothing wrong with my bill of lading.'

'You will send for me at once if that is likely to happen. I will not, of course, be sailing with you and neither will my man, Davy Locke.' He paused. 'Unless Miss Gilpin is on board when you sail, in which case, I shall take over the ship and we will return to London and English justice. Is that understood?'

'Yes, my lord. It shall be as you say.'

'And do not go bleating to Lord Falsham about our little talk. He will not help you. And I shall cite that as evidence of your complicity if the matter comes to court.' And with that he turned on his heel, made his way to the starboard entry and clambered down into the boat which he had instructed to wait for him.

Davy was waiting for him at the steps as he landed. 'The earl has gone to the British Club,' he told him. The British Club had been formed for ex-patriots, diplomats, naval officers and others with business in Portugal. Sometimes they arranged social evenings at which ladies were present, but for the most part it was used for drinking and gambling. Lord Falsham was no doubt indulging in his favourite vice and getting deeper into debt.

'Good, we will have a look round the villa again while he is out, though I doubt he is holding her there.'

He was right. The villa was in darkness, the gardener asleep on straw in the stable and there was no one in the house. They climbed in through a window carelessly left open and found themselves in the room used by Charlotte; the chest and drawers were full of lady's clothes, among them the gown she had worn at the ball. They left everything undisturbed and searched all the other rooms. There was no sign of Charlotte.

'I think it is time I had further discourse with the Earl of Falsham,' Alex said. 'You keep an eye on Grosswaite. The earl relies on him to do his dirty work and he might lead you to her.'

They walked down as far as the Rossio together where Davy left him to go to the waterfront and a certain tavern Grosswaite was known to frequent. Alex found his way to the Club in the Rue Sao Bernardo.

The earl looked up when he saw Alex enter the room. Throwing down his cards, he strode over to him. 'How dare you show yourself here, Lieutenant Fox?' he demanded, his face so close to Alex's he could smell the brandy on his breath. 'What have you done with her?'

'Done with whom, my lord?' he asked coolly, though the man's question had set up a string of others in his head. If Falsham did not know where she was, who did?

'Miss Gilpin, my fiancée.' The earl turned to the others in the room, all of whom had stopped their play to look and listen. 'This man has abducted my fiancée, taken her from my protection. No doubt he is about to demand a ransom.' He laughed harshly. 'You will be unlucky there, Fox. Until I receive a certain communication from Mr Gilpin, the coffers are empty. Or were you planning to extract a ransom from him?'

Alex took a deep breath. 'I have no idea where Miss Gilpin is, Lord Falsham, but I am heartily glad she has escaped your clutches.'

One or two of the onlookers murmured, 'Shame.' Others advised the earl to call the upstart out and demand satisfaction. Alex was quite prepared to take him on if he did. Being the one challenged, he could choose the weapons.

'I would not lower myself to duel with anyone who is not a gentleman,' the earl said, looking down his nose at Alex. 'But I will offer a reward for anyone returning Miss Gilpin safely to me and ensuring this man is thrown in jail.'

Alex laughed. 'If your coffers are empty, as you say, my lord, how will you pay a reward? Mr Gilpin again, I suppose.'

Falsham's face turned purple and he took a step towards Alex, his hand raised, but seeing the implacable look on Alex's face, he changed his mind and dropped it to his side. 'I will not sully my hands with you.' He went back to the card table. 'I will give you twenty-four hours to bring her to me, Lieutenant Fox, or it will be the worse for you.' He picked up his cards. 'Let us continue with our game, gentlemen.'

For two pins Alex would have grabbed him by his collar and administered the beating he deserved, but he did not think that would help to find Charlotte, even if it did give him the satisfaction of seeing the man grovel. He turned on his heel and left.

The Earl of Falsham was as anxious to find Charlotte as he was and he had to find her first. But where to look? She wasn't at the villa, she wasn't at the Residency and she wasn't at the coachworks. Who else had an interest in her fortune? Grosswaite? He set off to find Davy.

'Grosswaite don't know where she is,' Davy told him. 'And he's in bad cess with the earl for not keeping a closer eye on her. He had a nasty bruise on his cheek. Feeling a mite resentful he was, blaming the servant at the villa for helping her to escape.'

'Do you think she did?'

Davy, shrugged. 'Could be. Apparently the girl was besotted by the Earl and didn't like the competition by half.'

'Davy you are a genius. Let us go and call on her while his lordship is busy with his cards. What's her name?'

'Madeleine Salvador.'

Charlotte felt ill, so weak she could not rise from the bed, let alone think of escape. She had been very sick and her head was so muzzy, trying to think made it ache. An idea would come into her brain, but before she could take a hold on it, it was gone to be replaced by another, equally ephemeral, and for long periods she drifted into unconsciousness.

Madeleine had left to return to the earl, leaving her in the care of her mother and brother. Madame brought her meals and took away her chamber pot, but that was the extent of her ministrations. She never saw Carlos, though she had heard him talking to his mother in the corridor outside. The old lady sniffed when Charlotte tried to tell her she was feeling unwell and required a doctor. She fell to wishing Madeleine would come back; at least she understood English.

She felt she was going to breathe her last, here in this tiny prison with no one to care whether she lived or died. Perhaps that was Madeleine's intention, that she should die. Was she being poisoned? The food had tasted strange lately. She had refused the next meal, but she was already too weak to take it. And she was so very thirsty, her mouth felt like cold ashes. Madame made her a drink which tasted of oranges and she gulped it down greedily only to feel even worse. How long had she been here? She had lost track of time.

She had nightmares, dreadful nightmares full of dark figures who stood over her, but did nothing to help her. And there was the earl and Alex and her father all mixed up together and seas crashing on rocks and dead bodies swirling about and she knew one of the bodies was hers. And men and women shouting, though she could not understand what they were saying. She thrashed from side to side, trying to throw off the nightmare. There were hands holding her down. She struggled against them, crying out for Alex.

'I am here.' The voice was quietly soothing. 'Do not fight me, please. Let yourself go.'

Let herself go? Did he mean don't struggle to live any more? Was the voice coming from the other side of the grave? She was too tired to wrestle any longer and lay back, unable to open her eyes, unable to stir.

'Dare we move her?' Davy asked.

Alex was kneeling beside the bed stroking the matted hair from Charlotte's face. She was bathed in sweat, the midshipman's shirt she was wearing soaked and sticking to her body. He knew it had to come off and she must be bathed and put into clean linen. Even then he wondered if they might have arrived too late and she was dying. His heart caught in his throat. That this lovely, innocent girl should suffer because of the greed and lust of one man and the jealousy of a wicked woman, and his own failure to protect her was tearing his insides to shreds.

'We cannot leave her here,' he said, anguish in his voice.

'Moving her might kill her.'

'Leaving her here will kill her. They have deliberately made her ill.'

'I did not.' The voice came from behind them. Madeleine, who had brought them here, stood in the doorway, watching them. 'It was my mother. After I left.'

The girl had not been in the villa when they returned there and it was dawn before she put in an appearance. Already angry and frustrated, Alex had not treated her kindly. He had threatened her with the law if she did not divulge where

Miss Gilpin was. 'Kidnap is a crime in anyone's country,' he had told her. 'You will go to gaol unless you tell me this instant where she is.' God help him, he had even raised his hand to her. He hadn't hit her; he would never hit a woman, but the threat was enough to make her co-operate.

Alex turned angrily towards her. 'What did your mother do? Did she give her something in her food?'

'She only wanted to calm her. She was making such a noise, shouting and banging on the door and walls. My mother was afraid the neighbours would hear her.'

'No doubt that was Miss Gilpin's intention,' Alex said grimly. 'What did your mother give her?'

'Laudanum.'

'Often enough and strong enough to kill her,' Alex snapped. 'It was attempted murder. If she does not recover, it will be murder.'

'No.' Madeleine put her hand to her mouth in horror. 'It was only enough to keep her quiet. She would not stop screaming and making a noise.'

'Well, you had better try to make amends. Find her something clean to wear and bring me a bowl of water and some cloths.'

'My lord…' Davy protested as the girl went to obey.

'This is no time for niceties,' he said. 'And it

is no more than I did for her when she was sick on board the *Vixen*. I will not trust her with anyone else in this house. You go and fetch the carriage. Bring it as close to the house as possible. And bring the blankets off my bed. There doesn't seem to be a scrap of anything decent here.'

'Will you be all right left here on your own?'

'Of course I will. Now, go and do as you are told.'

Davy passed Madeleine as he went out. She was carrying a bowl of water and had the other things Alex had asked for draped over her arm.

'Good,' Alex said, standing up to take everything from her. 'Now leave. I don't want you anywhere near her.'

'What are you going to do?' she asked fearfully.

'Do? I am going to make Miss Gilpin clean and comfortable and then I am going to take her away from here.'

'I meant what are you going to do about Mama?'

'I don't know. I haven't decided. I must get Miss Gilpin well first. If she should die…' He stopped to calm himself. 'You had better pray that she does not.'

'I will do that this instant.' She turned and fled, leaving Alex alone with Charlotte.

She was quieter now and he feared for one terrible moment that she had slipped away while he had been talking to Madeleine. He put the bowl on a table beside the bed and fell to his knees beside her. He took her hand in both his own and looked down at her pale face. Even her mouth had lost most of its colour and her eyes remained shut. He stroked her cheek with the back of his finger. 'Charlotte,' he murmured, fighting back tears he had not shed since he was a small boy. 'Charlotte, my love, don't leave me.'

His gaze went from her face to her body and saw the tiny movement of her bosom under the shirt. She still lived. He gave a huge sigh of relief, but it was still touch and go. 'Charlotte, you must live,' he murmured. 'You must live for everyone who loves and needs you: your papa, all the people at Gilpin's, the little orphan babies, your friends in England and me. Me especially.'

She gave no sign of having heard him. He dipped a small square of cloth into the water, squeezed it out and began gently washing and drying her face. He lifted her to take off the soaking shirt, then tenderly laid her back on the bed, trying not to let the sight and feel of her body rouse him. He washed her hands and arms and then her rounded breasts with their pink tips. She was not fighting him and he wondered if she knew he was there, that it was his broad man's hands that caressed her with cooling water before carefully drying her. She lay perfectly still, no longer tossing about.

His ministrations moved down to her flat belly and across her pubic hair, dampening, drying. He was glad no one else was in the room for they would surely have seen how this was affecting him. One day, God willing, and if she would have him, he would do this again and she would be conscious and fully aware of his desire. If she would have him. He leaned over and washed and dried one shapely leg, then the other, making himself hurry for he did not want Davy to come back before she was decently covered.

He found a cotton shift among the things Madeleine had brought and lifted her to slip it over her head. 'You will get better, my love,' he whispered as he put her arms into it and pulled it down to cover her nakedness. 'Trust me.'

'Alex.' Her voice was barely audible.

He looked at her face, wondering if she had been aware of what he had been doing, after all, but her eyes remained closed, though she was breathing a little easier. Had she been dreaming of him? He sat watching, willing her to recover, determined not to let her out of his sight again, whether she willed it or no.

Davy returned with blankets. 'The carriage is at the end of the alley,' he said. 'It is turned round and ready to go. I paid a young urchin to mind the horse.'

'Good.' Alex took one of the blankets and wrapped it round Charlotte before picking her up in his arms. 'Lead the way, Davy.'

He went downstairs and through the living room with his burden, watched by Madeleine and her mother, who was weeping noisily.

'You will not have my mother arrested, will you?' Madeleine implored, catching his arm.

'Not if the lady lives. You may tell her that.'

'And me? What of me?'

'I will leave your punishment to the Earl of Falsham.' He marched on behind Davy, ignoring the sobs he left behind him.

He put Charlotte in the carriage, covered her with a second blanket and climbed in to sit beside her and support her head.

'Where to?' Davy asked. 'Where are we taking her?'

'Home, of course. I will get a doctor to her and nurse her myself.'

'If you say so, my lord.' Davy obviously did not agree with this, but what else could he do? He didn't trust anyone with his love.

It was while they were on the way, threading through the morning traffic, that he changed his mind. Such an action would make him as dishonourable as the earl and she had been compromised enough. Besides, he was not a nurse and perhaps he did not have the skill needed. Nor did he think the earl would give up, there was too much at stake, and he and Davy alone could not keep her safe.

He wrapped on the roof. 'I've changed my mind,' he called to Davy. 'We will go to the Residency. It is the safest place for her.'

Edward was in the hall on the way out to an official engagement when Alex was admitted, carrying the still-unconscious Charlotte in his arms. 'My God, man, what have you there?'

'Miss Gilpin, sir.'

'What have you done with her? Is she ill?'

'I fear so. She was being held by Lord Falsham's servant in a tenement in the Alfama and dosed with so much laudanum, I fear for her life.' Alex sank into a chair with Charlotte on his lap.

The Minister was clearly discomforted by this impropriety, especially in front of his servants. 'You mean you spirited her away?'

'What else could I do? I beg you to give her sanctuary and fetch a doctor to her.'

'I am not sure I can condone what you have done, Alex. My invitation for her to stay was to observe the proprieties and allow her to be properly chaperoned until her father came to take charge of her. This latest development has altered the case. You have gone beyond the bounds of your remit. I will have the earl banging on my door the minute he realises where she is. I do not wish my home made into battleground while two men fight over a woman whose virtue is already in doubt.'

Alex had been looking down at Charlotte, at her paper-white face and pale lips, worrying that she had shown no signs of life except a slight fluttering of her breath which now and again came out as a sigh. He looked up at this, the muscles in his face working with frustrated anger, though he tried to control it for the sake of the precious burden in his arms. 'I cannot believe you mean to turn her away. Where is your common humanity, Edward? She needs help and sanctuary, not denial. Where do you suggest I take her? I cannot take her to my lodgings, can I? I took the rooms when we first landed with the intention of rescuing her from the earl and letting her live there independently with a female companion until such time as I could secure a berth on a vessel going to England. It was never my intention to live with her there.'

'No, I can see that would be not be a good idea. I suggest you take her to the nuns. They will nurse her and keep her safe. I will write the Mother Superior a note.'

He left Alex sitting where he was, nursing

Charlotte who was beginning to show signs of stirring. She ought to be in a comfortable bed, being properly looked after. All this hanging about would not help her recovery. If she died, he would never forgive himself. He tucked the blanket more firmly about her. 'Shush, my love,' he whispered. 'You will soon be more comfortable.'

Her eyes flickered. 'Alex?'

'I am here. You are safe.'

She sighed and her eyes closed again as if it were just too much trouble to keep them open.

Edward came back and handed Alex a letter on the outside of which was the name and address of the convent. 'I must leave you,' he said. 'I am already late for my engagement. Come back this evening and we will talk again. My best wishes to Miss Gilpin when she recovers.' And with that he was gone.

Chapter Ten

Charlotte stirred and opened her eyes. She had been having a lovely dream that Alex had her in his arms and was whispering loving words to her and she had not wanted to wake from it for fear of finding herself back in that grubby tenement with Madeleine's mother.

She turned her head. She was in a bed in small cell-like room. The walls were of stone and there was only a small window too high up to see out of. Was she in prison? But did they provide sheets and blankets in Portuguese prisons? There was a table on the wall opposite her bed and it was covered with a sparkling white cloth and on it stood a crucifix. And sitting on a stool beside it, reading from a small book, was a nun in a grey habit.

'Where am I?' Her voice came out as a croak.

The nun put the book down on the table and

walked towards her, her movements slow and deliberate. 'You are awake, the Lord be praised,' she said in English, standing over Charlotte and smiling at her. 'For a long time we feared for your life.'

'Am I in a hospital?'

'No, this is the Convent of Santa Marinha.'

'A convent. How did I get here?'

'You were brought here by a gentleman. You were very ill and he wished us to make you well again and keep you safe.'

'Gentleman. Was his name Alex?'

The nun smiled. 'You remember?'

'Only in fits and starts. I remember a room in a house and people keeping me confined. I was unwell.'

'Yes, you were, but you are better now the poison has worked its way out of your body.'

'Poison?' she queried. 'Was I poisoned?'

'Yes. You were given large overdoses of tincture of poppy. It made you sleepy and weak and gave you hallucinations. It is only your healthy constitution and determination that allowed you to survive.'

'And your nursing, I am sure.'

The nun put her hands together, as if in prayer, and bowed towards her. 'We did what we could. Many of the sisters are skilled in nursing and we have all prayed for you.'

'How many people know I am here?'

'The man who brought you and his driver and the British Minister who recommended you to our care.'

'The man, was it...?' She paused, wondering what name Alex might have used, but as far as she knew he had never admitted to being Captain Carstairs since boarding the *Vixen*. 'Lieutenant Fox?'

'Yes, that was the name he gave us.'

'Has anyone else come in search of me?'

'No.' She paused. 'You are afraid?'

'Yes. Did Alex... Lieutenant Fox tell you why he brought me to you? Besides making me well again, I mean.'

'He spoke a little of it. It is a strange tale of kidnapping and imprisonment that is hardly credible.'

'It is true none the less. The lieutenant was sent by my father to rescue me. Where is he? I should like to thank him.'

The nun smiled. 'He has been here every day, asking after you. When you are well enough to leave your bed and dress, then we will think about allowing a visit and you may express your gratitude.'

'Every day? How long have I been here?'

'A week.

'As long as that?'

'Yes, you almost died.'

'Then I have you to thank for my life.'

'And the young man who brought you to us.' The nun smiled. 'He is a little in love with you, I think.'

Charlotte brightened. 'Do you think so? I think he was only doing his duty for my father.'

'Love and duty are inextricably entwined, my dear.'

'What shall I call you?' she asked.

'I am Sister Charity.'

'You speak very good English, Sister Charity.'

'I was brought up in England, my family were London wine merchants. I came home to Lisbon to take my vows.'

'And have you ever regretted your decision?'

'Never. But the life is not for everyone. Now I shall go and tell Mother Superior and Sister Bernadette you are awake. And then I will arrange for food to be brought to you. We must build up your strength if you are to see that young man again.'

Charlotte smiled at the thought of seeing Alex and finding out how he had rescued her. She had vague memories of crying out for him and then his soft voice reassuring her and someone washing her, very, very gently, as if she were made of gossamer and might easily break. Had that been Alex, or one of her hallucinations? If it was a dream, it was very different from the dark terrors that had preceded it.

She ate the food they brought her, took the medicine designed to build her strength and longed for the day when she could see Alex's dear face again. The nuns were gentle and kind, but firm in their resolution that he would not be allowed into her sick room and she must wait until she could dress and go downstairs to greet him.

Day by day she grew stronger and more impatient. The day she left her bed was a milestone, but her legs were so shaky she could not stand for more than a few moments and the idea that she would go downstairs was abandoned. She was nothing if not determined and spent time walking about her room, from door to bed to window, and back again, over and over again until Sister Charity made her go back to bed. 'You will exhaust yourself, Charlotte. We cannot have all our good work come to naught simply because you are too impatient to allow time to heal. It will come all in good time.'

'Has Lieutenant Fox been again today?'

'Yes, he comes every day.'

'Has anyone else asked for me?'

'No. Rest easy. You are safe here.'

* * *

The next day she walked to the head of the stairs with Sister Charity supporting her, but she was not allowed to descend. 'Tomorrow, perhaps,' the nun said. 'We must find you some clothes. You had none when you arrived.'

She looked down at the plain cambric night-gown she was wearing. It covered her from neck to feet. 'What was I wearing when I arrived?'

'A shift and a blanket.'

'Nothing else?'

'Nothing else. They have been laundered and given back to Lieutenant Fox.'

'Oh.' This piece of information gave her pause for thought. Alex had rescued her like that. A vague memory stirred of being picked up and carried. Alex. It must have been Alex.

'Back to your room now or you will be too tired to try the stairs tomorrow.'

'Miss Gilpin is almost fully recovered,' Alex was told when he arrived at the convent the following day. 'She is dressed and sitting in the garden. I will take you to her.'

The nun who conducted him into the garden was the same one who had taken Charlotte in, calling others to bring a stretcher to carry her away into the bowels of the convent. He had been stopped from following. 'We will attend to the young lady,' he had been told in excellent English. 'Mother Superior will wish to speak to you. I will take you to her office.'

The Mother Superior was tall and upright, covered from head to foot in her habit, but her face was serene and she had not judged him as he told his tale. 'We cannot tell the rights and wrongs of it,' she had told him in French, the only language they had in common. 'The *mademoiselle* is undoubtedly seriously ill, but we will do our best to make her well again and, if it is God's will, she will recover.'

'Amen to that,' he said. 'But I entreat you not to let anyone from outside see her. Do not even divulge that she is here. I fear for her.'

She had reassured him the no man would ever be allowed to penetrate the nuns' quarters, not even he, so he had taken his leave. The responsibility did not leave him however. He had called every afternoon to ask after her and enquire if anyone else had done so. She was recovering slowly, he had been assured. 'And no one other than you, man or woman, has enquired for her.'

The *Vixen* had sailed without the earl, much to Captain Brookside's fury because he had not been paid the money promised him by Falsham, and he had to take on replacement crew for Alex and Davy. Alex told him he was lucky he was being allowed to continue in view of his complicity in Miss Gilpin's abduction.

Falsham went on with his dissolute ways, still telling anyone who would listen that Lieutenant Fox had kidnapped the woman to whom he was betrothed and if only he could find him and her, he would exact retribution. This Alex had learned from Davy who kept his ear to the ground on his behalf.

'He has had a letter from England,' Davy had told him only the day before. 'Probably from Mr Gilpin.'

'How do you know that?'

'Madeleine told me.'

'The maidservant? You are on terms with her?'

'I persuaded her to co-operate on pain of telling the earl what she had done. She was more afraid of his lordship's wrath than of the threat of prison and has been careful not to let him know what she did. She tells me what I want to know.'

'Did she say what was in the letter?'

'She did not know. The earl put it in his writing desk and keeps that locked. I do not think she dare try to open it.' He paused. 'I could try.'

'No, definitely not. I forbid it.'

'Mr Gilpin might have agreed to the wedding. After all, it's been a long time and he might have thought…' His voice tailed away.

'Do you think I have not considered that? I have written to Mr Gilpin myself and put all the facts before him. I have assured him no one has violated Miss Gilpin's virtue and she is safe with the nuns. He need not give in to the earl's demands, but that is not to say he won't. I wish he would set aside his business affairs and come out here. Charlotte needs him. Falsham would not dare to touch her if her father were with her.'

'Perhaps he is on his way.'

'Perhaps,' he said, but he was not at all sure. What sort of man put his business before the well-being of his daughter? If he had a daughter as lovely and sweet as Charlotte, her happiness would mean everything to him and he would abandon everything to go to her. But perhaps he was doing Henry Gilpin an injustice and he would come.

He had left Davy at their lodgings and made his way to the convent and this time he was going to be allowed to see Charlotte. He followed the nun into a small garden enclosed by a high wall and was shown where Charlotte was sitting on a bench beside a pool, contemplating the fountain which splashed sparkling droplets into the water.

She was very thin, he noticed, and the shapeless cotton gown they had dressed her in hung loosely on her. Her hair had been washed and brushed and hung to her shoulders in soft waves, held in place by a small lace cap. He stood and watched her for a moment. She looked sad, lost in thought. She had not seen him and he approached quietly so as not to startle her.

'Charlotte.' He spoke her name softly.

She turned towards him, her grey eyes coming alive and a smile lighting her face. 'Alex, you came.' She moved along the bench so that he could sit beside her.

He sat down and took both her hands in his, wishing he could take her in his arms and kiss her until she was breathless, but she was as fragile as the thinnest porcelain, no longer the healthy young lady who had left England six weeks before. It was hardly surprising; she had been ill on board ship which had left her weak and then all the worry of escaping from Falsham and working as a painter and, to top it all, being poisoned until she was near to death would have been the end of most ladies. He was thankful that she was recovering and that had to be enough for the time being. 'Naturally, I came. Did you think I would not?'

'Sister Charity said you have been here every day.'

'So I have but they would not let me in. I have been very worried about you.' He looked closely into her face. Her cheeks were hollow and there were dark rings below her eyes, but she looked a hundred times better than when he had brought her here. 'How are you?'

'I am getting better every day. The nuns have been good to me, given me nourishing broth and new baked bread and herbal medicines. When I have some money, I must repay their kindness with a donation to the convent.'

'I have done that on your behalf.'

'But I have no money.'

He grinned a little sheepishly. 'Yes, you have. Davy relieved Mr Grosswaite of almost five hundred guineas before he left the *Vixen*.'

She laughed. 'Oh, that is good to hear. Papa nearly died because of that and I hated the idea of that man having it. Does he know Mr Locke took it?'

'He may have guessed, but there wasn't a thing he could do about it.'

'I hope Papa is well. I had hoped he would have written to me by now to say he was coming, but I have moved about so much, a letter could easily have been lost.'

He decided not to worry her with the news that the earl had heard from her father. She might think that writing to him and not her meant that he condoned what the man had done and had given his permission for him to address his daughter. The very thought of that made Alex's blood boil. 'Perhaps, or perhaps he relies on me to fulfil my mission and take you home. I hope to have word from him myself before long. In the meantime, you are safe here.'

'Do you think Lord Falsham knows where I am? If he should come...'

'If he knew where you were, he would have come before now, but in any case, the nuns would not let him in.' He did not tell her the earl had made public his accusation that she had been kidnapped and his offer of a reward to anyone giving him information leading to her recovery and the apprehension of the culprit, believed to be Lieutenant Fox. 'They would not even allow me in.'

'I am sorry for that. I wanted to see you. Every day I asked and they said I must be well enough to be dressed and come downstairs before I could receive you. As if—' She stopped suddenly. She had been going to say, 'As if you had not seen me in nothing but a shift before.' It brought the colour flaming into her cheeks and she looked down at their clasped hands. 'Alex, tell me what happened. How did you find me? My memory is so vague.'

'What do you remember?'

'I remember being forced into a carriage by Madeleine, the Earl of Falsham's servant, though I believe she is also his mistress, and a man she said was her brother. Carlos, I think. Yes, Carlos. They conveyed me to a house up on the hill towards the castle and locked me in a room at the top of the house. After that I am not sure what happened. I was desperate to escape, but I did not feel well.'

'Senhora Salvador was slowly poisoning you.'

'That is what Sister Charity told me, but why would she do that? Whatever had I done to her?'

He smiled and absentmindedly stroked the back of her hands with his thumbs. 'You stood between her daughter and her daughter's happiness. They both had great hopes of the earl. The foolish girl imagined that if you were not there the earl would marry her and she would become a countess and they would never be poor again.'

'I doubt Lord Falsham would marry her.'

'Of course he would not. He has set his mind on your fortune.'

'He shall not have it. I will die first.'

'You very nearly did. Did you not realise there was something wrong with the food they gave you?'

'Not at first. When I arrived, I had a meal in the kitchen with everyone else, but after that it was brought to my room by the *senhora*. When I became too ill to eat it she gave me a cordial drink made of oranges. It was refreshing and I drank it all. I do not remember much after that.' She paused to look into the pool where their two reflections were mirrored, side by side. The droplets from the fountain shimmered and distorted them and she returned her gaze to his face. There was no distortion there, he was the same handsome man she had known in London, but thinner and more serious. 'Yes. Go on with what you were telling me. How did you find me?'

'I went back to the coachworks to fetch you only to discover you had gone.'

'I was waiting outside for you and when a carriage drew up beside me, I foolishly thought it was you and opened the door. They dragged me inside and bound and gagged me. If I had had my wits about me, I should have known it was not the landaulet you bought from Senhor Rodrigues.'

'I thought it must have been something like that.'

'They must have found out where I was and laid in wait for me.'

'We searched everywhere, Davy and I. You were not at the earl's villa, nor at the Minister's Residency, nor even on board the *Vixen*, ready to sail with her. Captain Brookside denied all knowledge of your whereabouts. I tackled Lord Falsham, but it was clear he had no idea of where you were either. He was angry and accused me of kidnapping you.'

'That coming from him! He is the kidnapper, not you.'

'It was Davy who had the idea of talking to his maidservant.'

'She admitted where I was?'

He smiled grimly. 'With a little persuasion.'

'And so you found me.'

'Yes. You were so ill I thought you were dying, but I could not leave you there.'

She shuddered. 'Would they really have let me die?'

'I do not think Madeleine knew what her mother had done until we arrived at the house, and her mother said she was trying to stop you shouting and banging and alerting the neighbours.' He paused to smile at her, his brown eyes looking at her so tenderly her heart flipped. Was Sister Charity right? Could he be a little in love with her? Oh, if only that were true. 'You must have been making a fearful din.'

'I could not escape, so I hoped someone would come to me. The houses are close packed in that district.'

'I shall never forget the sight of you,' he said. 'You were unconscious, close to death and bathed in sweat, your lovely hair plastered to your scalp and your face was as white as a sheet. I thought we had come too late.'

'And then?' she prompted.

'I carried you out to my carriage and took you

to the Residency. Mr Hay suggested you would be safest with the nuns.'

'I think you have left something out,' she said, smiling at him. 'I was wearing the midshipman's shirt the whole time I was in that room. I arrived here in a shift I had never seen before.'

'You remember?'

'I remember gentle hands touching me and feeling better for it. I do not think they belonged to Madeleine or her mother for they would not have been so careful of me. It was you, wasn't it?'

'You needed to be washed to cool your skin and put into clean clothes. It was urgent and I would not trust anyone else with the task.'

'I wish I had been awake.'

He smiled. 'I am glad you were not. You would have been mortified.'

'I am grateful for all you have done for me, all you are doing.'

'I do not need your gratitude, Charlotte. I did what was required of me with a glad heart.' His heart was full to bursting with love, but he held back from telling her so. She was weak, not her usual self, and she might agree to marry him simply out of gratitude and that was the last thing he wanted. No, he would wait until she was her usual robust, independent, outspoken self before he asked her to become his wife. He would risk more humiliation. And there was still the not-so-little matter of freeing her from the Earl of Falsham's clutches and taking her back to England and the life she knew. Once there, she might very well reject him because her father refused to sanction their union. If he could be sure she loved the lowly sea captain, then would be the time to reveal himself as the Marquis of Foxlees.

He looked at her now, smiling at him, her lips slightly parted, almost inviting him to kiss her. The temptation was almost overwhelming, but he was aware of nuns working in the garden around them. They appeared to be concentrating on their hoeing and weeding and gathering of blooms, but he knew they were keeping a watchful eye out for impropriety. If he blotted his copy book, they would not allow him to see her again. He forced himself to stop looking at her mouth, but shifting his gaze to her expressive grey eyes was just as unsettling. It was not only her lips that invited him to kiss her, her eyes repeated the invitation. He glanced down at their entwined hands and lifted them to his lips, one by one.

'What now?' she whispered.

He chose to misinterpret her words. 'You are right to remind me,' he said, his voice rough with the effort of controlling his seething emotions. 'We are not out of the wood yet and must think of ways of getting you home to your papa and everything you hold dear.'

'Not everything I hold dear is in London,' she murmured.

He did not know how to answer that without betraying himself. He released her hands and stood up to pace up and down. 'You must stay here until a British ship arrives on its way to London and I can arrange a passage for us. That is if you will trust yourself to the sea again. We could go overland, but it would be more trouble to arrange for we should have to hire horses and carriages and stay in inns and it would take several weeks to reach Calais and take a packet to Dover. I do not think your papa would like that.'

'We will do whatever you say,' she said, realising he was not going to utter the words she longed to hear and which she thought she had seen in his eyes. If he had, she would have said she didn't care how long the journey took as long as they were together. His failure to speak and his impatient pacing up and down cast her into despondency. How could he be so tender and loving one minute and change in the flash of a second into a hard practical man who could think only of how speedily he could relieve himself of responsibility for her? 'After everything that has happened to me since, I do not think I shall be sea sick again. If I am, I am—I shall recover as I did before.'

He stopped his pacing to turn towards her.

'I will employ a maid for you. You will need clothes and other things a lady needs before we go. I cannot take you back to your father looking like a waif.'

'Is that what I look like, a waif?' she asked, trying to make him smile again. When he smiled his face was alight, his eyes a soft light brown. When he was sombre or angry his eyes turned to green, hard as emeralds. She had noticed it before, but it had not been quite so obvious as it was now when she was alive to his every mood.

He looked at the simple garment she was wearing. It had no decoration of any kind and covered her completely from neck to feet, and yet it could not detract from her desirability. He wanted to strip it off her and feel again her smooth white skin beneath his searching fingers, to cover her with kisses. 'A waif,' he said firmly.

'Are you going to take me shopping for clothes like the earl did?'

'I am not the earl, nor anything like him,' he said gruffly. 'And you will not be taken shopping. It is unwise for you to leave here until a ship is about to sail for England and we can get you on board without being seen.'

'I am surprised Lord Falsham still wants me if he thinks I have been with you all this time.'

'Your fortune will allow him to be magnanimous and forgive your lapse,' he said wryly.

'Well he might, but I shall never forgive him.'

'I will ask Mrs Hay if she will be kind enough to purchase clothes for you.'

'I do not want anything fine,' she said. 'After all, there is no opportunity to dress up on board ship and I have plenty of clothes at home.'

'I shall tell her that.'

'I rather liked being a midshipman,' she said wistfully.

'And a very poor midshipman you made.'

'Did you recompense the boy for the loss of his clothes?'

'I did.'

'Good. That is another thing for which I am in debt to you.'

'You are not in my debt, Miss Gilpin.'

'Oh, we are back to Miss Gilpin, are we? What happened to Charlotte?'

'I forgot myself. I beg your pardon.'

She shivered. The sun, which had been blazing down from a cobalt-blue sky, was suddenly hidden by a dark cloud and the courtyard became cool and full of shadows from the nearby buildings. The mist made by the fountain, which had been pleasantly cooling, turned cold. She stood up, noticing the nuns gathering up their tools and hurrying back into the convent. 'I think it is time to go indoors,' she said.

'Yes, I believe we might be in for a shower of

rain.' He fell into step beside her. 'It will be welcome; the ground is parched.'

The rain started just as they reached the door. He held it for her to go inside. 'You must come into the anteroom or you will be soaked,' she said.

'A drop of rain will not hurt me. And I have much to do before we leave for England.'

'But you will come back again?'

'I will be back.' He bowed formally and took her hand to raise it to his lips.

'And when you come, Alex, I would wish you to forget yourself again,' she whispered. And then she left him, running lightly into the dim interior of the convent, her white gown making a ghost of her, as she disappeared.

He groaned and went home, uncaring that he was being soaked by the rain which was running off the corners of his tricorne hat and trickling down his neck.

The sun was shining again the next morning and he was busy. His first call was to the harbour, where he discovered that a ship bound for England from the Cape was expected two days hence. Whether it would have room for passengers, he had no way of knowing until it arrived, but he would assume it had and make preparations accordingly.

Then he went to the British Minister's residence, making his way through the garden and in at a back door, startling a cook and several kitchen maids who were preparing food. He smiled and put his fingers to his lips to stop them crying out and went on through a door on the far side which led into a corridor and thence to the front of the house. Here he was accosted by a footman who made every endeavour to throw him out.

'I must see the Minister,' Alex demanded loudly enough for that gentleman to hear him if he were nearby.

'Not coming in like a thief in the night, you don't.'

'It is broad day and I am not a thief and I know if you were to tell Mr Hay I am here, he will see me.'

A door opened and an equerry came out. 'What is all this hullabaloo about?' he demanded, then, seeing Alex, 'Oh, it is you, Lieutenant Fox.'

Alex shrugged off the detaining hand of the footman. 'Yes, and I must speak with the Minister.'

'Let him come in,' Edward's voice called from inside the room the equerry had left.

Alex dusted down his clothes with his hand, handed his hat to the footman and strode into the room.

'What was all that about?' Edward asked. 'Why were you being denied admittance?

Alex carefully shut the door on the listening servants. 'Not wishing to be seen I came in through a back way and your footman took exception to it.'

'You are wise to be circumspect, Alex. I have had the Earl of Falsham here complaining bitterly that you have kidnapped his bride and demanding I do something about it.'

'You know differently.'

'Of course I do, but I could not say so without betraying I knew where Miss Gilpin is. How is she?'

'Recovering slowly. There is a merchantman due in on its way to England and I have a mind to take passage for myself and my man, Miss Gilpin and a female companion. Do you know of anyone suitable who might be wishing to go to England?'

'No, but I will ask my wife.'

'I was hoping to call on your good lady's offices to purchase some clothes for Miss Gilpin. The nuns have put her in a strange garment I think must have come from their charity box. She has no clothes of her own.'

'I am sure Mary will be glad to do that, but I must caution you to be on your guard. The Earl tells me he has had a letter from Miss Gilpin's father sanctioning the betrothal and desiring him to bring his daughter home so that all may be done properly.'

'I was afraid of that.'

'It seems your services are no longer required.'

'While Miss Gilpin needs me and while she insists she will never consent to marry the earl, I will stay with her. If, when we return to England, she is disposed to bow to her father's advice, then I will, of course, leave her, my work done.' He did not add how hard that would be. Not for a second would he contemplate telling Gilpin he outranked the earl and was easily able to maintain his daughter in the style he would wish, something he felt sure Lord Falsham could not do. His pride would not let him.

Edward summoned a servant to ask his wife to join them and while they waited, offered Alex a glass of Madeira. She appeared while they were drinking it.

'Alex, my dear boy,' she said, coming forward to take both his hands. 'How are you? You look tired?'

He bowed. 'I am well, madam, but, as you say, a little tired.'

'How is Miss Gilpin?'

'Being well looked after by the nuns.'

'You do not blame my husband for sending her there, do you? If she had been here when

Lord Falsham called, it could have been very awkward.'

'Yes, I understand. I have decided not to wait on Mr Gilpin. If he has written to Falsham, it must mean he does not intend to come out himself and I must take Miss Gilpin back to England. I came to enlist your help in buying clothes for her and finding a trustworthy lady to act as her maid and companion during the voyage.'

She smiled. 'Is it not a little too late to worry about propriety, Alex? After all, she arrived without a maid.'

'That was not her fault nor mine,' he answered tersely. 'She assures me the earl has not violated her and her virtue is intact. I would keep it that way.'

'Why don't you marry her yourself? You are not ineligible, are you?'

'No, I am not, but now is not the time or place to make an offer, even if I were contemplating matrimony.' He was reminded of the clumsy attempt he had made while Charlotte had been working for Rodrigues, telling her they could annul it when they returned to England and, when she turned him down, his angry rejoinder, that he would not ask her again. What a numbskull he had been!

'No, perhaps you are right when there is a cloud hanging over you.'

'A cloud, madam?'

'Yes, Lord Falsham's assertion you have kidnapped his bride and are holding her hostage for some imagined slight or other. He calls you an overgrown poppycock of a naval lieutenant and if you were a gentleman he would call you out and make you eat grass. It is all over town.'

'I was afraid of that. Is anyone listening to him?'

'His friends, who witnessed a contretemps between you and his lordship. He does have some support, not least from his servant, Madeleine Salvador.'

'Good Lord! What has she been saying?'

'That she rescued Miss Gilpin from your clutches and was keeping her safe, but you arrived and forcibly took her back.'

'She is saying that to save face with the earl. I wonder how he found out what she had done? She was certainly anxious that I should not tell him.'

'There is evidence from a Mr Grosswaite, too.'

'He is one of the earl's minions and the one who arranged Miss Gilpin's abduction in London. If he ever shows his face in England again, it will go ill with him. I know his henchmen. They are murderers and thieves who escaped from Newgate and are being sought by the Piccadilly Gentlemen. I wrote and alerted Viscount Leinster as soon as I arrived here. No doubt he has them safely behind bars again and they will be persuaded to talk. The sooner I get back to London with Miss Gilpin, the better.'

'I agree,' Edward said. 'But better leave her where she is until you are ready to go.'

'Then how are we to buy clothes for her?' his wife asked.

'I shall have to guess her size,' Alex said. He knew every inch of her, from her height, which was just below his chin, to the span of her waist and the curve of her breasts.

'Then we will go shopping tomorrow. We will go in my carriage. I will have it ready for ten in the morning.'

'Thank you.'

'And I will make enquiries about a suitable maid for your journey.'

Alex thanked them and left the way he had come, ignoring the glowering of the footman.

It was Captain Carstairs who arrived promptly as ten the following morning. Lieutenant Fox in his rather untidy uniform and white wig was gone and in his place was a sea captain in a dark-blue coat, white breeches and snowy shirt, cravat and hose. His own dark hair was held in a queue with a black ribbon.

'Oh, I am so glad you have thrown off that

untidy disguise and that dreadful wig,' Mrs Hay said when she saw him.

He smiled. 'I decided it would be expedient to keep the Lieutenant and the Captain separate, ma'am. You would not want to be seen with Lieutenant Fox in view of Lord Falsham's accusations. And it is as Captain Carstairs I mean to take Miss Gilpin home.' He chuckled. 'All very proper.'

'Then let us go and do the shopping. I have made out a list of what Miss Gilpin will require.'

'She has charged me not to be extravagant because there will be little opportunity for wearing finery on the voyage and she has plenty of clothes at home.'

'Three gowns, I think,' the lady said, as they sat side by side in the coach. 'Two day gowns, perhaps of light wool for it will seem chilly on board after the heat of Lisbon, and an evening gown for dining with the captain. Then she will need stays and undergarments, nightgowns, hose and shoes, a cap and a hat for when you land in England, powder, rouge, toilet water…'

Alex laughed. 'I am glad I have you with me, madam, I should never have thought of all that.'

'It is a pity Miss Gilpin could not come with us,' she said. 'I have no idea what her preference is as to colours.'

'I know what suits her,' Alex said firmly. 'She

looks well in any colour, but blue and rose and pale lemon, I think, will do very well, and a little lace and ribbon, but not overly decorated.'

'And her size?'

'Her head comes to my chin when she is standing beside me and I can almost span her waist with my hands.'

'Oh, Alex…' she laughed '…I will not ask you how you know that.'

'You forget I carried her from that dreadful room.'

'So you did.' She turned to look at him. 'I think you are perhaps in love with Miss Gilpin.'

'Who would not be?' he said. 'She is lovely, brave and altogether desirable.'

'Have you told her so?'

'No, I have not. Nor will I. There will be time enough for that when she is safely back with her father and he has given up the idea of persuading her to marry Falsham.'

'Why does he want the match?'

'For the title. He is determined she will marry a nobleman.'

'But you outrank Falsham.'

'Mr Gilpin does not know that.'

'Alex, you are too proud for your own good.'

'Perhaps. She is proud, too, you know.'

'Then I should like to bang your heads together to knock some sense into them.'

He laughed because he knew she meant no harm. They had turned into the Rossio and stopped outside the shop where he had paid the earl's account. 'Is this where you told the driver to come?'

'Yes, it is the best mantua maker in Lisbon and she will no doubt have some ready-made clothes which might suit. If not, her seamstresses work very swiftly and we can bespoke something.'

They spent a pleasant hour or two buying clothes and a large portmanteau to put them in, for which he paid in gold. He had hesitated when the mantua maker asked where they should be delivered. He did not want them sent to the convent, for fear word might get out that there was a lady staying there who needed fashionable clothes. 'They can be sent to the Residency,' Mrs Hay told him in an undertone.

'No, for that would mean I would have to bring Charlotte to you to change into them and we might not have time for that, once the ship has dropped anchor. I will take them with me in the portmanteau to my lodgings, ready to take to her at the convent when the brig is ready to sail.'

When they left the shop he was carrying the portmanteau. He saw Mrs Hay into her carriage, bade her adieu and strode off towards his lodgings, which were in the opposite direction from her house.

* * *

He had eaten the meal Davy had prepared and then set off for the convent. He was looking forward to telling Charlotte how their plans were progressing and, with luck, they would be on board a ship bound for England the very next day. But he never reached her.

A black windowless carriage drew up beside him and two men jumped out and bundled him into it. He gave one startled yell before the door was shut and they moved off.

Chapter Eleven

~~~~~~

Charlotte had spent most of the night sleeplessly going over and over every word Alex had said in the garden. She recalled the sweetness of his look, the gentleness of his hands as he clasped hers, his softly spoken words, all of which she savoured and clung on to like a drowning man clutching at straws. But there were other signs that disturbed her and made her sad: his sudden change of mood, as if she had said something to displease him; his springing to his feet and pacing about and his refusal to come into the anteroom when it rained. It was a public room, one that anyone visiting the convent could enter while their business was being dealt with. Instead he had preferred to go out into the storm.

But he said he would come again and they were going back to England together. Home. How sweet that word sounded! Perhaps, during the voyage, or even when they were back in London, he would come to realise how much he meant to her, that his lack of a title was unimportant and that what was important was the man he was, the man she loved to distraction. If she could make him see that, then he might tell her what she most wanted to hear. He must feel something for her or he would not have been at such pains to rescue her from the Salvadors and look after her. He had seen her naked, washed her body and wrapped her in a blanket and he had carried her in his arms to keep her safe. That was surely not the action of an uncaring man and more than he need have done to fulfil his mission for the Pic-cadilly Gentlemen.

He had asked her to marry him and immediately regretted it. Oh, how she wished she had not laughed at the idea. Laughter had covered her hurt that he could talk of marriage and annulment in the same breath, but it had been unkind of her and it had hurt him. When he came, she would have it out with him and see if she could make him understand that they belonged together and no one, not the Earl of Falsham, not her father, not distance, nor disparity in wealth, nor her own silly determination not to marry, would make the smallest difference. If he laughed at her, it would be no more than she deserved and she would have to try to bear her disappointment stoically. At least she would know the worst.

She was waiting for him by the pool the next afternoon, rehearsing in her mind what she would say. The rain had gone and the sky was blue again. The puddles had evaporated from the paths and the cobbles were once more bone dry. No vestige of the storm remained and the day was tranquil, though a little cooler than it had been. Sister Charity had said perhaps she ought to wait in the anteroom, but she wanted to be outside, to sit with him by the fountain and try to bring back the quiet rapport they had had before the storm blew up.

'Very well,' Sister had said, putting a shawl about her shoulders. 'But you must come in at once if you grow chilled.'

She would not be cold surrounded by Alex's warmth and had made her way out to the bench and sat down to wait. She sat there a very long time. He did not come. He did not come the next day either or the day after that. The ship he talked of must have sailed by now. So much for her grand plans to make him understand how her love for him would overcome all barriers, even those she had put up herself. How foolish she had been.

'He would not leave Lisbon without you, Charlotte,' Sister Charity said, on the third day when she persuaded her to leave her vigil and return indoors for her evening meal. 'Something must have detained him.'

'But if that were so, why has he not sent word?'

'I do not know, my child, but you must have faith. All will turn out as God intends.'

'Do you think God intended me to be so miserable?'

'Adversity makes us stronger.'

'It is not making me stronger. I grow weaker every day I am without him.'

'Shall we go into the chapel after dinner and pray for him?'

She knew the good sister was trying to make her feel better when nothing but the sight of Alex would do that. Nevertheless, she agreed.

She walked into the garden the next afternoon, though her heart was heavy and she had almost given up hoping he would come. Instead of sitting by the pool she paced the paths, too distressed to sit still. It was as she turned at the end of the path to face the convent building a second time that she saw Sister Charity hurrying towards her accompanied by the British Minister's wife. She started to run, knowing something must have happened to Alex, something dreadful.

'Mrs Hay,' she cried, stopping beside the pool. 'What has happened? It's Alex, isn't it?'

'Shall we sit down?' Mrs Hay suggested.

Charlotte sat on the bench with the lady beside her. 'Tell me what has happened? He's not... not dead, is he?'

'No, my dear, he is not dead. He has been arrested.'

'Arrested? Whatever for?'

'For kidnapping you.'

Charlotte began to laugh, a high-pitched nervous sound. 'He didn't kidnap me. Whatever gave anyone that idea?'

'The Earl of Falsham. He has accused Alex of taking you from his protection. He is demanding Alex return you forthwith.'

'No, oh, no. He won't do it, will he?'

'I am not sure what the Portuguese law is on the matter and I cannot ask my husband because he has gone to Queluz, the King's summer palace, and is not due back for another week, but Lord Falsham has a letter from your father, which he says confirms that you are betrothed to him.'

'Lord Falsham is a fiend. I am not engaged to him and would never, never agree to it. Papa would not make me, I know he would not. I must go to the authorities and tell them so.' She jumped up impatiently, but Mrs Hay took her hand and pulled her down again. 'I do not advise that, my dear. While the Earl has no idea where you are, he will do nothing to Alex. If you show yourself, the Portuguese authorities might very well hand you back to the earl. It is important for you to stay hidden.'

'But how can I, when Alex needs me? He risked everything to save me from the earl and I cannot bear the thought of him being in prison on my account.'

'It is what he wishes, Charlotte.'

'You have seen him?'

'Yes. He was allowed to inform my husband what had happened and, in Edward's absence, they allowed me speak to him. He has been arrested as Lieutenant Fox, but he is insisting he is not the lieutenant and they have arrested the wrong man. He maintains he is Captain Alexander Carstairs of the British Navy. I confirmed that, but they seem disinclined to believe me. I have no doubt Lord Falsham is lining someone's pockets.'

'Does the earl know him as Captain Carstairs?'

'I do not think so.'

'What can we do?'

'We must wait until my husband returns. He will make representations to the Portuguese authorities that they have no right to imprison a British citizen.'

'And they will let Alex go?'

'I do not know. We must pray they do and that

nothing delays my husband and he arrives before Alex is tried.'

'The prosecution will surely have to prove he kidnapped me.'

'Yes, but it could be said he did. He did take you from the Salvadors' house.'

'But he was rescuing me, not abducting me. And he was being Lieutenant Fox then.'

'So he was, so they will have to prove Lieutenant Fox and Captain Carstairs are one and the same. That is one of the reasons why you must remain hidden. He begged me to impress that upon you.'

'What do the nuns know?'

'I have told them everything. They do not make judgements, naturally, but they tell me you have sanctuary here for as long as you need it. Even if Lord Falsham did find out where you were, he would not dare do anything while you are under the protection of the nuns.'

'I wish I were poor, or at least not so rich, then there would not be all this fighting over me. Someone might love me for myself alone.'

'I believe Alex does.'

'Do you?' Charlotte's sad expression suddenly lightened. 'Do you really?'

Mrs Hay smiled. 'The signs are all there, though perhaps he does not yet realise it himself. You must be patient.' She stood up to leave.

'I must go now. You will do as Alex asks and stay here until we know the outcome of his arrest, won't you?'

'Yes, though it will be hard. I am so impatient.'

As soon as her ladyship had gone, Charlotte asked Sister Charity to give her something useful to do. She needed to keep busy, to stop herself dwelling on the image of Alex locked in a prison cell and the dreadful prospect that he would be found guilty. How Lord Falsham would gloat! But she would never go back to him. If she had to stay in the convent for the rest of her life, she would do it rather than live with that dreadful man. There was only one man she wanted and no other would do.

Sister Charity took her to the children's section of the convent where they looked after the city's orphans. It reminded Charlotte of the Foundling Hospital in London and she quickly became immersed in the work of looking after them, washing and dressing the babies and feeding them, giving them a hug and singing to them. The older ones could talk, but as she could not understand Portuguese they communicated with signs and gestures which often caused hilarity when they were misunderstood.

Thus her days were filled, but it did not stop her brooding at night. Unable to sleep, she tossed and turned. Sometimes she would rise and stand on a stool to look out of the window. She was on the second storey, on a level with the tops of the trees, which moved gently in the breeze coming from the river. She could see the rooftops of other buildings and below her glimpsed a ribbon of road winding down to the lower level of the town. During the day there were people going about their business, carriages and carts, horse and donkeys being ridden, but at night it was almost deserted. High above her she could just glimpse the outline of the castle against the sky. Was that where Alex was being held? Was he thinking of her, as she was of him? What would she do if they found him guilty? What punishment could he expect? Execution? The thought of that made her heart falter. How could she save him? There was only one way that she could see and that was to give herself up to the Earl of Falsham in exchange for Alex's life. If the worst came to the worst that was what she would have to do.

She shivered, though whether from fear or the cool air coming in the open window, she did not know. She climbed down and went back to bed. He dreams were filled with nightmares, black shapes, yawning pits, the sea crashing on rocks battering Alex's body and her own inability to save him. She woke in a sweat, crying out his name. The moon was shining in the window on to the crucifix on the table. She tumbled out of bed and knelt before it, praying harder than she had ever done in her life.

Alex was angry with himself. He should have foreseen what would happen and taken more care not to be followed. It was fortunate he had been dressed as a sea captain and not wearing Lieutenant Fox's clothes; it gave him a breathing space, but not much. All the same, he wondered who had connected the captain with the lieutenant. He did not think it had been Falsham, but if the man came to the castle to see for himself, he would soon confirm there was only one man and not two.

It was the devil's luck that Edward had been called away or he might have had him out of this prison cell and under his jurisdiction the day he was taken. As it was he was not sure whether Edward could, or would, do, anything to help him, since he had warned him not to fall foul of Portuguese law. The only thing he had to be thankful for was that he had been taken before he reached the convent. Charlotte should still be safe. That is, if she did as she was told and stayed where she was and did nothing to draw attention to herself. Knowing her, he could not be sure she would.

His anger and misery was not only for his predicament, dire though it was, but for the way he had left Charlotte the last time he had seen her. He had been almost brusque, fighting a desire within himself to admit he had fallen in love with her and the memory of her laughter when she had turned down his offer of marriage. It had reminded him of his last meeting with Letitia and her incredulity that he would even think she would disobey her father to marry him. The hurt of that had bruised him so badly he had vowed never to risk it again. It was why he had told Charlotte it would only be a temporary union, not to be consummated. A marriage of convenience Charlotte had called it and he had agreed. Mrs Hay had been right, he was too proud, when a little humility would have served him better. There was a vast difference between humiliation and humility and it had taken Charlotte to make him realise it.

If only he could get out of here and go to her, tell her the truth, explain why he had made the proposal and ask her again. She meant more to him than his pride, more than his life, which he would gladly sacrifice for her. What would happen to her if his life was forfeit? Would Falsham find her and, with no one to help her, force her to submit? Day after day, he paced his small cell, back and forth, back and forth, unable to sit still, unable eat, unable to sleep.

The day was set for his trial. It would mean standing in open court, unable to speak the language, unable to defend himself. And the Earl of Falsham would be there to accuse him, along with Madeleine and Grosswaite and anyone else the earl could drum up as witnesses. His masquerade as two men would be exposed, and if Edward Gilpin's letter to Falsham was produced in court, which it undoubtedly would be, he had not a hope of acquittal. He began to consider means of escape.

He had a cell to himself which had been granted to him as a subject of his Britannic Majesty. It was a small box-like room in the bowels of the castle, with a tiny barred window high up on one wall. He had pulled his bed over to it and climbed up to see out, but all it revealed was a cobbled yard patrolled by uniformed militia whose feet were on a level with his head. The door was of heavy oak and had a secure lock and bolts on the outside. Forcing a way out was not possible; it would take cunning and subterfuge when the door was opened and he was allowed out. That would not be before the day of the trial.

He asked for paper, pen and ink to prepare his defence and this was granted. He spent the time before his trial writing down everything that had happened: the original kidnapping of Miss Gilpin in London, her being taken aboard the *Vixen* by Grosswaite and the reason he went on board himself, and everything that had occurred since then. He did not know whether it would be allowed as evidence, but Edward Hay would make sure everyone at home, including the Piccadilly Gentlemen, would know he had acted honourably.

When it was done, he wrote to Charlotte, telling her everything, including the fact that he was the Marchioness of Foxlees, and how, if he had not been condemned, he would have declared his undying love and his wish to make her happy, and if it pleased her, to marry her and spend his life helping her to forget the horror of what the earl had done to her. He asked her to forgive him for his faults and remember him as someone whose life meant nothing to him without her. Tears he had not shed since he was a small boy filled his eyes as he sealed it. He did not send it, but marked it to be delivered in the event of his death. Then he prepared to await his fate.

The morning of the trial was blustery and cooler than it had been; summer was on its way out. Guards came to take him to the court. The room was full of people: the judge, court officials, the prosecutor and witnesses and the public who had heard about the case through gossip and come out of curiosity. The Earl of Falsham was prominent, ostentatiously bedecked in plum-coloured satin with yards of cream lace about his neck and on his cuffs. He was wearing a full toupee with side and end curls and a tricorne hat with a cockade. A sword hung on his hip. He sat next to the prosecutor and glared at Alex, as if trying to intimidate him. Alex, sitting alone and in irons, returned his gaze without flinching.

The preliminaries were completed, during which an interpreter was appointed to translate the proceedings for Alex's benefit, and then the prosecutor called the earl to put his case. Speaking in English, which was translated for the benefit of the court, the earl identified Alex as the man he had known as Lieutenant Fox, but if he really was Captain Alexander Carstairs it would explain why he had behaved so abominably. 'He once had the effrontery to pay his respects to my late wife and has never forgiven me for taking her from him,' he said. 'It was an act of revenge.'

'Nonsense!' Alex protested. 'What happened years ago has no bearing on the case.'

'I agree,' the judge said. 'Stick to the matter in hand, my lord.'

The earl, having made his point, continued. He was fluent and convincing in his act of being aggrieved and desperate for the return of the lady he loved and to whom he was betrothed. He called witnesses, the first of whom was Grosswaite, who told the tale the earl had told at the British Minister's ball, that her father had been booked to travel with them but had been delayed by unexpected business and because his lordship could not put off his own departure, Miss Gilpin had chosen to travel with him and wait for her father in Lisbon.

Alex, who was obliged to defend himself, rose to repudiate the man's evidence. 'You kidnapped Miss Gilpin on behalf of the Earl of Falsham,' he said.

'No, sir, I did not.'

'But you paid others to do it, two men already wanted by the English law for robbery and murder. A ransom of five hundred guineas was demanded.'

The earl snorted with derision.

'I know of no such men,' Grosswaite said. 'Nor of a ransom. It is an invention on your part.'

'What happened in London is no part of this trial,' the judge warned Alex through the interpreter.

Alex bowed to him and continued. 'Miss Gilpin denied many times while she was aboard the *Vixen* on her way here that she ever was, or ever would be, betrothed to the Earl of Falsham and that you were responsible for her abduction in London.'

'I never heard her say that,' Grosswaite insisted.

Alex could think of no other questions for him; the man remained loyal to the earl and he was wasting his time trying to break him. If Charlotte were brought to court, she would confirm the truth and for a second, but no longer, he considered whether to do that, but decided not to bring her into the glare of the public gaze and subject her to cross-examination. If the verdict went against him, the earl would carry her off in triumph. While the man did not know where she was, there was hope.

The prosecutor called Madeleine Salvador. Her name echoed round the courtroom, but she did not appear. Alex looked round like everyone else, expecting her to be brought through one of the doors. He glanced up at the public, all engrossed in the proceedings, wondering if she might be there, and caught sight of Davy, who grinned at him and stuck his thumb in the air. What had Davy done? He hoped fervently his servant had not broken the law or he would be standing beside him in the dock.

Men were sent to find the missing witness and in the meantime the earl was asked to produce his other witnesses. They were his card-playing companions, undoubtedly owed money by the earl, which they would never see again if the man were disgraced. All they could say was that they had witnessed a confrontation between the earl and the accused, which Alex soon established could as easily prove his point as the earl's, and they were dismissed.

Alex was not allowed to bring witnesses. Instead he chose to question the earl. Their exchange was conducted in English, which had to be translated and slowed the process down, and he could not get him to change his story that he had Mr Gilpin's whole-hearted support for the marriage and that, although Miss Gilpin was a young, inexperienced young lady who did not know her own mind, she was an obedient daughter and the agreement reached between Mr Gilpin and himself would stand. They would have been married before now, if Lieutenant Fox or Captain Carstairs or whatever name he liked to call himself had not spirited her away.

'Where was she when I supposedly spirited her away?' Alex asked.

'You know well where she was.'

'Tell the court, if you please.'

'At the home of my servant, Madeleine Salvador, being looked after. It was not seemly to have the lady under my roof before the wedding.'

'But she was under your roof earlier. You took her there from the ship as soon as she dropped anchor and kept her there, until she took matters into her own hands and escaped.'

'She did not escape, you took her.'

'But you have just said I took her from your servant's house, not your villa. Which is it?'

The earl looked confused for a moment and then said triumphantly, 'Both. She escaped from you and returned to me before you took her a second time.'

'It is obvious that the lady was not inclined to marry you and would do anything to prevent that happening,' Alex said. 'When she was at your servant's house, she was being given opiates to make her compliant.'

'That was nothing to do with me,' the earl said angrily. 'I never gave any orders for that, nor would I need to. Miss Gilpin was not trying to escape from me. It is you who is the abductor, not I. I am not on trial.'

The judge pointed out that this was true and the defendant would do well to stick to defending himself and not accusing others. Alex took a deep breath, wishing he could call witnesses, but as the defendant this was denied him. Davy and Edward Hay and the nuns would all testify to Charlotte's state of mind and her health, so would Madeleine if she could be found and coerced. He would wager Davy knew where she was. Captain

Brookside would have made a good witness, but he was halfway to India by now.

He turned back to the earl. 'You said Mr Gilpin agreed to the betrothal,' he said.

'I did.'

'When?'

'In London before we sailed.'

'Will Mr Gilpin testify to that?'

'He would, but unfortunately the gentleman is no longer with us. He succumbed to a fever after falling into the River Thames after waving us goodbye. My dear fiancée does not know this for the news has only recently been conveyed to me.'

Alex was shocked to the core. Gilpin dead? Poor, poor Charlotte. He returned to his seat, nonplussed for the moment, while the court officials offered condolences to the earl. The implications for Charlotte would be overwhelming. She would need comfort, support and wise advice. If only he could get out of the mess he was in and go to her. The judge was speaking, but he could not take in what he was saying. Did it mean Charlotte was free or more securely bound than ever? Did it mean that he was no longer under Gilpin's instructions to find and restore his daughter to him? He feared it did. Had she inherited the Gilpin business as she had expected to? Falsham would be even more determined to secure it for himself.

He came back to the present to hear a translation of the judge's words. 'You will be returned to your cell and sentence will be postponed until Miss Gilpin is found. I advise you to notify the court of her whereabouts without further delay.'

Two militiamen took his arms and propelled him out of the court. He struggled to free himself, but the muzzle of a pistol in his back made him desist. He would be no use to Charlotte dead. He heard the earl laughing as he was escorted roughly along the corridor and back to his lonely cell.

As the key was turned in the lock and the bolts were pushed home, he sank back on the hard bed and groaned in despair. He had been sitting there no more than half an hour, discarding one idea after another, when he heard the door being unlocked again. He looked up as a warder pushed it open and Mrs Hay and Davy came in together.

He scrambled to his feet to bow to the lady. 'You have news? Is your husband returned?'

'No, but expected any day now,' she said.

There was no chair in the room. He indicated the bed. 'Please be seated, ma'am.'

When she had done so, he turned to his servant. 'What have you done with Madeleine, Davy?'

'Me?' he queried, pretending innocence.

'Yes, you. She did not answer her name in

court. I sincerely hope you have not frightened her out of giving evidence. It could go ill for you.'

'I have not frightened her. She is not easily scared, that one,' Davy said. 'The earl dismissed her, threw her out. There is no fury like a woman scorned, isn't that what they say?'

'Something like it. So what happened?'

'His lordship discovered what her mother had done to Miss Gilpin.'

'How did he discover it?' Alex asked. 'I am sure Madeleine would not have told him herself.'

'The garden boy divulged it.'

'And how did the garden boy hear of it?' Alex asked, suspicion mounting.

'A hint was dropped in his ear.'

'And as a result the girl is without employment. Davy, I despair of you. Where is she?'

'She is at the Residency,' Mrs Hay put in. 'I have her there for her own protection until my husband comes back.'

'I persuaded her not to give evidence against you,' Davy said. 'But she was adamant she would not face the earl and speak for you.'

'Perhaps it is enough. I am indebted to you, Davy.'

'She brought this with her when she left the villa,' Mrs Hay said, producing a letter from her reticule.

'And before you say a word, I did not ask for

it,' Davy said. 'It was her own idea. She wanted to read it and find out if the earl really was engaged to Miss Gilpin.'

'She could not understand the writing,' Mrs Hay said. 'She asked me to read it to her. It is not from Mr Gilpin.'

Alex took the letter, which came from a firm of lawyers. He scanned it quickly and learned the coachmaker had never recovered from his immersion in the noisome waters of the Thames. He had been in his bed for a week and finally succumbed.

'This is dreadful news,' Alex said. 'Charlotte must be told and I dread to think how she will receive it. She is all alone in the world now and I am incarcerated in here.' He flung the letter down and began pacing the room, banging one fist into the other palm. 'The earl told everyone he had had a letter from Mr Gilpin giving his consent to the marriage.'

'He was lying,' Davy said.

'Obviously and hoping no one would ask him to produce it. But if he finds out where Charlotte is…' He stopped, imagining the scene, a mourning and tearful Charlotte, with no one to turn to except the earl. Would she? And if she did, had he any right to interfere? He was no longer on the case. The man who had employed him was no more. He regretted, more than he could possibly express, that he had not told Charlotte of his love for her the last time he had seen her. At least then, she would know and it might have given her strength to fight Lord Falsham.

He turned to Mrs Hay. 'Madam, can nothing be done?'

'We must wait for my husband to return. He understands about Portuguese justice and will know what to do.'

'We'll get you out, my lord,' Davy said. 'Do not despair.'

'Thank you, my friend.'

'And don't disclose where Miss Gilpin is no matter how hard they try to get it out of you,' Davy added. 'While they do not know where she is, you will live.'

'I have already thought of that, Davy,' he said, with a half-smile.

'For that reason we have decided not to visit her, in case we are followed,' Mrs Hay said. 'It means she will not learn of her father's demise until you can tell her, but she is worried enough about you, so perhaps it is for the best.'

'Someone followed me after I left you, my lady.'

'Yes, it was one of the footmen who was tempted by the reward the earl offered. He has been dismissed.'

'It seems there are few people we can trust,'

Alex said. 'I am grateful for those who stand by me.'

'I have known you for many years, Alex, and I have always found you honest and thoughtful of others,' she said. 'I pray you will get out of this coil safely and take your Charlotte home to London. She will make you a splendid marchioness, I think.'

'If she will have me.'

'Oh, I do not doubt that for a moment.' She was smiling as she stood up and shook out her skirts. 'You have only to ask.'

The door was opened to let his visitors out. Alex sank back on the bed, unsure whether to be optimistic or not.

Charlotte, who knew this was the day of Alex's so-called trial, was on hot coals the whole day, wondering what was happening. Sister Charity had said none of the nuns would go to the court for fear a nun showing an interest in the proceedings would attract attention and though there were men employed at the convent to do the heavy work, they could not send them because no one knew who she was or why she was with them and it was best they did not. So how was she to find out if Alex had convinced them of his innocence or been condemned?

She washed and fed the babies, hugging them

to her for comfort, hers as well as theirs. No one came to her with news, not even the Minister's wife. She felt abandoned, just as the little ones for whom she cared had been abandoned, their survival dependent on the nuns who did their best for them, but it wasn't like having a loving family. Was that to be her fate too?

She tried telling herself that Alex would not leave her to her fate, but supposing he had no choice? Surely they would not condemn him on the word of that fiend, Lord Falsham? If only she could give evidence, she would soon convince the judge of the truth. Why was Alex trying to do this all on his own? And why had she not heard from Papa? Why would he write to the earl and not to her? Would the nuns stop her if she tried to leave?

And then an idea came to her. Nuns were covered from head to foot and no one would dare molest one of them, would they? She began to lay plans.

Alex jumped up from contemplating the floor when Edward Hay was admitted to his cell. 'Edward, thank goodness, you have come,' he said. 'Can you get me out of here?'

'I have spoken to the Count of Oeires, his Majesty's Chief Minister, and he has intervened on your behalf. He is anxious to maintain good relations with the British Government and he does not want this affair to escalate into a political storm. On certain conditions, you will be released into my custody.'

'Conditions? I will wager one of them is that I reveal the whereabouts of Miss Gilpin.'

'That is hardly necessary, since I know where she is.'

'And you have told the Portuguese, I suppose. How could you do that? Falsham will grab her back as soon as he learns it.'

'No, for she is to reside with me until she can be repatriated with a suitable escort and a female companion. Falsham would not dare defy my ruling on the matter.'

'You know her father is dead?'

'Yes, and I am sorry for it.'

'She will need comfort and support.'

'It will be provided.'

'Is she already at your house?'

'No. I came straight here as soon as my wife told me what had happened. I will fetch her after I've left you.'

'What are these conditions, then?'

'You do not attempt to see Miss Gilpin and you do not confront the Earl of Falsham. You will leave Lisbon on the first available vessel going to England.'

Alex's face, which had hitherto been sombre,

lit with a smile. 'And will it also be the one Miss Gilpin travels on?'

Edward shrugged, but he was smiling. 'Who is to tell? We shall have to wait and see.'

'Does Falsham know of these conditions?'

'He will be informed.'

'Then I wonder what he will do. I cannot see him giving up.'

'He will have no choice, and now there is no Mr Gilpin for him to fall back on, I do not see what he can do. Unless, of course, Miss Gilpin decides to accept his suit, but I cannot see that happening, can you?'

'I sincerely hope not.'

'If he asks for her and she agrees, I will let him see her for a few moments, in my presence, so that she may confirm to him and to me that she will not marry him.'

'Thank you.'

'Now, come with me. My carriage is outside. I will take you to your lodgings. Your man is waiting for you there. You will stay there until I send you word.'

Half an hour later he was being greeted by a jubilant Davy. 'Good to see you, my lord. I knew they would have to let you out.'

Alex smiled wearily. 'It is a start, but I am

under house arrest and may not attempt to see Miss Gilpin.'

'I reckon she's safe enough where she is.'

'Mr Hay is going to fetch her to stay with him.'

'It makes a difference, her pa being dead, don't it?'

'Yes. It means she is independent and may conduct her own affairs and marry or not marry as she chooses.'

'Then your work is done.'

'In a way, yes.'

'What do you mean "in a way"?'

'Do you think I could leave her here, alone and unprotected?'

'But the British Minister will protect her.'

'So he will, but he is a diplomat and he won't do anything to upset the Portuguese authorities. I don't feel happy about it. Something in my bones tells me we are not at the end of the road yet.'

'You are too glum, my lord. I heard there was a ship due in soon from the Cape on its way to London.'

'Good. I shall not breathe easily until it weighs anchor and we are all safely on our way to England.'

Alex's premonition was borne out when Edward returned half an hour later. 'I have just come from the convent,' he said. 'Miss Gilpin has slipped her leash and disappeared. You wouldn't know anything about that, would you, Alex?'

Alex, who was having a meal Davy had brought in from one of the nearby eating houses, jumped up in alarm, his cutlery clattering onto his plate. 'No, I do not. How can she have gone? I asked Mrs Hay to impress upon her the importance of not leaving the sanctuary of the convent.'

'She evidently did not think that advice worth heeding.'

Alex was both alarmed and angry. Why was she so independent, so stubborn, but so courageous? 'We have to find her before Falsham does.'

'He cannot harm her now,' Edward said. 'He has shot his bolt.'

'She doesn't know that,' Davy pointed out. 'She thinks the captain's still in gaol. She'll be off to persuade them to let him out.'

'In a nun's habit,' Edward put in. 'She stole one from a laundry basket. She left a note promising to return it.'

'We must go to the gaol then and intercept her, otherwise they may hand her over to Falsham.' Alex was already halfway to the door. 'The judge was not sympathetic to my case and I think he believed the earl's story.'

'Get in my carriage,' Edward said. 'It will not take many minutes.'

Davy climbed up on the box beside the driver and Alex tumbled into the carriage with Edward. He was anxious and afraid. Portuguese justice was not like British justice, although sometimes even that could be bought, though not so easily since the blind magistrate, Sir John Fielding, had taken over and the Piccadilly Gentleman's Club was becoming a force to be reckoned with. There was no one like that in Portugal.

The horses were toiling up the hill towards the castle and could not go fast enough for Alex. 'Just when it seemed everything was going right for a change, the foolish girl had to go and take matters into her own hands,' he said. 'I shall have strong words to say to her when I see her.'

That would not happen as soon as he had hoped. When they reached the castle they discovered the lady had been and gone.

Chapter Twelve

After a wait of two hours in the vestibule of the castle governor's quarters, Charlotte had been shown into his presence, only to discover he did not speak English and could not understand her questions. The odd few phrases of Portuguese she had learned from the nuns was not sufficient to make herself understood. She found herself repeating 'Captain Carstairs, where is he?' over and over, until he realised she must be talking about the trial.

He had shrugged. 'Gone.'

She had understood that word; one of the orphans had used it in a game they had been playing. 'Where? *Onde?*'

He spread his hands wide. *'Não sei.'*

'But you must know. Find someone who speaks English.'

He had called his clerk from the outer office and held a lengthy and voluble conversation with him, while she waited impatiently. 'The prisoner was taken away in a carriage,' the clerk told her.

'Where was he taken?'

'I have no idea. He was fetched.'

'By whom?'

'An English gentleman. I do not know his name.'

Realising she was getting nowhere, she had turned away. There were many English people in Lisbon, including the Earl of Falsham, but Alex would never go in a carriage with him, unless he had been told she wanted to see him. Would Alex believe that? There was the British Minister, of course, but he was out of town, and there was Grosswaite and Davy Locke. Davy would have the landaulet Alex had hired from Manuel Rodrigues, but would the prison authorities allow him to take Alex away? It had to be Lord Falsham and there was nothing for it but to confront him.

It was a long walk to the villa, especially as she did not know any of the short cuts and was obliged to go down into the lower town, cross the Rossio and climb the hill to the house. She was anonymous in the nun's garb, but it was a warm day and she was growing hot and sticky. She was plodding up the last and steepest part of the hill when she was aware of a carriage coming up behind her. She stepped into the shadows to watch it pass and it was then she noticed the Minister's coat of arms on the door. He was back in Lisbon and he would help her. Eagerly she stepped out into the road, but the driver took no notice of her and the coach rolled past. She stood in the middle of the road, looking at the back of it, weeping with frustration and disappointment.

And then it slowed to a stop. She began to run after it.

'My lord, there is a nun on the road,' Davy said, turning almost upside down to look into the carriage. 'She is running after us.'

Alex was out of the carriage in an instant, just as Charlotte reached them. Her cheeks were pink and she was panting for breath. Her wimple, which she had not known how to fasten properly, had slipped and her rich brown hair was tumbling about her shoulders. When she saw who it was standing in the road, she cried his name and fell into his arms.

'In with you,' he said, picking her up and depositing her on the seat beside Edward. He climbed in to sit opposite her. He was so tense with anxiety, so annoyed with her for frightening him so badly, he wanted to kiss her and spank her both at the same time. If Edward had not been there, he might very well have done so. He waited for her to regain her breath while the driver found a place in the road wide enough for him to turn the carriage back the way they had come.

'Where did you think you were going?' Alex demanded after Edward had told the driver to take them to the Residency and they were once more on their way.

'To see the Earl of Falsham. I wanted to plead with him to drop the case against you.'

'Do you think he would listen?'

'He would if I made it worth his while.'

'By doing what?'

'Agreeing to marry him.'

'Good God!' He found it hard to believe she would make such a sacrifice for him. What had he done to deserve it? 'Why on earth would you do that, after assuring me you never would?'

'Because I could not bear the thought of you being locked away, perhaps losing your life, on my account. It was too much to ask of you.'

'You did not ask it of me,' he said stiffly. 'I am responsible for my own actions.'

'He would not have forfeited his life,' Edward put in. 'The British government would have had something to say about executing a British citizen and the Portuguese authorities know it.'

'I did not know that, did I? No one came to tell me what happened at the trial. I had to do something. You are very unkind to be so cross with me.'

'I am not cross,' Alex said, softening at last. 'I am horrified to think what might have happened to you if we had not come upon you before you reached the earl.'

'I am so glad you did,' she said softly. 'Now are you going to tell me what happened at the trial?'

Alex recounted everything, who was there, what was said and the delay while he was supposed to make up his mind to tell the court where she was.

'But you would not?'

'No. I could not be sure they would not hand you over to Falsham, but it gave me a breathing space and then Mr Hay turned up. It was through his good offices I was released.

'Into my custody,' Edward reminded him.

Alex smiled at him. 'As you say. You have my eternal gratitude.'

'And am I also in your custody, Mr Hay?' she asked him, smiling.

'You will be my guest until arrangements can be made for you to return to England'.

'We are going home! Oh, how wonderful! I am so looking forward to seeing Papa again.'

The men looked at each other and were saved from commentating because they had arrived outside the Residency and the carriage was coming to a stop.

'Here we are,' Edward said. 'Let us go in and tell my wife all is well. She has been worrying about you both.'

As they left the coach, Alex turned to Davy. 'Go back to our lodgings, Davy, and bring the brown portmanteau I left in my bedchamber. Miss Gilpin will need her clothes.'

'Take the coach,' Edward said.

It rolled away and Edward led the way into the house where Mrs Hay hurried forwards to greet them, taking a hand of each. 'Oh, you have got them both back safe and sound, how relieved I am. But, my dear Charlotte, what are you doing dressed like that?'

'Let us go into the drawing room,' Edward said. 'Mary, order some refreshments for our guests, if you please. And then you shall hear the whole story.'

She turned to speak to a hovering footman and then followed them into the elegantly furnished drawing room. Alex and Charlotte sat together on a sofa, Edward took a wing-backed chair and Mrs Hay another sofa. 'I am all agog,' the lady said. 'Which one of you will tell the tale?'

Alex began and was interrupted now and again by Edward, who told what he had done while Alex had been pacing about his prison cell trying to think of a way out, and then Charlotte took over with her story, until all three came together at the end. 'Alex was very cross with me,' she said. 'I do believe he still is.'

'You should not have left the convent,' he said. 'You put Mr Hay to great inconvenience, driving all over town looking for you, not to mention upsetting the nuns who looked after you so well, especially Sister Charity.'

'I am sorry for that, truly I am,' she said, near to tears because their reunion had not been all she had hoped for. 'But I could not just do nothing.'

The refreshments arrived, tea and little almond cakes, meant to sustain them until dinner a little later in the day. When she had drunk her tea, Mary Hay stood up. 'Edward, there is something I need to show you.'

He looked up startled, a cake halfway to his mouth. 'What, now?'

'Yes, this instant.' She jerked her head towards the door.

'Oh, very well.' He got up and they left together.

Alex smiled. 'Not very subtle, is she? But then Edward would not have taken the hint if she had been. There is something important I have to say to you.'

'Oh.' Her breath caught in her throat. He was

going to propose again and this time she would not give him time to retract before she said yes.

He caught her hand in his. 'You remember Lord Falsham saying he had had a letter from your father that gave his consent to the marriage.'

'Yes, but I do not believe he did because Papa would have written to me, too, and it would not have made any difference if he had. I was ready to defy him.'

'You were right not to believe it. Falsham did have a letter from London, but it was not from your father.'

'Oh, who sent it then? And how do you know about it?'

'Madeleine stole it and gave it to Davy.'

'Madeleine! Why would she do that?'

'Because the earl found out about her holding you prisoner and poisoning you. He obviously wanted you alive. He dismissed her and before she left she stole the letter.'

'I see. So it was nothing to do with Papa?'

'Yes, it was. I have it here.' He took it from his pocket. 'I will sit with you while you read it.'

She read it once, then again. 'Oh, Alex,' she said, her eyes filling with tears. 'I am so sorry I was not there to comfort him and ease his going. What am I going to do without him?'

He put his arm about her shoulders and pulled

her against him, letting her cry. 'I am sorry, Charlotte. I wish I could have prevented it.'

'It wasn't your fault.' Her voice was muffled in his coat. 'Martin Grosswaite murdered him just as surely as if he had taken a dagger to his heart. Oh, poor, poor Papa. I am so angry.'

'Be angry if it helps. I am angry, too.'

'With me?'

'No, sweetheart, not with you.' Above her head, he gave a wry smile. Henry and Charlotte were alike in one thing. Neither listened to good advice, but must dash off and take matters into their own hands. He had warned Gilpin not to go alone to hand over the ransom but he had been so anxious about his daughter, he could not wait, just as Charlotte could not wait with the nuns until he went for her. But that was part of the woman she was and he was immeasurably heartened to think she felt enough for him to sacrifice herself to that fiend, Falsham. He thanked God she had not succeeded.

'I must go home as soon as possible,' she said, as he handed her his handkerchief to wipe her face.

'Of course. As soon as it can be arranged.'

'Will you be coming, too?'

'Yes.'

'The earl won't do anything to stop us, will he?'

'He dare not defy his Majesty's Minister Plenipotentiary to Portugal, especially when he has the wholehearted support of the Portuguese Chief Minister.'

'No more Earl of Falsham?'

'No. I doubt he dare show his face in England again.'

'All the same, I shall not be easy until we are on our way.'

'Be patient. Stay close to Mrs Hay. I have to go to my lodgings.'

'You are not staying here?'

'No, it would not be fitting. Edward must be seen to be following the letter of his arrangement with Count Oeires. But as soon as a ship arrives and passage has been booked, we will meet again on board.'

'When will that be?'

'Soon, I hope.'

Mrs Hay peeped round the door. 'May I come in?' She did not wait for a reply, but came in and sat down opposite them. 'I see Alex has told you,' she said, nodding at the letter screwed up in Charlotte's hand.

'Yes.' Her voice was still watery. 'I cannot quite believe it. Life without Papa will be hard. We were so close.'

'But you do have Alex.' She saw Alex shaking his head and fell silent.

'Yes, Alex has been my rock. Without him I

should not have survived all that has happened to me. One day I will find a way to thank him.'

'Not today,' he said quickly. 'You are worn out and must rest.'

'Alex is right,' Mrs Hay said. 'I will show you up to your room. Davy Locke has brought your clothes.'

'What clothes?' she asked. 'I have none.'

'We bought you some, Alex and I,' she said. 'If they are not to your liking, you must blame him.'

'You are both so kind.'

'Kind, be damned,' Alex muttered and though Charlotte looked curiously at him, she did not comment.

'I am worried about the business,' she said. 'There is no one to look after it with Papa gone. The workers will be lost and worried about their jobs. The sooner I can get back and take over, the better.'

'Yes, of course,' Mrs Hay soothed, taking Charlotte's arm and leading her away. 'Your father's lawyers will have done everything that is necessary. Do not worry about it.'

Alex sat in contemplation. He could not have told her how much he loved her and wanted to marry her while she was grieving for her father. She was grateful to him for what he had done, which had been done out of love, not duty, but that appeared to be all it was. Gratitude. He did not want gratitude, he wanted her love. He had read the signs wrongly; her first concern, after her initial shock and grief over her father had abated a little, had been about the coachmaking business.

Charlotte lay in a fresh dimity nightdress in the most comfortable bed she had had since leaving home and sobbed her heart out. Alex had tried to comfort her, but nothing at that moment would ease the pain of her loss. Papa had been father and mother to her, bringing her up to be strong and independent, not to take wealth for granted and to think of those less fortunate. He had given her an education many a young man might envy, providing her with teachers to instruct her in riding, dancing and the appreciation of good music. He had taught her the intricacies and ethics of the coachmaking business, introducing her to book-keeping and accounting. Until the Earl of Falsham had sent Grosswaite to kidnap her, it had been her whole world. Love and marriage were something for the distant future, if at all.

Now what? Without her what would the lawyers have done? Shut Gilpin's down? Put it up for sale? Had Joe Smithson kept it going until she could get back? And overriding all that was the ache in her heart from wanting Alex so much.

He was angry with her and that wasn't fair. She had only left the convent to try to help him, but had he taken that into consideration? No, he had not. If only he had spoken of love, of wanting and needing her for herself alone, she would have been able to bear her grief the better.

He was proud, he had told her so, too proud to accept her wealth perhaps. Was that what was holding him back? She would give it all away and live in poverty with him if that was what it took. But how could she do that when her wealth was tied up in a coachmaking business with over two hundred employees? She had a responsibility to them she could not shirk. Alex must be made to understand that.

Two days later a private yacht dropped anchor in Lisbon harbour. Lord Trentham came ashore and went straight to see Edward Hay where he asked him to send for Alex. All three were closeted in the library for some time before joining Mrs Hay and Charlotte in the drawing room.

'Ladies, may I present Admiral Lord Trentham,' Edward said. 'My lord, this is my wife, Mary, and Miss Charlotte Gilpin.'

His lordship bowed to them both. Charlotte, bending knee and head in acknowledgement, was very aware of the tall form of Alex standing behind the Admiral. When she straightened up she saw him looking at her, but she could not read his expression. Was it sorrow? Was it tenderness? Or was he still dwelling on their differences?

'His lordship has come in his own yacht to take you home, Charlotte,' Edward said.

Charlotte's face lit with pleasure. 'Oh, that is good of you, my lord. But how did you know I was here and anxious to return?'

'I have kept abreast of matters as far as it has been possible,' his lordship said, as they all sat down. 'Alex has reported to the Society for the Discovery and Apprehending of Criminals, as often as he was able. The first time was on the night you were taken, the second the day you arrived in Lisbon.'

'Oh, are you one of the Piccadilly Gentleman?'

He smiled. 'Not exactly one of them, but I sponsor them and smooth their path with the authorities when necessary. After Alex's second letter, setting out what had happened and what he proposed to do about it, I decided he would need help and so I rearranged my appointments, had my yacht readied and set sail. And here I am.'

'So everyone in London knew what was happening to me? Even my father?'

'Miss Gilpin knows of the demise of her father,' Edward put in.

'Oh, I hoped it would not be necessary for her to know that. How did it come about?'

'What do you mean not necessary for me to know?' Charlotte cried out. 'Of course I had to know.'

'No, my dear. Mr Gilpin is not dead.'

'Not dead?' She could hardly take it in.

'No, he has been exceedingly ill and we despaired of him for some time, but he is recovering slowly and the sight of you, well and unharmed, will no doubt accelerate that.'

'But why did Lord Falsham's letter say he was dead? I do not understand.'

'Mr Gilpin's illness, caused by his immersion in the Thames, was made worse by worry over you and what Lord Falsham would do to you. He had received a letter from his lordship, telling him that he proposed to marry you and he expected his whole-hearted support for the sake of your reputation. There was more about a dowry and the cancellation of his debts, but I won't trouble you with that. I visited him at the time and it came to us that if Mr Gilpin were to die, you would be independent and Falsham would not be able to use him as a hold over you. At that time Mr Gilpin was very near to death and did not expect to survive, so, with his agreement, we had the lawyers send the letter. The wonderful thing is that as soon as it was posted your father rallied.'

'Oh, thank God.' She was shaking with nerves

and could not quite take it in. She looked across the room at Alex, longing to be closer to him, to feel his arms about her, his warmth breath fanning her face, and his quiet gentle voice telling her all was well. If he said it, she might believe it.

'You will be anxious to go home and see him for yourself,' Lord Trentham said.

'Yes, oh, yes. How soon can we go?'

'Tomorrow, if wind and tide are favourable.'

'And will Alex come, too?'

'Of course.' It was said with an understanding smile. 'We cannot leave him behind, can we?'

They all went on board the yacht the following morning. It was not a large craft, but it was comfortable, or as comfortable as sea-going vessels ever were. A young English girl whose parents were sending her back to England to be educated had been hired as a maid, which Charlotte felt bound to accept, though she would much rather have had Alex helping her to dress and undress. The gowns he had chosen for her were exactly what she would have chosen herself, clean colours and designs, easy to get in and out of. She took the first opportunity to thank him.

'How did you know my size?' she asked. They were standing together at the rail as the little ship sailed north towards the Bay of Biscay. Already the air was colder and she was glad of the warm petticoats and the long pelisse she had found in the portmanteau.

He was not called upon to do any sailing duties and so they had ample time to talk. 'Do you need to ask that? I know every inch of you.'

She felt the colour rise in her cheeks. 'I suppose you do, but I don't remember it.'

'None of it?' he queried, lifting one eyebrow.

'Very little. I remember feeling safe while you held me, that nothing bad would happen to me while you were there.'

'I should like you to feel like that all the time,' he said. 'For ever more, day by day, until death do us part.'

Her breath caught in her throat. 'Alex, what are you saying?'

'I thought it was plain enough.' He took both her hands in his own. 'Charlotte, I am asking you to marry me. I cannot imagine my life without you in it. I love you.'

'Oh, Alex, how I have longed for you to tell me that, but you always held back. I was in despair and thought you looked upon rescuing me as your duty to the Piccadilly Gentlemen.'

'It started out that way, but it was not long before I realised it was not duty, but love.'

'Sister Charity said duty and love are intertwined.'

'Sister Charity is very wise.'

'I am so glad I was able to go and see her before we left. I intend to make a large donation to the convent when I get home. I would give away all my wealth if it meant you would love me and want to marry me, except that it is tied up with Gilpin's and I am not free to spend it.'

'Can't you forget the coachmaking business for a minute?' He did not mean to speak sharply, but he could not help himself. Competing with a business was infinitely worse than competing with a jealous rival.

'Alex, my father worked years of long hours to build the business up and he did it for me. I am his only child, son and daughter in one. How can I forget it?'

'I understand that, sweetheart, and I did not mean you should dismiss it as unimportant, but can you stop being the son and concentrate on being the daughter for a moment. Your father is on the road to recovery, he has years ahead of him yet.'

'But, according to Lord Trentham, he is still ill. How is he managing? Is Joe Smithson keeping it going so the men have enough work to do? They have families who need their support. If you have employees, Alex, you have a responsibility to them.'

'Do you think I do not know that? I have an

estate to run and I, too, employ labour. Running about solving crime is not my only occupation.'

'I did not know that.'

'I have been endeavouring to tell you, if you will only stop tormenting yourself over building coaches long enough to listen.'

'I am listening,' she said meekly.

'Do you love me?' he asked.

'Yes. Why do you think I have been so tormented? There is nothing I want more than to marry you, but when I think of Papa, struggling along without me, I feel I cannot leave him. Do you not think you could work in the business with him, then we could work side by side?'

'No, Charlotte.' He spoke firmly so as to brook no argument. 'Your father has reliable, skilled employees, he does not need a clumsy oaf like me pretending to help him and getting in the way.'

'You are not a clumsy oaf. You are gentle and kind and I owe you my life, more than once, too.'

'I don't want your gratitude, Charlotte, I want much more than that. I want your love.'

'You have it, always and for ever. But I cannot abandon my father when he needs me.'

'Of course not. And I love you the more for saying so. But you know he was expecting you to marry some day and so he must have accepted that you would leave him to live with your husband.'

'Yes, a man with a title.' She smiled suddenly. 'I do not know if captain is a proper title, but it is good enough for me.'

'You mean you will marry me?'

'Yes.'

'Oh, Charlotte!' He pulled her to him and subjected her to a long and searching kiss which left her breathless and wanting more.

'Alex, there are people about.'

'I don't care. What made you decide to accept?'

'I realised if I didn't climb down, I would lose you, and that I could not have borne. So, Captain Carstairs, you have yourself a bride.'

'Thank heaven for that. I never thought proposing and being accepted would be such hard work. I suppose that was why I was so clumsy the first time, when I foolishly offered you a way out.'

'Did you love me then?'

'Oh, yes, and I did want to marry you, but you looked so shocked, I realised I had blundered. That's why I said the marriage could be annulled. That wasn't what I wanted at all.'

She laughed. 'And I was hurt and disappointed that you wanted to be rid of me as soon as we were back in England.'

'It is all behind us now. Shall I tell you about Foxlees?'

'Foxlees, what is that?'

'It is my estate in Norfolk. I recently inherited it. It was badly run down, but I am having it restored. It will be our marital home, if you like it.'

'Do you mean you are not a poor sea captain on half-pay, making ends meet working for the Piccadilly Gentlemen's Club?'

'The Piccadilly Gentlemen are all just that: gentlemen. They do not work for pay, but to try to improve the society in which we live. I am a sea captain on half-pay, but that is not all I am. While I was serving in the late war I earned substantial prize money and when my father died I came into a considerable inheritance. And that has been added to with the demise of my uncle.' He stepped back to watch her face. 'You see before you the Marquis of Foxlees.'

She stared at him and then began to laugh. It was wonderful to see her and it made him smile. The sailors stopped their work to look at them and they began to smile, too, though they did not know the reason for it. She laughed so much her hat fell off into the sea and went bobbing away on the current. 'Oh, Alex, you are funning me.'

'No, I am not.' He saw Davy standing beside Charlotte's maid a little way off. 'Davy, come here, if you please.' And when he obeyed, added, 'Tell Miss Gilpin who I am.'

'Captain Alexander Carstairs, late of His Majesty's navy.'

'My full title, if you please.'

'But you said I was not to say anything of it.'

'You may say it now.'

Davy grinned, turning from him to Charlotte. 'He is the Marquis of Foxlees, Miss Gilpin, but he don't like the title above half and won't use it.'

'I do not care whether he uses it or not,' she said. 'He is the same man whatever name he goes by.'

'Am I to congratulate you, my lord?'

'Yes, for Miss Gilpin has consented to marry me.'

Lord Trentham, who was pacing the deck with his captain, overheard and hurried to offer his felicitations.

'I have yet to speak to Mr Gilpin and ask his blessing,' Alex said.

'A mere formality, my boy, a mere formality.'

His words proved true. After an almost smooth crossing of the Bay of Biscay and a run up the channel with the wind behind them, they made good time and docked in London as the leaves began falling from the trees. The summer was gone and they felt the nip of autumn in the air, but it could not dampen their spirits. Once they had disembarked Alex hired a cab and they were conveyed to Piccadilly. Leaving Lord Trentham outside his own house, Alex and Charlotte carried on to Gilpin House.

Henry was almost his old self, though much thinner than he had been. He was sitting by the fire in the drawing room, wrapped in a shawl and reading a newspaper when they came in. 'Charlotte!' He jumped to his feet and opened his arms. 'My precious child.'

Charlotte ran to embrace him. 'Oh, Papa, I am so glad to be back.'

He hugged her. 'No more glad than I am to have you back safe and sound. I was so afraid…'

'You need not have been, I had Alex taking care of me.'

'Alex?' He looked over her head at Alex, who was standing just inside the door, not wishing to intrude on their reunion. 'You have done well, Captain Carstairs. My daughter is restored to me.'

'Not for ever,' she said. 'Alex has asked me to marry him and I have said yes.'

'I hope we have your blessing, sir,' Alex added.

'Yes, whatever my daughter wants she shall have and you have proved yourself a true knight errant. I had hoped for a title for her, but that is unimportant if she is determined to have you.'

'But I shall have a title, Papa. Alex is a marquis and I shall be a marchioness, but I do not

care about that at all. All that matters is that Alex
loves me and I love him.'

'Then let us have supper and you can tell me
all your adventures.'

They did this, but both were very careful to
conceal the worst of Charlotte's ordeals for fear
of making him ill again.

It was very late when Alex left to go to Mount
Street, only to find all the Gentlemen there waiting to congratulate him on a difficult job well
done and to congratulate him on his engagement.

'I told you it would happen, didn't I?' Harry
said, raising a glass to him. 'If you join the Piccadilly Gentlemen, you are bound to fall in love.
Nothing is more sure.'

* * * * *

A sneaky peek at next month...

HISTORICAL

IGNITE YOUR IMAGINATION, STEP INTO THE PAST...

My wish list for next month's titles...

In stores from 7th December 2012:

☐ Some Like It Wicked – Carole Mortimer

☐ Born to Scandal – Diane Gaston

☐ Beneath the Major's Scars – Sarah Mallory

☐ Warriors in Winter – Michelle Willingham

☐ A Stranger's Touch – Anne Herries

☐ Oklahoma Wedding Bells – Carol Finch

Available at WHSmith, Tesco, Asda, Eason, Amazon and Apple

Just can't wait?

MILLS & BOON® Book Club

2 Free Books!

Get your free books now at
www.millsandboon.co.uk/freebookoffer

Or fill in the form below and post it back to us

THE MILLS & BOON® BOOK CLUB™—HERE'S HOW IT WORKS: Accepting your free books places you under no obligation to buy anything. You may keep the books and return the despatch note marked 'Cancel'. If we do not hear from you, about a month later we'll send you 4 brand-new stories from the Historical series priced at £4.50* each. There is no extra charge for post and packaging. You may cancel at any time, otherwise we will send you 4 stories a month which you may purchase or return to us—the choice is yours. *Terms and prices subject to change without notice. Offer valid in UK only. Applicants must be 18 or over. Offer expires 31st January 2013. **For full terms and conditions, please go to www.millsandboon.co.uk/freebookoffer**

Mrs/Miss/Ms/Mr (please circle)
_____

First Name
_____

Surname
_____

Address
_____

_____

_____ Postcode _____

E-mail
_____

Send this completed page to: Mills & Boon Book Club, Free Book Offer, FREEPOST NAT 10298, Richmond, Surrey, TW9 1BR

Find out more at
www.millsandboon.co.uk/freebookoffer

Visit us Online

0712/H2YEA

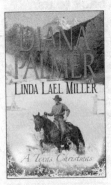  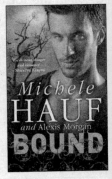